# The Earl's Angel

## Cary Harter

# Prickle Forrest Books

Wooster Ohio  USA

# COPYRIGHT



First edition September 2024

Book Cover design by GetCovers
Editing by Christina Benchoff

ISBN (paperback)978-1-965780-00-8
ISBN (Ebook)978-1-965780-01-5
ISBN (Large Print)

Author Website caryharter.com

# DEDICATION

For Michael, who spent thirty-five years showing me what
true love is, I miss you

.

.

# ACKNOWLEDGMENTS

I would like to acknowledge:

My family for their patience and for not complaining too much when they had to spend their hard-earned money on DoorDash.

The Wayne County Novelist Guild for their encouragement and support during the many bouts of insecurity I had. Especially, John Newton for help with formatting, Cyndi Brec for marketing ideas and brainstorming, and Christina Benchoff my go to girl for everything, including editing. So, if my book sucks, you can blame her. Conversely, if you like my book, it is due in a large part to her help.

Deb Grey, who is not a writer herself, but listened to me rattle on about imaginary people and would say, "You can do this," whenever I would call in a panic.

Last, but not least, I would like to acknowledge my mother, who besides bearing and raising me (not an easy task) retyped a number of half-finished manuscripts, including this one, after a major computer crash. Thanks, Mum, what would I do without you?

# Chapter 1



Edward Montgomery leaned back in his chair and gazed through half closed eyes at the blond woman winding her way through the crowd with a carafe of wine in her hands. Her dress had been dampened to show her every curve. He felt his pulse quicken. It had been too long since he had been with a woman. He raised his cup in a salute toward her and watched as she made her way over to his table.

"Would you like some?" the woman asked

leaning over, her breasts spilling out of her low-cut gown.

"Definitely," he said placing his wine glass directly above her bosom.

She began to pour the liquid into his glass. As she did, she looked at him from beneath her lashes. He smiled at her and when he drew his glass away, he tilted it just a bit to let a few drops fall from his glass.

"Oh, I'm sorry," he said. The wine was the same color as the tops of her rouged nipples which peeked out from the low neckline of her dress. He leaned forward even closer. "Here, let me help."

He ran his tongue across her exposed flesh lapping up the spilled wine. She leaned in closer giving him freer access.

She bent her head alongside his. "I could find someone else to pour the wine if you would like to go upstairs," she murmured in his ear.

"That sounds like a wonderful idea."

She straightened and scanned the room. Spotting a small brunette, she waved her over.

"Ariella, would you mind pouring the wine for a while?"

"Not at all," said the girl whose real name was probably Ella. *Or Sally*, he nodded to himself, *she looks like a Sally.*

He looked back over at the blond woman who smiled and took his hand, pulling him up out of his chair and toward the stairs leading to the private rooms.

"What's your name?" he asked as she led him up the stairs and down a dimly lit hall.

"Maribel," she said opening a door near the end of the hall.

He looked at her through alcohol blurred eyes. *Probably just plain Mary.*

'What's yours?" she asked stepping into the room.

Edward smiled, *when in Rome, do as the Roman's do.* "Rupert," he said following her, "My name's Rupert," and closed the door behind them.

Caroline Aldridge sat by herself in the room full of chattering guests and glanced at the clock on the mantel for what seemed like the hundredth time this evening. He was almost an hour late. She began to doubt that he was coming at all. She lifted the end of her sash and began to pick at it absentmindedly.

The party was another attempt by her parents to introduce the reluctant bridegroom to his bride. It was a match that had been talked about since her childhood. It was an accepted fact of life that she was going to marry Edward Montgomery. Just like the fact that breakfast was served every morning at precisely nine o'clock, and always contained a plate of kippers and poached eggs, but now that the day loomed closer and she still had no more than a glimpse of her soon to be husband, it moved from an everyday fact to an unknown. What was the man she was going to marry like?

"I think it's terrible," she heard a high-pitched, female voice behind her say, tearing her away from her thoughts.

"Yes, but typical.  The poor girl deserves better," another voice chimed in.

"Where do you think he is?"

"I'm sure I don't want to know. You know what kind of reputation he has."

"Why is she marrying him anyway?  She seems so quiet and meek, the poor thing." the first woman asked.

A third voice chimed in, "It's only because of his title, you know. Some people will overlook almost anything just to become Lady Something," she said in nasally over refined tones.

"I heard that it was all arranged years ago before his older brothers died. If so, the family had no idea he would be the next Earl of Rockmorton," the second voice offered.

"That's what they say. No one wants to sound as if that's the reason, you know. As for Lord Montgomery, I heard that the current earl has threatened to cut him off and leave his inheritance to his nephew Rupert if he doesn't go along with the marriage.  The earl probably thinks marriage will curb some of his son's excesses, but men like that never change."

"Perhaps with a little kindness..." the soft spoken first woman started to say.

"No. They don't change," said the nasal voice with a finality that comes from experience.

Caroline felt tears begin to form in her eyes. Her parents wouldn't lead her into an unhappy marriage, would they? She blinked them away as the voices continued.

"I wonder if she knows about—"

"Letitia!" the second voice interrupted. This was followed by a slight gasp and a low, "Do you think she heard?" as the voices moved away.

*What was it the woman had been about to say?* She felt a flutter in her chest as a tiny seed of fear planted itself there.

Caroline looked down and realized that she had begun to unravel the edges of her sash with her picking. She folded it underneath to hide the frayed edges just as her friend Emily came to sit beside her. Emily Whithers was one of the friends she had made in her short season. A tiny girl with mousy brown hair and large brown eyes, Emily was easily overlooked and a bit hard to get to know, but Caroline was glad to have made the effort. She was a good person and a loyal friend.

"How are you?" Emily asked.

"As well as any girl whose fiancé did not show to their own party would be, I suppose."

Emily smiled at her and patted her hand. "I'm

sure he must have a good reason."

"Just like he had all the other times he did not come to see me?  When he came to discuss the wedding agreement with my father, I assumed he would see me then, but I waited all morning and all I got for my troubles was the view of the top of his hat and his back as he walked away." Caroline took a deep breath.  "I'm sorry, I shouldn't speak so.  I'm sure you are right and he has a very good reason."

"Don't apologize, it must be frustrating.  Do you mean to say you have *never* seen him face to face, never talked to him?"

Caroline shook her head.  "Not since I was too young to remember."

Emily's eyes grew wide.  "I can't imagine not knowing anything about the man I was to marry."

Caroline took another deep breath and smiled a bit wanly.  "I'm sure everything will work out fine.  My parents would never do anything that would hurt me.  I trust their judgement."
They both sat side by side in silence for a few minutes, and then Emily said, "I hope your marriage will not affect our friendship.  Although I have not known you long, I feel a deep affection for you and would miss you terribly were we to break contact."

Caroline smiled and put her hand over her friend's.  "Of course not, I feel the same way.  As soon as I'm a married woman, I'll be on the lookout for a good husband for you."

Emily grimaced. "Oh, please, no. You're beginning to sound like my cousin, Sarah. She is coming to stay with us soon and has expressed her desire to find me a husband. At least your choice would be more acceptable. You would try to find someone I would be compatible with. I shudder to think of who cousin Sarah would choose for me. All she cares for is money...and a title of course. But honestly, I have no desire to find a husband."

Caroline gave her friend a puzzle look. "Then why are you here for the season?"

Emily sighed, "My mother. I was happy with my life just the way it was. She convinced my father that I needed to have a season. All my protestations fell on deaf ears and so, here I am."

They both fell into an awkward silence. They both watched as an older man rushed across the room and began speaking urgently to Caroline's parents.

"Is that the Earl of Rockmorten?" Emily asked nodding her head toward the man. "He looks pretty upset."

As she said this, the man's face began to turn red and he began to gesture with his hands.

"Well, who wouldn't be. This dinner was practically given in honor of his son and he didn't even bother to show," Caroline's frustration showed in her voice.

Just then a stern looking, dark-haired man

walked up to the group. He laid his hand on Lord Rockmorten's arm and said a few words. Even from this distance you could see the earl start to relax.

"Who is that man speaking with the earl?" Emily asked.

"Lord Lydford, he's Lord Montgomery's best man for the wedding."

"He looks awful grim. What is he like?"

Caroline shrugged. "He introduced himself pleasantly enough, but other than that I couldn't say."

"Well, I think he looks rather fierce. I don't think I would want him as my enemy," Emily said. They both watched as the gentleman made a quick bow to both of Caroline's parents and strode from the room. "It looks like he's leaving before dinner, how rude."

Caroline shook her head. "It does not surprise me. I think if anything could go wrong during this party it will."

Just then Doyle, the butler, came in and spoke to her mother. She glanced over at Caroline and then turned back to Doyle, said a few words, and hurried over to Caroline.

"What now?" Caroline asked under her breath.

"Oh, Caroline," she said, "I don't know what could be keeping Lord Montgomery. Lord Lydford has kindly gone to check on him, but I do not think we can wait any longer. Doyle has just informed me that the French chef we borrowed from Lady Blackwood is having an apoplexy. He is threatening to throw everything out and start again. He says his creations will be past their peak if we do not eat now and he will not serve food which does not meet his standards. I keep picturing duck and buttered lobster lying in the gutter! Oh, the waste! Oh, the expense!"

"Do whatever you think is best, mama. I don't believe Lord Montgomery is going to show and I would hate to see such a lovely dinner go to waste."

Mrs. Aldridge smiled and patted her daughter on her hand which was lying on the arm of the setee. "You are such a good girl." Then she wrinkled her brow. "I do not know what could have kept him." She walked off, toward the waiting Doyle, shaking her head.

Caroline sighed.

Emily patted her hand. "Don't worry, after people have packed themselves full of French food, they'll all go home and forget that Lord Montgomery was even supposed to come."

Caroline cast doubtful eyes at her friend as Doyle announced dinner and they all began to walk from the sitting room. Caroline was one of the last to leave, even though she would have been at the head being escorted by her future husband had he shown. Instead, she was to be escorted by old Mr. Givens who was deeply in a discussion with Mr. Currans and did not seem to be willing to let him go despite the longing glances the other man was casting toward the door to the dining room.

As she was waiting for Mr. Givens to claim her hand, she heard Mr. Warwick say to Lord Southerland, "Ten to one he doesn't show to the wedding either."

"I'll take that one. I think he likes his money too much to give it up. He'd do about anything to stay in funds. I heard his father threatened to cut him off if he didn't go through with it."

"I think he hates the idea of marriage so much he'd rather be penniless," said Warwick, "And I'm willing to put fifty guineas on it."

"It's a wager. Come with me to White's afterward and we'll put it in the book."

Caroline felt her face burn. Her marriage had become a thing to bet on, and if she were a betting woman, she wasn't sure which way she'd put her money.

The days leading to her wedding passed quickly, days that brought no sign of her fiancé. She lay in bed the night before she was to be married, and realized that tomorrow she would be sharing a bed with a complete stranger. Her heart lurched in her chest. The seed that had been planted the night of the party had been growing ever since and had now burst into full flower.

Where had he been that night? What didn't she know? She felt her breath speed up. Why had he never come to see her? Was there something terribly wrong with him? Was he disfigured? Did he fly into uncontrolled rages? What would he do to her? Could she really go through with this? The thud of her racing heart sounded in her ears. The wedding was tomorrow. What should she do?

"Stop," Caroline said out loud, surprising herself.

She let out a shaky breath. Her imagination was getting out of control. Even if he was not the most handsome man, her husband would not be a beast. Her father had met him, had talked with him. Her father loved her. She was his only child. He would never marry her off to a monster. She took a deep breath and forced herself to calm her mind and turn all those other thoughts away. She didn't need to ask, she knew what she would do. She would walk down the aisle of St. George's church tomorrow morning. The question was, would there be a groom waiting at the end of the aisle?

# Chapter 2


*It doesn't much matter whom one marries,*
*For one is sure to find next morning*
*That it was someone else.*
*-Samuel Rogers*

The church seemed unusually dark and gloomy the morning that Caroline put her hand on her father's arm and began the walk down the aisle of St. George's. There was not even a dim light from the windows which she found strange. Only every fourth candle was lit in the massive chandelier above, which left the edges of the room in darkness. Though there were few candles burning, drops of hot wax were raining down as if the very tapers were weeping at the thought of her impending vows.

She couldn't see the face of the man she was going to marry. She could barely make out dim figures at the end of the aisle which seemed to stretch on forever. It seemed that every echoing step she took brought her no closer to her fate. The oddness of it all made her look around. She was surprised to find that the church was empty except for the three men waiting at the end of the aisle. Where was everyone? Where was her mother? She began to feel a sense of panic growing inside her.

Finally, she reached the end of the long walk and stood before a man who was not the rector of St. George's at all, but a small wizened old man who kept leering at her and rubbing his hands together. He smelled of old sweat and something sweet and musky she couldn't quite place. Her stomach turned in distaste. There was something about the old man that made her feel horribly dirty.

She looked away from him hoping to find solace in the gaze of her soon to be husband. He was still shrouded in darkness, but when he stepped forward to take her hand, she let out a gasp and stepped back toward her father. His face was an unnatural pale as if he was a walking corpse, but it was his eyes that commanded her attention. They were not the brown eyes she had expected, but an unearthly shade of red that seemed to burn through her. She felt her throat tighten and begin to burn from the bile that surged from her stomach.

She turned away from his fiery gaze to look to her father for salvation. He just stood there and smiled as if it were wonderful that he was about to marry his only daughter to Lucifer himself.

The old man presiding over the ceremony rubbed his gnarled hands together and cackled before he began to recite the words of the wedding ceremony. No! She couldn't let this happen. Suddenly her leaden limbs found strength and she began to run as fast as she could back to the doors she had entered. Wedding guests, who had suddenly appeared from nowhere, kept trying to stop her, reaching out and grabbing at her, their clawed hands snatching at her filmy, white overdress. She wrenched away from one monster's grasp only to fall into the clutches of yet another. Sobbing and panting, she finally reached the doors and threw them open to find total blackness outside.

She looked back. The wedding party had almost reached her. She had to make a choice. She glanced at the evil look in the eyes of the man she was supposed to marry, and then out into the deepest darkness she had ever seen. It took only a second to make her decision. She threw herself out the doors and into the unknown. The moment she did, she was falling. Her heart flew up into her throat, the fear almost gagging her as she heard a voice call out, "Miss! Miss! You must wake up! You can't be late for your own wedding!" That was when she crashed, or her world crashed around her she wasn't sure which.

Caroline's eyes flew open. She was staring directly into a pair of brown eyes hovering over her. She gasped her arms flailing out involuntarily to grasp the covers on either side of her.

"Are you alright, Miss?"

Caroline blinked a couple of times and let out the breath she had been unaware of holding. The eyes belonged to Sally, her lady's maid and longtime friend. Sally was standing beside her bed. She was still lying in it. Everything was alright. She took a deep breath and tried to relax, but the images of her dream were still with her and her breath trembled a bit as she exhaled.

"Are you awake now? You must have been having an awful dream, you were thrashing around so."

"Yes," Caroline said, pulling herself into a sitting position. "I'm fine now."

"Well then, you'd best get up. I brought you some tea and toast. It's on your dressing table."

"Thank you," said Caroline rising and walking over to it.

Sally gave her an odd look and began to bustle around the room, moving things around that didn't really need moved and glancing at her from under her lashes. Caroline knew she wasn't telling her something, but she also knew Sally, and she knew that she could never keep that something in for long.

She sat at the table and took a bite of toast, but her mouth was so dry she had trouble swallowing it and when she did her stomach did not want to accept it. So, she concentrated on her tea instead. Sally began to get louder in her ministrations until finally she stopped and stood in front of Caroline.

"I know it is not my place, I'm just a maid after all, but I just can't help it. You can't grow up with someone all their lives and not say something," she burst out.

"Sally, you know that you are not just a maid. I think of you as a bit of a big sister too."

Sally smiled and some of the tension left her. "Well, yes, and a big sister could not just sit by and let her little sister make a mistake, could she?"

"What are you suggesting?"

"Perhaps this dream is an omen, Miss. It can't be good to have a nightmare on the morning of your wedding. Perhaps it is a warning of some kind."

"Don't be silly," Caroline said though her heart jumped at the prospect.

"I just don't think this marriage the best thing for you. I have heard some gossip and I don't like what I have heard. I'm sure you have heard some things too. Do you really want to marry Lord

Montgomery?"

Caroline did not know what she thought.  How could she know?  She had never met him.  She was afraid, her dream had proved that, but she had never gone against her parents in anything.   In the seventeen years of her life, she had never had to make a decision of her own and she had never even thought of doing so.  Her parents had always done that for her and everything had always turned out fine.     Surely her fears were ungrounded, just the silly imaginings of a young girl.  She would be a married woman soon.  It was time to grow up.

Caroline straightened her shoulders, forced her lips into a smile, and replied airily, "Of course I am sure.  It has been settled forever.  I always knew that when I came of age, I would be marrying Lord Montgomery.  Do you think I would even for one moment consider crying off such a long-standing engagement, let alone on the morning of the wedding?   My goodness, Sally, think of the scandal.  Even though I know little about my intended, I'm sure Papa would never marry me off to a complete blackguard.  I wouldn't worry if I were you."

"Yes, Miss," Sally said as she turned back to her work, grumbling under her breath about a body being able to worry about whatever she pleased.

Caroline smiled a bit at her friend's concern as she sipped her tea.  She was glad that Sally would be going with her to her new home.  It would be good to have at least one familiar face around her. Lord knew it wouldn't be her husband's. She felt her stomach drop as the thought came to her.

Caroline sat at her dressing table and Sally began to brush her hair.  She felt very small.  At only eighteen, she felt not old enough to be someone's wife, but she was soon to be Lady Montgomery. It certainly was strange how things turned out.

She heard the sound of Sally's voice chattering on as she finished with her hair and began dressing her.  She moved automatically her mind still occupied with thoughts of this odd marriage.

"All done Miss, and you look lovelier than I've ever seen you, if I may say so," Sally said pulling Caroline over to the glass, "See for yourself."

Caroline blinked as if coming out of a dream. She almost didn't recognize herself as she gazed at the young woman before her in the looking glass. Sally had certainly outdone herself.  Her hair was an intricate arrangement of braids and curls interwoven with white ribbon and interspersed with pearls.  Her cream dress fit her perfectly, making her look more like a woman than she felt. The neckline was lower than she was used to, but still high enough not to be immodest by today's standards. The capped sleeves were so sheer it seemed that if she pressed the material between her fingers, it would melt away like frost on a leaf.

Her skirt fell straight to the ground from the sash tied just beneath her breasts. She touched the band of embroidered leaves and tiny beaded flowers which was worked in white on the sheer cuffs and was repeated along the hem then looked back at the image before her. She caught the eye of Sally in the reflection standing behind her.

"Thank you, Sally. You have made me beautiful."

Sally flushed with pleasure. "Thank you, Miss, but I didn't do anything except fix your hair. You are beautiful on your own."

A tap sounded on the door. Caroline was glad of the interruption, for the way Sally was looking at her was beginning to make her cry.

"The carriage is ready and waiting, Miss" came the voice of a footman from outside.

Caroline blinked back her tears as she opened the door.

"I'm ready," she said and stepped out the door not feeling ready at all. She threw an unsure smile at Sally as she left the room. Her stomach flew to her throat once more as she was hurried down the stairs, bundled into a gaily decorated carriage and started on her journey to the church. Her parents sat silently on the seat opposite her. Her father looking even more stern than usual and her mother with a smile that seemed painted on her face and eyes that were too bright. Were they tears?

"Are you all right, mama?" Caroline asked.

Her mother started, as if any break in her concentration would melt her carefully constructed façade. Her eyes flicked quickly toward her daughter and then away, and then she took a deep breath, smiled even more brightly and said, "Why whatever could be wrong, dearest?"

"I'm not sure, mama. Everyone just seems so strained today. In fact, it's felt odd all week, and I had the strangest dream. Do you think it means anything?"

"I'm sure it must be all the excitement," her mother said and turned away quickly, leaving Caroline even more puzzled and unsure.

All too soon the church came into view. The driver brought the carriage to a halt at the front entrance. Before her mother got out of the carriage she turned back toward her daughter and grabbed her in a quick embrace. As she did so she whispered, "It won't be that bad dearest, but remember, if you ever need my help, I'm always here for you." Then she squeezed her tightly, turned and exited the carriage.

Caroline stared blankly for a moment. It won't be that bad? It won't be that bad! What did her mother mean! The fear that started in her dream began to feel like it was choking her. She looked frantically around the carriage, her eyes darting around, like a rabbit trying to find its way out of a trap, until settling ,at last, on the one solid thing in her life, her father.

"Now Caroline," her father said firmly, "you need to go in there.  Everyone is waiting.  Just think, you will be an earl's wife someday and have all the privileges that come with it.  Although that came as a pleasant surprise, this marriage was not.   There has been an understanding since practically the day you were born and Edward was just a lad of ten."

"I know papa," she said quietly looking down at her hands lying in her lap.

Her father leaned over and gathered her hands in his.  "Caro, everything will be alright.  I never told you why we arranged this marriage for you.  I think you need to know. Plenty of parents arrange marriages for a title, but you know that wasn't our purpose.  We had no idea Edward would inherit the title."

He brought one of his hands away from hers, placed it under her chin and tilted it up so that he could look into her eyes.  "We love you, Caro.  We want only the best for you.  We didn't want to see you crushed by a man who thinks of you only as his possession.  A man is formed by his parents and the example they give him.  Edward grew up with loving parents.   Until the day of Lady Rockmorten's death, they were inseparable.  That was how he saw a marriage, and that is what he will expect for himself.   I truly believe he will make you a good husband.  If I did not, I could never give you to him. It was in him when he was a little boy. He was a kind boy, a little more rambunctious than most, but he had a kind heart. I don't know what rumours you have heard, or the veracity of them, but all you need to know, or think about, is that he had a kind heart. He needs your help, Caro, to find it again."

Caroline wasn't certain what to think. She knew that her father would only do what he thought was best for her, but he had only known Lord Montgomery as a boy. What kind of man he had grown into he did not claim to know. What about these rumours? Were they true? What sort of man was she marrying? What was it that was so horrible no one would tell her?

"Caroline?"

Caroline blinked.

"Ready to go?" Her father had exited the carriage and was holding his hand out to help her down.

"Yes, Papa," she said forcing a smile on her face. She put her hand in his and ducked her head as she got out of the carriage.

Once she was down, her father offered her his arm and they walked to the door. As she stepped through it and into the entry of St. George's, the only thought in her buzzing head was, *soon I shall see the man with whom I will be spending the rest of my life. I hope he is not awful.* The music started as Caroline and her father began the long procession down the aisle toward her future.

·

# Chapter 3

*...very few husbands love their wives;*
*and I confess,*
*the moment one is obliged to marry any person*
*it is enough to render them hateful.*
*-Caroline, Princess of Wales*

As they made their way down the aisle Caroline was relieved to see that her future did not look as horrible as she had feared. She let out the breath she had been holding and her heart leapt as hope began to enter it. She was marrying a very handsome man. Dark hair, slightly long, and arranged in artistic disarray, curled around his face. It was a cherubic face, rounded cheeks, full lips, but with a nose too strong to be angelic.      No, rather like Michelangelo's 'David'. That's it, I have my own David, and from what my father said his eyes are probably full of mischief.  She started to smile to herself at the thought, but her smile faded as she drew closer and saw the signs of dissipation that had begun to show their mark on that beautiful visage.

His cheeks, upon closer examination, were more flabby than full.  His skin, like marble from afar, was upon closer inspection more a sickly pale, as if he were not used to the light of day.  A bit of a paunch was noticeable beneath the well-cut coat he wore.  She watched him as his eyes swept over her body in a lascivious manner which turned her stomach.  Then they swept back up and looked straight into her eyes.  His eyes were a beautiful, piercing blue.  Not full of mischief as she had imagined, or full of an unearthly fire as in her dreams, but completely dead, cold.  So cold she actually shivered as she walked the last few steps to him and her father placed her hand on his.  To her relief he quickly turned those eyes toward the bishop.  She felt as if she would have swooned if he had kept that expressionless gaze on her one moment more.

The ceremony went by in a blur, but apparently, she spoke at all the right times and said all the right things, for all too soon that cold look was upon her once more. As he turned to kiss her with a smile which didn't reach his eyes, Caroline thought she would be sick, but it was over in a second as he gave her a quick peck and turned them both to be introduced for the first time as Lord and Lady Montgomery.  Then they made their way down the center aisle and out of the church.

As she stepped out from the dim interior of the church, the sun shone brightly down upon her face.  This was said to be a good omen, but she began to doubt the veracity of this claim as she was practically dragged by her husband down the church steps.  He hurriedly helped her into the waiting carriage and got in behind her.  Then they were on their way to the wedding breakfast.

Edward lounged back in his seat and looked at her from under drooping eyelids.

"I imagine that went as well as could be expected."

"Yes," Caroline answered quietly still rather shaken from the experience.

"Ah yes, but there is still the wedding breakfast to get through," he said with a bored sigh. "All that – 'wish you well' and 'so happy for you' as if they didn't know we'd never set eyes on each other before the moment we stood in front of the altar, unless of course you count the time when you were two."

Caroline pressed her lips together. *Whose fault is that? We invited you to come for a weekend in the country.  You never came. We had a dinner party in your honor which you chose not to attend.  You never even spared an afternoon to call on your betrothed.  When the marriage settlement was finalized, you discussed it with my father and then left, never even caring to see your bride to be.  You never thought of my feelings at all.  I was just a business transaction. Did you not think I may have wanted to see more of my intended than the back of a male walking away from my house?*

She said nothing except, "Yes," and looked down at her hands.

"Not very talkative, are you?  Ah well, at least you won't be nattering at me night and day.  I never could stomach a garrulous woman.  There are times I do like a woman to be more vocal though," he said, raising his eyebrows and looking at her with a leer on his face as he reached for her.

Caroline nearly flew off the seat jerking away from him.  She quickly glanced at him, eyes filled with fear and revulsion, before dropping her eyes once more to her hands clenched in her lap.

"Oh, is that the way it is" he sneered.  Gone was the bored aristocrat.  Now his cold eyes were flashing hot with anger. "I hate to break it to you dear wife but that title you just bought back there needs to be paid for. You need to supply me with an heir.  That does involve a certain amount of touching, most of it in a much more intimate manner than I just attempted with you.  Do not think I find it any more to my liking than you do, I am not partial to milk and water misses of which you so obviously are.  I like women with more spirit."

Then it was as if he put a mask on and he went back to his former lounging position, his eyes drooping closed once more. "Ah, but we have to learn to make do with what we have, don't we?" With that comment he turned his head and gazed lazily at the passing scene ignoring her completely.

Caroline could not believe what she had heard. Had he really insulted her so fully?  Her emotions were churning and changing so fast she didn't even know how she felt.  Shock, anger, fear, and hopelessness all warred for a front position in her mind.  She sat completely mute until, at last, they reached her father's house.

When the driver stopped, Edward jumped down and reached his hand up to her to help her down.  She hesitated, taking it only because if she did not, she would probably have tripped on her dress and fallen flat on her face in front of her guests.  He quickly released her hand, almost throwing it down as soon as she reached the pavement, and looked as if he was going to stalk off before he checked himself and offered her his arm to escort her inside.

The wedding breakfast was a nightmare.

People seemed to be everywhere. Faces flashed before her wishing her well. Her husband quickly distanced himself from her. She felt lost and a little dizzy after all the pressures of the morning. She had only nibbled on the toast Sally had brought her this morning and was grateful to find herself ushered into a seat at the table.

Caroline found herself seated next to Lady Kittredge an outspoken lady from the last generation. She had always felt intimidated by this great aunt of her new husband. She closed her eyes and sighed. The fates must indeed be against her.

"Well dear, you certainly have done well for yourself, haven't you?" Lady Kittredge croaked as if her voice had given up years ago, beaten into submission by her iron will.

"Yes, Lady Kittredge"

"Ah yes, a future earl," she looked at Edward who was asking for more wine, "and a fine specimen of manhood too if I might add. Of course, you might not believe it now, but my Fitzwilliam was too, before the drink got to him."

Caroline looked at the fat, florid-faced man leering at the maid serving him pheasant. Her stomach turned over, as she had the dreadful feeling she was looking at her own future.

"...best to plan the next day's activities. It's rather like killing two birds with one stone." Lady Kittredge finished laughing at her joke. Caroline blinked as Lady Kittredge's laugh brought her back from her dismal thoughts.

"Excuse me?  I'm sorry I... I ..." Caroline stuttered unsure of what to say.

"Oh, of course, I'm sorry if I offended your sensibilities," was the biting reply. "You younger generation, nothing but a bunch of milk and water misses."

Caroline pressed her lips together in frustration. It was the second time she had been called a milk and water miss that day.  Her eyes flashed in a moment of defiance. She was no milk and water miss!  She was not going to stand for this.

She pulled herself up straight, looked Lady Kittredge straight in the eyes and said in a strong, firm voice, "I am sorry Lady Kittredge I was not attending to what you were saying.  If you would care to repeat yourself, I am sure I would love to know what it is you were telling me,"

Lady Kittredge raised her eyebrows.  There was a good deal of mirth in her eyes as she said, "In that case my dear, I shall be glad to repeat it for you.  I was letting you know that I had found it helpful during conjugal activities to plan the next day's menus and schedules.  I've heard some say 'think of England' and all such mush, but I've always found it more practical to do my planning. You can accomplish two things at once." She broke off and her face lit up with a devilish grin before she added, "Of course, one must commit the list to memory as it is not practical to actually write it."

Her cackling laugh filled Caroline's ears as she blushed to the roots of her hair. Why had she opened her mouth? She would much rather have remained the milk and water miss Lady Kittredge supposed her to be.

She bowed her head and looked from under her lashes at the man beside her. Her stomach tightened and she almost brought up the three mouthfuls of food she had managed to keep down in the last fifteen minutes. It was apparent that her husband had not eaten much either. He had been filling himself with much more drink than food. His laughter was becoming more and more raucous, his words slurring.

When would this breakfast end? No! She didn't want it to end. Then she would have to go home with this loathsome creature. God help me! What have I done?

After the horrid discussion with Lady Kittredge, Caroline decided her best defense was to retreat back into the incoherent numbness she felt during the ceremony. The rest of the breakfast went by in a blur. By the time Edward stumbled over to claim his bride, Caroline was ready to swoon from lack of nourishment and the strain of it all. The last thing she saw as she numbly allowed him to lead her unsteadily out of the breakfast to her new home was her mother's worried expression.

The drive was a silent affair, as the groom was so intoxicated he could barely keep himself upright, and the bride was so terrified all she could do was sit and stare at nothing. All too soon Caroline saw the Montgomery town house come into view. She knew it was his because her parents had pointed it out to her. It was quite large as townhouses go, much larger than the one her parents had rented for the season. Caroline would have been impressed, but very little penetrated the shell she had built around herself, so the house went unappreciated.

The staff was assembled in the hall awaiting the arrival of their master and new mistress. Their faces were a blur, as a shocked Caroline was dragged past with no introductions at all except a few incoherent mumbles from her husband. He pulled her through the hall and up the stairs before she knew what was happening, and suddenly she found herself thrust into the master's chambers.

Edward began removing his coat and cravat. Caroline heard a rip as he struggled drunkenly with the tight-fitting coat. She tried to melt into the shadows along the walls of the room. Whatever was he doing? Whatever would he do to her?   Caroline knew little about the relations between man and wife except that she heard it was painful and that it was a duty every wife must bear, no matter how distasteful.  Was this what her mother had meant when she said it shouldn't be that bad? She felt a wave of dizziness wash over her. She did not think, after the strain of the day, she would be able to bear it.

Her private musings were interrupted by the vision of a large, stumbling, grim looking man approaching.  Caroline panicked.  She tried to scramble away, tripping on her dress in the process. Edward's hands reached to grab her and all her fear burst into action. She fought for all she was worth, clawing and scratching at anything within reach.

Edward released her with a curse, and she looked up to see him towering over her with clenched fists and a face full of rage.  Fear and hopelessness filled her as she suddenly realized her fate.  She looked into his eyes and saw something unknown flicker there for a moment before he turned away.

"I don't need this," he growled, "I can find plenty of women who will give me what I want. You're not worth the effort. You will give me an heir though, so get that through your pretty little vacuous head while I am gone. I will be back, and you will behave and give me what is rightfully mine! Enjoy your reprieve, wife."

He grabbed his coat and cravat and stalked out the door, slamming it behind him.

Caroline sank to the floor, finally completely overcome, covered her face with her hands, and wept. She wasn't sure how long she remained in this position before she heard a light tap at the door. Caroline stood and tried to put herself in some semblance of order before answering, "Yes?"

The door opened to reveal Sally with a face full of compassion. Apparently, the news of her embarrassing wedding night had reached the ears of the servants. Caroline's fragile hold on her newly won control broke, and with a burst of tears she reached out to Sally.

"It's alright, Sally's here," the maid said, closing the door quickly and walking to her mistress. She led her to a small settee by the fire and held her in her arms rocking her back and forth murmuring soft words of comfort until Caroline began to calm. When she was as limp as a rag doll, Sally helped her up and supported her until she could stand on her own.

"Come Miss, we need to get you to bed," she said, leading her from the master bedroom to Caroline's own suite through the adjoining door. At the sound of the word 'bed' Caroline shivered, but she was too drained to do any more than that, and passively allowed Sally to lead her to her room. Once there, Sally helped her undress, pulled her nightgown over her head and tucked her between the cool, crisp sheets.  Her duties finished Sally turned to go.

"Please, stay with me," begged Caroline's voice from the bed like a scared child.

"Surely Miss, as long as you'd like," she said pulling a comfortable chair beside the bed.

"Thank you, I just don't think I could bear to be alone."

Sally sat down and patted her mistress's hand. "You get some sleep now," she said and smoothing Caroline's hair back from her forehead, she began to hum a song her mother sang to her as a child. Caroline nodded slightly and within minutes was sound asleep.

# Chapter 4



*Manner is all in all, what e'er is writ,*
*The substitute for genius, sense, and wit.*
*-William Cowper*

After three days, her husband was not back. Things were slowly getting better for Caroline. The first day was the worst. She did not even want to get out of bed that morning, but Sally, who had slept in the chair at her bedside all night, insisted she must.

"My Lady," she said using Caroline's new title for the first time, "you must set a precedent with the servants on your first day. The unfortunate way you were presented, or rather *not* presented, to them yesterday by Lord Montgomery must be overcome."

So Caroline let a chattering Sally bathe and dress her and fix her hair, while she sat mute and staring, moving only when prompted by her maid.

"My Lady!" Sally's sharp voice broke through her numbness, and she forced herself to focus, finding herself looking directly into the eyes of her maid. "You must pull yourself together. You must show them that though you are young, you are strong, and deserve their respect. How you begin in your dealings with these servants is how it will remain. Unless you want your wishes to be completely disregarded, you must not show weakness. You know this is true."

This short speech of Sally's struck a chord deep within Caroline. She knew her friend was right. She had to summon the strength to let the servants know that it was she who was in charge. She took a deep breath, pulled her shoulders back and with head perfectly erect stood and walked regally to the door.

"Thank you, Sally, I am ready," she said and opened the door to her new life as Lady Montgomery.

Over the next few days, she found that the servants treated her with the appropriate respect. There were a few incidents. Conversations that stopped abruptly when she came into a room, and once she thought she saw a footman smirk at her, but when she looked sharply at him his face was appropriately expressionless once more.

Mrs. Hutchinson, the housekeeper, was extremely cordial.  She showed her the books, which were in perfect order, introduced her properly to the staff in the absence of the master of the house, and took her on a tour of her new house pointing out things of interest.  As she showed her around, she talked about the family which she had been with for many years.

"Here is the ballroom," she said with pride. "There are not many who can boast of having a ballroom in their London residence, but Lady Rockmorten loved to dance.  She loved people, and Lord Rockmorten loved her and so they threw magnificent parties.  Those two were a pair.  I've never seen two people so much in love.  They were completely dedicated to each other until the day she passed.  And Lord Rockmorten was dedicated to her even after that.  He never remarried.  He finished raising those boys on his own.  It broke what was left of his heart when he received the news of his middle son's death at the battle of Assaye and if that were not enough, just weeks later he lost his eldest son to the influenza.  Those were dark times.  Of course, Edward had already been trying to kill himself by--," she stopped in embarrassment remembering who it was she was talking to.

"Oh, how I can go on.  Now dearie, don't you

worry.  That boy has always been a bit of a wild one, especially when he got older, but he hasn't got a truly mean bone in his body.  He's always had to be a tough one, first to prove something to his older brothers and then to prove something to himself, but I suspect there's a lot of gentleness in there just waiting to come out.  We always thought marriage would do the trick, but that don't seem –," she stopped her musing and looked at Caroline with wide eyes, then infusing her voice with an optimism she obviously didn't feel, she ended with, "but it's early days yet.  There's no telling what a good lady in his life will do.  It sure would be good to see Master Edward, Lord Montgomery now, smile a real smile again."

Caroline didn't care.  She didn't care if Master Edward never smiled a real smile for the rest of his life.  He could leer at every woman in London if he wanted, as long as he left her alone.

"Yes. Mrs. Hutchinson, did you say something about linens earlier?"

"Oh my, yes, right this way, my lady," Mrs. Hutchinson said as she led her to the third floor obviously relieved to be back to a safe subject like household goods.

Caroline spent a lot of time with Mrs. Hutchinson over the next few days as she became very involved with the workings of the house and even began redecorating some of the rooms in her mind.  Of course, she would have to ask her husband for permission first, but that was merely a formality. She doubted he cared what she did. He had become a shadowy figure in the back of her mind. Yet she could not get too hasty with her decorating, lest he send her to the country. But, oh, wouldn't that be wonderful, a house all to herself to do whatever she pleased with. The freedom to do whatever she wanted, whenever she wanted. Such were Caroline's dreams as the days passed.

Five days after her marriage to Lord Montgomery, her mother came to call. After being seated in the drawing room she looked searchingly at her daughter and asked, "How do you find married life, dear?"

"Fine, mama," Caroline answered.

Her mother's brows rose a bit at this answer, but she continued, "I have not seen you at any of the entertainments I attended. I wanted to give you and Edward time together, but I just had to check and see how you were faring."

"I have been doing fine, as I said, mama. I have been spending my time learning the management of the house. Mrs. Hutchinson and I have spent many hours together and I have a much better understanding of its workings. I am amazed at the decisions that have to be made. I never realized how much you did. I fear I took it all for granted."

Her mother smiled. "It is good to see that you are taking your position seriously, my dear, but you do not need to accomplish everything in one day. I'm sure your husband will be impressed by your abilities in time. You need to spend some of your time in more enjoyable pursuits."

"Oh, but I do enjoy it. It keeps my mind busy during the day."

"That's not quite what I meant, dear," she paused and looked around. "Where is Lord Montgomery?"

"Oh, somewhere about, he has much to keep him busy too," she said airily, inwardly cringing as she thought about what those things might be.

Her mother's eyes narrowed as she asked, "Are you certain everything is alright?"

"Do you think I would lie?" Caroline asked, feeling slightly guilty at her protest as she had been stretching the truth quite a bit, but it was only to spare her mother worry.

Mrs. Aldridge sighed, "No, of course not dear, I suppose I have not accustomed myself to your being married." She looked a bit sheepish as she continued, "I'm sorry if I seemed slightly melodramatic on the morning of your wedding. It is quite affecting to give your only daughter away. I had never realized how much. Your only daughter's wedding night...well...and your father and I had recently heard rumours of Edward drinking heavily and we were concerned. His behavior at the wedding breakfast did nothing to ease our fears, in fact it only made them worse.

Tell me, his drinking hasn't been a problem has it dearest?"

"I can honestly say that since our wedding night Lord Montgomery's drinking has not affected me in the least."

"Truly?"

"Truly, mother, I have not seen him take a single drink since that night." Every word of which was true as she had not set eyes on him since that dreadful night.

Her mother smiled. "That is a relief. From what we had heard we were afraid we had inadvertently married you off to a drunkard. So everything is alright with you?"

"Yes, everything is wonderful. It is much better than I thought it would be," thinking that this also was true as she had not had to deal with a husband at all. "Why do you ask?"

Her mother smiled and sighed as if a great weight had been lifted from her shoulders. "Well, I had to make sure everything was alright with you before I could decide." Her face became serious once more, "Everything *is* alright?"

"Yes, for goodness sake, yes. Now what decision is it that you have to make?"

Her mother's face lit up as she said, "Your father wants to take me abroad for a while."

"Abroad?"

"Yes, abroad, to tour the continent. I don't know if I ever told you, but I've always wanted to travel. Once you married, it seemed that there was really nothing to keep us here, so your father made some arrangements and now, off we go! I didn't even know until yesterday. He had planned it as a surprise. He knew it would be hard for me to see my only child go and thought this would be just the thing to cheer me up, but I told him I would not leave if you needed us."

Having not seen her husband for days, Caroline had acquired a sense of security. Had her mother visited her the day after her marriage, she would have been greeted by a much different daughter. This daughter had been dreaming dreams of an independent life, and so had the confidence to assure her mother of her contentedness.

"Mother, I am perfectly fine, and now even better knowing how happy you will be too. I have always known of your desire to travel. I remember hearing it in your voice as you told me tales from different lands. You loved Marco Polo and Scheherazade and all the adventures the tales described. Now you can have your own adventure. Perhaps you can bring home the talking bird, just remember to take some cotton to stuff in your ears," she said with a smile.

Laughter tinkled from her mother's lips. "Well, I don't believe Africa or India were on our itinerary."

"Even so, mama, I am so excited for you. Now tell me when does this adventure start?"

"That is the most surprising part, for your father has booked us a passage next Thursday, so we will be leaving London on Tuesday to arrive in Dover in plenty of time before the ship sails."

"Tuesday! However will you be ready in time?"

Her mother's eyes twinkled as she rose from her seat. "By beginning as soon as I arrive home. I have to go tell your father that all my concerns were for nothing, and that we shall be able to go according to his plans. Oh, I must say it feels like a dream," she said and grabbed her daughter in a great hug. "We shall be leaving very early Tuesday morning so I may not see you before then, but if you need anything before we leave, don't hesitate to ask. You know that you mean much more to your father and me than any trip we could take."

"I know, mama, I love you too," Caroline said and hugged her mother once more. "Now, I expect you to write from every place you visit and tell me what you have seen and done. Don't forget, for I shall be traveling vicariously through your letters and don't want to miss a thing." Caroline walked her mother to the door where they shared a last hug. "I will try to visit you before you leave, but I am not sure if Lord Montgomery has plans," she said, suddenly unsure of what the man she was now wed to would do when, or if, he returned before her parent's departure.

"Of course dear, things are so hectic at this time

of year and you have just compounded it by entering into marriage. You need time with your husband more than time with your mother. You have a lot to get used to. By the time we return you will have it all figured out, and who knows, perhaps you will be on the way to becoming a mother yourself."

She squeezed Caroline's hand in hers and gave her a quick peck on the cheek before leaving the house wreathed in smiles, too absorbed in her own happy thoughts to notice the stricken look that came over her daughter's face at the mention of motherhood.

The next afternoon, Caroline was in the sitting room with Lady Stahlwood and Lady Wharton who had come to pay their respects and see how the new bride was getting along. Caroline knew they were nosey biddies just looking for some gossip, but they were good ton and it was never good to refuse a call from someone of their standing.

Lady Stahlwood was a plump motherly looking woman. Her brown curling hair threaded with grey, and her innocent looking blue eyes, gave the impression of someone you could share your troubles with, and that is exactly the way she liked it. If you had not heard of her reputation and didn't notice the sharpness that came into her soft eyes as you poured out your troubles, you would never believe that she was the one behind the fact that everyone knew your story by the next morning.

Lady Wharton was as thin as her friend was plump. She had a sharp angular face, long nose and protruding grey eyes. Her lips were thin, and seemed to be set in an expression of perpetual disapproval. She sat stiffly erect in contrast to her friends slightly rounded shoulders. She was not someone you would share things with, but she had the advantage of being quiet. She would almost seem to disappear as a poor unsuspecting female would pour out her troubles to the seemingly empathetic Lady Stahlwood. In fact, many times when the ladies got up to leave, their hostess would look at her other visitor in surprise having forgotten her very presence.

They were here to sniff out the story from this young new bride and were feeling rather disappointed to find everything perfectly normal and their host happy and at ease. In fact, they were just preparing to tell their host that they regretfully had other calls to make, when suddenly there was a thud coming from the entrance hall. This was followed by a scraping sound and a loud bump, like something hitting the other side of the wall. The older ladies jumped slightly and looked at each other, eyes gleaming in gleeful surprise.

They might have time to stay just a while longer. The lamentingly uneventful visit might turn out to be interesting after all.

There was definitely something strange about this marriage.  Hadn't Lord Montgomery been seen on his wedding night at White's Gentleman's Club?  What man goes to White's on his wedding night?   And two nights later hadn't Lady Dalrimple said she had seen him forcibly ejected from the Hendy's townhouse after trying to gain entrance to their party in an extremely intoxicated state?  Now, here was his wife who was clearly trying to act as if nothing was wrong, but looking increasingly uncomfortable about the ruckus in the hall.  They may be privy to one of the most delectable on dits of the season.  They couldn't wait to see what would happen next.

"Excuse me for just one moment," Caroline said rising after the second bump sounded about a foot away from the first.

"Certainly," Lady Stahlwood replied, her eyes wide and innocent, "Honoria and I will just visit and partake of your wonderful tea."

As Caroline moved toward the door, she heard another bump followed by a loud groan.  She looked back at the ladies who had paused with their cups of tea halfway to their mouths which were hanging open, tried to smile, though she was sure it was more of a grimace, and quickly exited the room before anything more could happen.

"What is going –," she began but never finished, for the sight before her eyes rendered her speechless.  Her husband, half naked, with wet hair plastered to his head, his face crimson, and eyes nothing but slits was being held up, just barely, by the previously smirking footman.  The footman was definitely not smirking now as it took all of his strength to keep the nearly insensible man off the floor.  As the footman staggered under his weight, Roth, Edward's valet, appeared at his master's side.  He threw Edward's arm over his shoulder and grabbed his waist just before his legs collapsed completely and he hung there between the two men.

"Take him to his room," she spit out, her disgust showing plainly in her voice.  She began to turn back to the sitting room and her guests when she stopped.  Wrinkling her nose she added, "And do something about that horrible smell."

She walked to the door of the sitting room and stood there with her eyes closed, her hand resting on the knob breathing deeply and trying to gain control of herself.

How could he do this to her?  Leave one night drunk and six days later come staggering into his front hall so drunk he could not even stand on his own, and with two of London's notorious gossips in his sitting room, just on the other side of the wall.  She was sure that all of London would know about this by tonight.  Was this to be her life, her drunken husband giving the gossip mill another story every week?  Banishment to the country could not come fast enough.  Unfortunately, now she needed to go back into the sitting room and try to diffuse the situation.  She knew they probably would not believe anything she told them anyway, but she had to say something.  She took a deep breath, pasted a smile on her face, and opened the door to the lion's den.

The ladies were still seated, but she had the distinct feeling that they had been leaning toward the door and snapped to an upright position as she entered.

"I'm so sorry about the disturbance.  Such a ruckus about nothing," she lied. "It seems that the footman knocked against a table and the vase on top fell.  He tried to catch it, but apparently tripped over his own feet, for he fell against the wall.  I am glad to say the footman is alright, but the vase is a total loss.  It should be cleaned up by the time we've finished with our tea."

The falsehoods fairly flew out of her mouth. She had never been much of a liar before, but felt she was becoming quite adept at them since her marriage.  As she finished her speech, she sat down, picked up her now cold tea, and ventured a look at the ladies' reaction over the rim of her cup. Lady Wharton shot her a dubious look before she took a sip of her tea, but said nothing. The rest of the visit went by without incident.

As she was seeing the ladies out, she caught Lady Wharton looking at the table against the wall. There in all its splendor was the very vase she had declared destroyed by the footman. Apparently, lying did not come to her as easily as she had thought. The ladies gave each other a knowing look as they walked out the door, probably already making plans to stop at the nearest gossip's house to spread their story.

Caroline could do nothing about it so she headed back to the sitting room to gather her sewing and proceed to the room she felt the most comfortable in, the morning room. Danvers entered the room just as she had picked up her basket and cleared his throat.

"Yes, Danvers?"

"I just wanted to inform you, my lady, that the physician has been summoned and will probably wish to speak to you shortly."

"Physician!" Caroline said, her surprise showing on her face, "Surely there is no need to call a physician for his condition. Won't he just sleep it off?"

"Mrs. Hutchinson believed it was imperative as his fever is so high."

"Fever?" Caroline repeated dumbly.

"Yes, my lady, as I said, it is quite high. That is why we summoned the physician. I would have consulted you first, but I thought it would be unwise considering the company you were entertaining."

*So, he knew what kind of gossips they are too. How incredibly callous I must have seemed, but how was I to know he was ill? When he left, he was drunk. Given my limited experience with the man, was it so wrong to think him to be even more so when he finally returned?* She passed her hand over her eyes and faced Danvers.

"Yes Danvers, you were perfectly right not to disturb us again. You know that I trust Mrs. Hutchinson's judgment completely, so if she thought the doctor needed to be summoned, I am sure she was absolutely right in doing so. Please direct the physician to me after his examination. I shall be in the morning room."

"Yes, my lady," Danvers said and held the door for her. She finished gathering her sewing and quit the room heading for the morning room on the second floor.

The morning room had quickly become her favorite place in the house. The bluish-green walls seemed to sooth her spirit, while the white woodwork and many windows overlooking a small walled garden made all but the dreariest days seem bright. If ever a soul needed soothed and brightened, right now, it was hers.

She sat in a chair by one of the windows, her sewing sitting disregarded in her lap. Guilt lay heavy on her. For not only had she been callous in her attitude toward her husband when he was ill, but she had actually found herself thinking when she had first learned of his fever, that it would be remarkably convenient if he would just die.  Immediately after thinking such horrible thoughts, she felt incredibly ashamed, but the fact remained that it seemed much more preferable to be a widow than the married life she had known in his presence thus far.

She was interrupted in her musings by Danvers who was showing the physician into the room. Caroline motioned to the chair across from her and invited him to sit down.

"Please have a seat."

"Thank you, but only for a moment," he said. "Unfortunately, there has been a spate of illness lately.  I am much in demand, but I did want to inform you of the seriousness of your husband's condition."  He searched Caroline's eyes as if trying to ascertain something, then nodded slightly as if coming to a decision before continuing. "My lady, the truth is, it does not look very good.  His fever is so high he is insensible. You will need to keep applying cold compresses to his head.  They will need to be changed constantly as the fever is so high that they heat up in less than a minute.  Contrary to popular opinion, I do not believe that bleeding is of any good use, but that in fact it weakens the system, so I have not bled him.  Willow bark is known to help, but at this point it is difficult just to get enough liquid in him to keep him alive. I have left a small packet with your housekeeper to administer as soon as you are able, but I am afraid that beyond that I cannot be of much use to you."

He glanced away for a moment and sighed before fixing her with his steady, probing gaze and continuing.

"I will be brutally honest with you, Lady Montgomery, I do not know if your husband will make it through this or not. He is young and strong, that is in his favor, but we will not know for a few days whether it is enough. The next few days are going to be very difficult. We need to try to keep him still. He may thrash around quite a bit in the throes of the fever. The most important things are to try to cool him down, keep liquids in him, and keep him as still as possible. Do the best you can and if things begin to turn for the worse do not hesitate to give me a call, though I'm not sure if there is much else I can do."

At the stricken look on Caroline's face, he added gently, "Do not worry, Lady Montgomery, your housekeeper knows what to do. You do not even need to be present in the sickroom. Your husband will probably not be aware of your presence there anyway. There really is not much you can do but wait. And now, I really must be going," he said rising.

Yes, I understand," said Caroline as she rose to show the physician out. "Thank you for your time and your honesty. We will inform you if his condition worsens."

After ringing for Danvers to show the physician out, Caroline forced herself to climb the steps to the door of her husband's room. She had avoided it in all the days he was gone. The memories there were horribly unpleasant. She had finally buried them deep in her mind and had no desire to resurrect them.

Not only that, but she had no idea what to do. She had never nursed anyone in her life. She knew that as a wife it was her duty to nurse her husband, but she hated the thought. Her family had been blessed with inordinately good health and so she had never seen anything beyond a sniffle before, certainly nothing this serious. He could actually die, possibly right in front of her very eyes. Feeling that his death would be convenient and experiencing that event first hand were two different things. She found herself praying that he would recover, or at least, if he had to die, for it to be when she was not present. With these thoughts in her head, she lifted her hand to tap lightly on the door.

"Come in," the motherly voice of Mrs. Hutchinson said immediately.

Caroline entered the room. Mrs. Hutchinson was sitting in a straight-backed chair at the bedside wringing a wet cloth out into a bowl of water. She took one look at the apprehensive expression on Caroline's face and exclaimed, "Oh, my lady, there is really no need for you to be here. I have everything under control and unfortunately his lordship will not even know if you are here or not."

Here it was, her chance for escape. She need not trouble herself about anything. She could just leave all this unpleasantness in Mrs. Hutchinson's capable hands. She was just about to thank the housekeeper and leave when her eyes wandered to the figure in the bed. Without thought, she walked towards the inert form of her husband. For a man of twenty-eight, his face seemed remarkably childlike in repose, except for the stubble which darkened his chin, but like a child in the throes of a nightmare. Scowls and grimaces broke his normally peaceful expression periodically. Occasionally he would flail an arm or make a whimpering sound.

She walked closer, drawn to his innocent looks. How could such a large man seem like a child? Suddenly her father's words came back to her, "Caro, he was a kind boy." That must be what drew her, that part of him. Suddenly her mind was made up. She could not leave.

"I'm sure you have everything under control, Mrs. Hutchinson, but I think I'll stay here for now." She said reaching for the cloth and bowl of water. "Why don't you get things in order downstairs? From what the doctor said I'm sure we have quite a lot of work ahead of us."

"Yes, my lady, if you're sure," the housekeeper said uncertainly, fixing her with an intent look as she rose from her chair. Caroline's brisk nod brought a shine of approval to the older woman's eyes. "Well then, the water for his cloth is in this bowl. If the water gets too warm there is more cool water in the pitcher. Just ring if you need anything."

"Thank you, Mrs. Hutchinson, we should be fine for a while," Caroline said before taking her seat on the chair beside her husband's bed and applying the cool cloth to his head.

Caroline's declaration that the days ahead would be difficult proved to be an understatement. The occasional flailing arm turned, that night, into a full-fledged, fighting male. The footmen had to be called to hold him down, and for a while he actually had to be tied down to the bedposts. Caroline's heart ached for him as he strained against his restraints. Finally, he exhausted himself, or somewhere in his consciousness he realized that his struggles were fruitless. He calmed at last and they were able to release him.

Still the fever raged on. The days and nights seemed to run together, it always seemed dark in the sickroom.  Although she had lost track of what day it was, Caroline was certain her parents had left by now and that knowledge made her feel even more overwhelmed and alone.

She, Mrs. Hutchinson, and Roth, the valet, took turns with their bedside vigils, but more often than not Caroline sent Mrs. Hutchinson to care for the house and staff and took over the care of her husband herself.  She no longer wished him dead.  It no longer seemed convenient, but a tragedy to be prevented at all costs.  For, sometime during her long vigils, the depraved man she knew as her husband was slowly replaced in her mind by the vulnerable, kind boy who was now grown.

During her tending, Caroline had come to know him in an intimate way.  She had never before seen a man in a state of undress.  At first, she could hardly bear to look at her husband in this state without embarrassment, but as she performed her ministrations, she overcame her original reservations.  As the days passed, she began to grow familiar with the planes of his face and the form of his torso.  Slowly her embarrassment and revulsion were replaced with tenderness.  She began to feel her heart soften toward the man inside, a man who, even when ravaged by illness, became more attractive to her every day.

One night, after falling asleep in the chair next to his bed, Caroline was awoken by his cry.  He was saying something.  She straightened in her chair and leaned toward him trying to catch what he said.

"Sarah!" he suddenly cried, "Sarah, no!" It was said with such anguish she longed to do something to comfort him. She tried to touch his hand, but he began to toss, moving his arms and legs as though trying to run.

"Sarah... Sarah," he continued to call over and over.

*Who was this Sarah and what had happened to her? It was apparently something that hurt her husband deeply. He did not have a sister. Oh, perhaps it was his first love. Perhaps she died. The pain of losing someone you loved so deeply must be horrible.* The more she thought about it the more emotional she became. Finally. she could take it no longer. She had to do something. She grabbed his hand and said firmly, "Edward, it's alright Edward." He clung to her hand like a lifeline. She was amazed at his strength after being so sick.

"Sarah?" he said and she could hear the pleading in his voice.

"It's alright now," she repeated and with her free hand she smoothed the creases in his forehead.

He calmed immediately and soon dropped into a peaceful sleep, still clinging to her hand with a half-smile playing on his lips.

That was the moment she realized she knew

nothing about this man. She knew nothing of his life before her and the pain he had to live through. She also realized that she had lost a part of her heart to this man. The part that hurt to hear her husband call the name of another woman, even if she was dead, with such raw emotion. It was the part that vowed that someday her name would fall from this man's lips in the same way.

The following night Caroline was sleeping as usual, in the chair next to his bed. At three o'clock she jerked awake. The room seemed too still. Her eyes flew to the motionless body in the bed. No more restless movements, no movements at all! Her heart jumped and she gasped as she sat upright. Was all her care for nothing? Would her vow be in vain? Would she be a widow before she was ever really a wife?

His face looked pale in the candlelight. Was he dead? She was afraid to touch him, but had to know. She clenched her teeth as she reached her hand out to touch his cheek. It was cool, but not cold. She tentatively moved her hand down to rest on his chest and could feel the slow, steady rhythm of his heartbeat. She let out the breath she had not realized she had been holding and closed her eyes. A tear ran out of the corner where it had been gathering. He was alright. It was over now. The fever had broken.

*Chapter 5*

*One can drink too much,*
*but one can never drink enough.*
*-Gotthold Lessing*

Edward woke up with an extremely dry mouth and eyes too heavy to open. He lay there for a while thinking that this was the worst hangover he had ever had in his life, and he had had quite a few. He felt so weak he couldn't even lift his hand off the bed. Whose bed was he in anyway, his own? He tried to remember what happened, but everything was just too fuzzy. The last thought he had before drifting off to sleep once more was, didn't I get married?

Hours, or maybe days later, he wasn't sure

which, Edward awoke once more.  This time he managed to open his eyes a bit.  He was in a dimly lit room, and yes, it was his room.  The draperies were closed, but he supposed it was daytime as he thought he could perceive light trying to steal its way in around their edges.  A footman was stationed in a chair beside his bed.  A footman!  Whatever for?  He was glad to find him there though, because his arms still wouldn't cooperate and he was thirsty as the devil.

"Water," he croaked.

The footman seemed surprised at the sound of his voice.  "Yes, my lord," he said and moved quickly to fetch him some water from the pitcher and help him to drink.  Its cool wetness felt heavenly, but after only a few swallows Edward let his head fall back, too weak to drink any more.

"What's happened?" he struggled to say.

"Why, you've been sick, my lord, pretty bad for a while.  I sure am glad to see you on the mend."

So that was it, he'd been sick.  He tried to remember what had led up to his illness, but his mind wouldn't cooperate.  Soon the siren call of sleep became irresistible and he succumbed once more.

The next time he awoke it was night.  A single candle was burning on his bed stand and his valet, Roth, was dozing in the chair which had contained the footman earlier.  The raging thirst was still with him, but he felt cooler than before and hesitated to wake his valet to ask for more water.  First, he needed time alone to collect his thoughts.

Just as he did when trying to find an article he had lost, he decided to think of the last thing he could remember.  He did get married.  He remembered it clearly now.  Waiting at the altar for the silly chit his father had promised him to.  He could have cried off, but his father had threatened to disinherit him if he didn't get married, and as much as he hated to admit it, he didn't like the thought of giving up his currant lifestyle.  He had to get married at some point anyway to continue the line, why not to the paragon his father had chosen?  One woman was as good as another.  As for settling down, he supposed that his behavior didn't have to change as much as his father wished it too.  He just needed to produce a bloody heir and then life could go back to the way he knew it.

He gritted his teeth remembering his father praising her to the skies in practically the same breath he used to deride his behavior.  To be honest he really didn't care what she was like.  It was a business deal anyway.  As he saw it, he was purchasing a brood mare for the price of a title.

She was a rather pretty chit though.  As she walked down the aisle with her father, he found he enjoyed watching her graceful walk and the proud set of her head.  As she came closer, he saw her golden curls and blue eyes, eyes that seemed soft as she looked at him.  A slight smile played on her lips.  His gaze swept down the length of her body.  Producing an heir may turn out to be a pleasurable experience after all.

His eyes traveled back to hers, seeking the warm softness he had seen in them before, but in its place, he found a harshly assessing gaze which clearly showed she had looked and found him wanting.  The warm feelings he had felt just moments ago all disappeared and he was left with a cold rage.  Who did this chit think she was to find him, Edward Robert Pierce Montgomery, the third Viscount Montgomery of Woolbreck, someday to be Earl of Rockmorten, unworthy of her, a mere baronet's daughter?

As soon as her hand was placed in his, he turned to the bishop wanting to get the whole thing over as quickly as possible before his anger exploded.  When the service was finally over, he kissed her dispassionately and hurried out.  Of course, the silly peahen had nothing to say on the way to the breakfast, what could there possibly be in her empty head to talk about?  He had to admit he had not even tried to make her comfortable. Actually, he had done the opposite.  After the way she had looked at him during the ceremony and then avoided his eyes after that, he had the overwhelming desire to get even in some way.  But for her to actually jump away from his touch and look at him with such revulsion was almost more than he could take.  So he decided to put the chit in her place, and once at the wedding breakfast proceeded to drink himself into a stupor, which had the added bonus of infuriating his father.

Beyond that, things became hazy.  He really couldn't remember much of anything until the hellcat attacked him.  Right here in his chamber, scratching and clawing in a complete frenzy.  He had seen nothing wrong with his behavior at the time, but now that he was sober, he was appalled at the thought that he had been about to force himself on her.  Then he had looked into her eyes.  In them he saw blatant fear that melted into desolate resignation.  He knew those feelings too well to want to be the cause of them in someone else, so he left before he could do something he would regret forever.

He grabbed his coat and cravat and went out the door slamming it behind him.  Then he charged down the stairs, through the hall, and out the front door.  He was too riled to wait for his horse to be brought around, so he walked off with long strides toward his club.  Unfortunately, he hadn't thought of how hard it was to don a coat and tie a cravat while walking at a fast pace.  The latter was practically impossible.  He arrived at his club looking quite disheveled but too frustrated to care.

"Hey old boy, didn't you just get married today?  What brings you to White's so soon, honeymoon over already?"  Someone said behind him with a chuckle.  Edward gritted his teeth and turned to see St. James with a wide grin on his face.  He pasted a smile on his own.

"Well, when a man's worn a woman out there's not much more to do with her," he said with derision.  "She was sleeping, so I figured it was as good a time as any for a drink with friends."

"I believe *any* time is a good time for a drink with friends.  Now that your duty is done you can begin the celebration.  It's good to know that just because you're leg shackled nothing will change," St. James said laughing and slapping him on the back. "I'm at the table with Lydford, go on over. I'll get us a bottle and meet you there."

Richard Blakemoor, Lord Lydford, was Edward's closest friend.  They had known each other since they started at Eton at the ripe age of thirteen.  Lydford knew all his secrets to this point, but he didn't feel like adding another to the list tonight.  Lydford looked up in surprise as he pulled out a chair and sat down.

"Montgomery, I certainly didn't expect to see you here tonight."

"I didn't expect to be."

Lydford looked at him, his questions written plainly in his eyes.

Edward shook his head tersely. "Not now, I just want a drink."

Lydford nodded. "Have you heard of the upcoming match between Gully and Gregson?" he asked hoping the change of subject would lighten his friend's mood. "I've heard they are fixing the odds at six to four in favor of Gully."

St. James had come up with a bottle of brandy during this comment and added his own views as he sat down. "I think they can say all they want about skill, but, if a man has the advantages of both size and brute strength as Gregson does, the fight will go to him."

"I disagree. I think skill is of the utmost. Just take a look at David and Goliath," Lydford counterpointed.

St. James who had begun to pour the liquor in their glasses snorted. "I do think you have it wrong there. The credit is not given to David for his skill, but as I said, to the greater power." He said with a grin, raising his eyes heavenward. "What do you say Montgomery, skill or power?" Both men turned toward Edward.

"Gentleman, I could really care less. What I do care about is that brandy which you are certainly taking your time in pouring. If you don't get on with it, I may just be in the mood to take Gregson on myself."

St. James shot a quick look at Lydford and finished pouring the drinks in silence. The first two drinks went down swiftly and before Edward knew it, the bottle was at his elbow.  Lydford and St. James continued their debate and made plans to go to the fight as he continued to drink in silence.  After that, things became sketchy once more.

At some point, he seemed to remember looking up at a woman with green eyes and red curls falling around her face.  Her breasts were straining against the fabric of her low-cut bodice, threatening to pop out the top.  His hands reached up to help them as she touched him in an extremely personal place in an extraordinarily personal way.

Somewhere in the back of his mind he seemed to recall a footman throwing him into the gutter, and he was fairly certain that at some point he had been jumped by footpads and relieved of anything he had of any worth.

He remembered walking through a downpour, having a heated one-sided discussion with the creator about why the hell he had made England such a cold, wet place.  Then nothing, until he awoke somewhere cold, hard, and smelly with his head pounding and his body aching all over.  His only thought was that he had to get home.

He forced himself to his feet and began to walk out of what must have been an alley in one of the seedier parts of London.  He began to shed clothes as he went.  It was hot.  It was so hot he would have sworn he was in India, except that the sky was greyer than any Indian sky would be. Then a light drizzle began to fall. At first, he welcomed it because it cooled his heated skin, but soon a chill set in and he became so cold he began to shake. Still, he walked, one foot in front of the other, one foot in front of the other, until he was so numb he didn't even feel connected to his body anymore, but floated above it looking down. Finally. the tenuous hold he had on consciousness slipped and he felt himself falling until he landed on something soft.

In that moment, he was suddenly twelve years old again running through the back meadow with Sarah. Being the third son of an earl had its advantages. He was not that important, so he could slip away to cavort with the girl next door practically whenever he wanted. Hoyden that she was, she would run circles around him. Running up ahead and then turning around to smile at her success. He would scowl and accuse her of cheating, but even at the tender age of twelve he was already beginning to fall half in love with her.

Then suddenly he was sixteen, returned home from school on break, struck by the changes that had occurred in his longtime friend. She had blossomed during his absence and he found her breathtakingly beautiful. Instead of the romps through the meadow, they now shared picnics under the oak tree.  After one such picnic, she had allowed him to hold her hand and he had pledged his undying love.

That summer was an idyllic one spent in the company of his Sarah.  They rarely let a day pass without seeing each other.  Edward had to contend with all the teasing his brothers inflicted on him, but it was worth every moment.  That fall when he went back to school, it was with the knowledge that Sarah would be there for him when he came home.  That soon she would be old enough for them to begin their lives together.

Abruptly the scene changed.  He was now twenty.  He would never forget that age, for that was when his nightmare began.  He was in the sitting room in Sarah's house.  He had finally managed to get her alone for a few minutes.  It was so long since those carefree days together.  She had come out that spring.  He had wanted to approach her then, but he hadn't, because he knew how much a season meant to a girl.  He was secure in her love.  What were a few months to wait in a lifetime together.  Now was the time to start that life.  They were sitting side by side on the settee.  He slid off onto one knee and grasped her hand.

"Edward, don't be silly!" she said with a smile, playfully slapping his shoulder with her fan.

He smiled back.  "Sarah, would you give me the honor of becoming my wife?"

"Oh Edward."  Laughter was shining in her eyes until she saw the look in his and her smile faded.  "You -- you're serious, aren't you?"

"I have never been more serious in my life."

She pulled her hand from his and raised it to her mouth.  "Oh, Edward," she repeated, the playfulness in her voice replaced with dismay.  "I thought you knew."

"Knew?"

She looked at him sadly.  "Yes.  Edward, I could never marry you.  You're a third son.  I thought you were already promised to someone anyway."

"Someone I have never seen.  I love *you*," he said passionately.  "You are the one I want for a wife.  I told you years ago.  We had an understanding."

"Edward, I was thirteen, you were an older boy and my friend.  Of course I was flattered, but that doesn't change the way things are."

"Are you saying you don't care for me?" he asked rising to his feet.

"I never said that."

He knelt back down beside her and grabbed her hand once more.  "I know that I am only a third son, but I'm not completely destitute.  I do have a small holding which will be mine when I turn twenty-one, and enough money to support you in style.  We may not have everything, but we certainly won't go hungry.  Just say we can be together forever.  Say you'll become my wife."

She pulled her hand from his and sat straighter in her seat, a prim expression on her face.  "I can't."

"What?  What do you mean? Why?"  His heart began to sink within him.

"Just what I said, I can't.  Edward, I can no longer play childhood games.  I care for you, but I want more from life than the things you can give me.  I want the prestige of being a member of the ton, the jewels, the dresses, the envious looks that come with being a part of the upper circles."  As she talked her face began to take on an unholy glow, and Edward's heart sunk lower and lower.  "A third son could never give me all that.  I have decided to marry Lord Owen."

Edward's heart hit the ground at this point. "Lord Owen! But he is old enough to be your father!"

"Yes, but he is a viscount.  No matter what my feelings are for him, or for you for that matter, he is the one who can give me the life I was born to, the life I deserve."

Now his heart was completely gone.  It had become part of the stone beneath his feet.  He rose from his humiliating position and adjusted his coat.  "I'm sorry if I inconvenienced you in any way, Miss Preston, it won't happen again."

"Edward –," she began.

"I do hope you get everything you deserve," he

interrupted. Then turned on his heel and left the room without looking back.

Six weeks later, he read that she had married Lord Owen, and his heart, which he had supposed had turned to stone, turned out not to be so indestructible. For it now shattered like a fragile vase dropped on a marble floor. He had cried out her name in anguish, the pain filling him once again. Yet through the pain he felt a ray of hope. A voice called him by name and told him it was going to be alright. He felt the hand of an angel which held his and pulled him up from the dark abyss of loss, soothing his pain and filling him with a long-forgotten feeling of peace. He smiled to himself the memory of that peace filling him again. The strain of remembering fell away and he drifted off to sleep once more.

# Chapter 6



*'Tis safest in matrimony to begin with a little
aversion.*
*-Richard Sheridan*

Once Edward regained consciousness the days passed slowly for Caroline. She couldn't bring herself to see him once he awoke, unsure of what to say. She needed to sort out her feelings before she faced him. Her information about his recovery came from the servants who continued to nurse him and the visits she made when she knew he was asleep. It had been three days since the fever broke. He would be completely recovered soon. What would happen then?

That was the question she asked herself as she

stood watching him sleep by the light of her candle. She hadn't been able to sleep and had lain in bed for hours wanting to see with her own eyes how her husband was doing. Finally, she had given in to her longings and lit the candle at her bedside and gone through the adjoining door to his room. As she looked down at his face, her breathing quickened and she felt her heart surge in her chest. She longed to reach out and sweep aside the curls which had fallen across his forehead as she had so many times before. Her hand was halfway to the task when she jerked it back. What was she thinking! He was no longer ill.

She looked down at him once more. He looked so peaceful in his repose, so angelic, so *kind*. *Her* Edward, *her* husband, the thought made her heart swell within her breast. She smiled down at him and began to reach out towards him once more. Her hand was inches away from his face when she came to her senses and straightened with a snap. She snatched her hand back and hurried from the room. When she reached her own room, she closed the door then leaned against it, her eyes wide and breathing uneven. What in the world was happening to her?

The next morning, after breakfast, she made

her way to the library to find a book to pass the time. She walked in and over to a set of shelves before she sensed a presence in the room. Slowly she turned to find her husband sitting in a chair by the fire. As she stood there in shock, he rose and walked slowly toward her, stopping halfway across the room to lean back against the table behind the settee and cross his arms across his chest.

"Edward," she breathed and rushed to him, arms outstretched. He straightened up and dropped his arms as she threw herself against his chest. "It's so good to see you looking so well. When you were so ill I..." she stopped in mid-sentence. He had wrapped his arms around her and began caressing her back in a very familiar way.

"Well, well, what have we here?" he drawled. "Apparently my wife has had a change of heart." Caroline looked up at him confused by the tone of his voice. The expression on his face was not the Edward she knew. It was definitely not *nice*, in fact, it was predatory. What was she doing running into his arms like this? This lecher was not the man she had taken care of all those nights. This was the terrible rake she had heard rumours about. Her hands were resting against his chest so she began to push away from him.

"Not so fast," he said, pulling her closer, "I find this rather nice."

Caroline started to struggle, but caught sight of the look in his eyes and froze. She felt like a mouse caught in the stare of a snake. Slowly his head tilted toward her and the glitter in his eyes increased. She knew he was going to kiss her. Bile rose in her throat. She didn't want it to be this way. She didn't want *him* to be this way. He crushed her to him. Then his mouth was on hers, demanding, pushing aside her lips with his tongue. She tried to grit her teeth to prevent further intrusion, but suddenly his hands seemed everywhere at once and she gasped which allowed him access to her mouth. Her head was reeling, her body feeling sensations it had never felt before, but surrounding it all was a feeling of panic. He eased her away from him, just enough to give him access to her breast.

As his hand pushed aside her bodice and he cupped her naked breast, she pushed at his chest with all her might. Fortunately, he was still somewhat weak from his illness. He fell back against the table and she was propelled two feet away. She walked backwards to increase the distance by several more while putting her dress in order.

"How dare you," she said in a low voice her wide eyes filled with indignation.

"How dare I?" he asked with a sneer, cocking his right eyebrow. "I seem to recall that it was *you* who threw yourself at *me*. Trying to act the good wife and make your future earl happy without sharing all of your charms?  Well, my dear, I am not some slavering pup who will give you all and be happy with crumbs.  If you want all the trappings of an earl's wife, you'll have to pay for it. I'll consider this to be your down payment, but you have quite a bit more to go."

Caroline stared at him.  "You are not who I thought you were," she ground out between clenched teeth.

"He threw his head back and barked a laugh. "Just who did you think I was?  Was there someone else you meant to throw yourself at in the library?  A footman perhaps?"

"How dare you!  I never throw myself at anybody."

"I hate to disagree with you, wife, but, having been the recipient of said action, I must."

Caroline's face reddened.  "I was concerned. You were so ill I thought you might die.  To see you standing there after the way you looked a week ago, I just-" she broke off, unwilling to share any more of her feelings with this stranger.

Edward stared at her looking confused for a moment.  Then he grinned at her, but his expression was anything but friendly.  In fact, he looked like the devil himself.  He shrugged slightly and held his hands out palms up.  "As you can see, I am now in perfect health."  He paused for a second then raised his eyebrows as his smile grew even more wicked. "Of course, if you would like to make a more thorough examination, it would be my pleasure."

"No, thank you. I am beginning to think it would be better to be wearing widow's weeds right now than to be talking with you!"

"Darling, unless you intend to take matters into your own hands, I plan on being here for quite a long while. I would get used to that fact if I were you. If you want me to give you the life I'm sure you think you deserve, you should consider giving me an heir as soon as possible. You might as well get the unpleasantness over with. It is the reason for this marriage after all."

Caroline stood with her mouth hanging open, the blood draining from her face. Then she stiffened her spine, spun on her heel and walked from the room without another word. As she walked away, tears filling her eyes, she heard his words follow her, "Remember, I get what I want, you get what you want, darling."

"Yes, *darling,*" she muttered to herself as the tears spilled down her cheeks. She hated the way he said that word. It made her feel dirty, like a Covent Garden doxy. She didn't understand why he treated her like this. Where was *her* Edward? The one she had come dangerously close to giving her entire heart to. When she looked at him it was the same face she had cared for, but it was twisted into a mocking smile. It made her heart ache. She made her way to her chambers. The tears were coming faster now. She wondered if she should put on her widow's weeds. Her Edward was surely dead.

As soon as his wife left the room, Edward collapsed onto the settee. He closed his eyes, took a deep breath, and drew his fingers across his brow to pinch the bridge of his nose. He needed a drink, but it was tiring enough to go down to the library. The thought of hauling himself down another flight of steps to his study seemed overwhelming.

He unclenched his teeth and moved his jaw from side to side, trying to relieve the tension coiled up inside him. All he had wanted was to get out of that damn bedroom for a little while. He was feeling better ensconced in his library with a book, until she had to come in to ruin his peaceful morning.

He ran his hands through his hair. Grasping the slightly damp curls, he propped his elbow against the back of the settee. It had felt so good to bathe this morning. Roth had disapproved so soon after his illness, but he couldn't stand the sour smell of sickness any longer. By the time he went back upstairs his sheets would be changed and his room aired. He just wished his strength could be brought back to normal as easily, not to mention his entire life.

He shook his head and sighed. He probably had handled the encounter with his wife badly, but in all fairness, the only experience he had with women in the last nine years was with widows or lightskirts. Never did he entertain a married woman. He valued the bonds of matrimony even if they didn't. But all he knew is that if a lady of the night threw herself at you in that way, she expected much more than a chaste embrace, and after his long illness his strength may not be up to any physical activity but his mind, and certain parts of his body, were.

Not that he thought his wife was a lady of the night, his father would be more discriminating than that, but his wife apparently did not know what she was playing at. He was not a lovesick boy which is what she obviously expected. In the past, she was probably used to being coddled and getting her way. As he knew from his experiences as a boy, children with no siblings seemed to master the art of manipulation. Well, he would not be manipulated. He hoped that this confrontation with his wife established the fact that it was dangerous to play games with him.

He drew his eyebrows down in concentration. Was she playing games with him? She seemed sincere. Of course, so did Sarah all those years ago, until she told him she was marrying another man. It was not as if his wife actually knew him. The only time she had ever even set eyes on him before today was at that disaster of a wedding. It had to be only his title she cared about, what else could it be? She married him without even talking to him. That just proved that she did not care to know him at all. The creases in his forehead eased as he slipped back in to his haughty mask. It was a business transaction, nothing more. He would not fall for her lies. He would never make himself vulnerable to a woman again.

He sighed as his eyes began to close. How could he be so angry and so tired at the same time? He yawned. None of this mattered anyway, they were married. Yes, they were married and he needed to be able to tolerate being in the same room with her. He had been letting his anger get the best of him. He hadn't been thinking clearly. You can't have a brood mare till you break the filly. He yawned once more. Maybe he'd try again tomorrow.

The next morning found Caroline in the morning room perusing the stack of invitations which had accumulated during her husband's illness. It was hard to keep her mind on task as she had little sleep the night before, even after locking her doors. Her stomach was tight with dreadful anticipation.     At any moment her husband could appear.  It was like waiting for the proverbial shoe to drop.

She closed her eyes and sighed.  She rolled her shoulders backward and arched her back trying to dispel some of the stiffness.  Suddenly she felt the hair on the back of her neck rise.  She turned her head slightly and opened her eyes to see her husband standing just within the threshold. Quickly straightening, she dropped her hands in her lap. She bowed her head but her eyes followed her husband as he made his way into the room. He stopped beside her and looked at the invitation in her hand.

"Ah, invitations, I suppose we have received quite a few since I have felt well enough to look at them"

"Yes, my lord," she answered not looking at him.

"Are there any that interest you?"

"Most have already passed, my lord."

Edward sighed, "You don't need to 'my lord' me to death.  We are married."

Caroline turned wide scared eyes toward him before looking back down at her hands, "Yes, my-- Montgomery."

"Better."

They remained as they were, in uncomfortable silence, until Edward began to feel irritated standing next to an unmoving, silent girl.

"If you find anything that interests you, put them on the desk in my study. I will accompany you when I am able."

Caroline lifted her head and studied him intently a moment before replying, "I will Montgomery."

Edward nodded and strode out of the room. Caroline watched him go and sat staring at the door he exited for quite some time before turning back pensively to the invitations before her.

Caroline was in the morning room the next day trying to read the newspaper, but her mind kept wandering to the conversation, if you could call it that, with her husband the previous day. He hadn't seemed the ogre she had imagined after the other altercations with him. Could it be that her Edward was in there somewhere? She wondered.

She turned her attention back to the newspaper and was muddling through the social columns when she felt the now familiar awareness of her husband's presence. She looked over her left shoulder to find that he had indeed entered the room.

He cleared his throat and stood uncertainly for a moment. "Mrs. Hutchinson said you had the newspaper."

Her mouth fell open a bit. "Uh... yes."

Edward waited for her to say more. The silence stretched between them. "Well, when you are done if you could please give it to Roth I'd like to catch up on things." He turned to go.

She began to panic. Who was her husband? Here was a chance to see a little more of what kind of man he was and she was letting it slip through her fingers. She needed to keep him here. She needed to know him better. What might interest him?

"Gully," she burst out, surprising herself as much as him.

He turned back around. "Excuse me?"

She felt her face redden. "The fight, I figured that was what you wanted to know. Gully won."

He tilted his head to the side and looked at her with something akin to humor lighting his eyes. "Is that so?  I had no idea I had a wife whose interests ventured into pugilism.  How many rounds did they go?"

Caroline's mind went blank.  What was wrong with her?  She had read the whole story. Not that she would ever go see such a thing, but any match of skill held interest for her.  Now, for the life of her, she could not remember a single detail.  She sat mutely staring into space trying to remember any small fact.

Her husband's face showed his disappointment. "That's alright, I can--"

"A certain Miss A was seen dancing with Mr. W

three times at Lady H's ball last night," she interrupted.

Caroline watched as her husband's eyes widened. *Where did that even come from? I sound like a complete idiot.* She looked away from her husband and down to her lap where the newspaper lay crumpled in her hands. She pressed her lips together realizing what happened. She had been reading the society pages when he walked in. It was the only thing that had come to her mind.

"Here," she said jumping up from her seat to give the offending article to him. Unfortunately, in her haste, she caught her foot on the leg of the small table beside her chair. She heard the sound of breaking china as the remains of her lunch hit the floor at the same time she did.

Edward crossed the floor faster than she had thought possible in his weakened state. When she turned herself around and into a sitting position, he was already by her side with his hand outstretched.

"Oh," she said, "here." She thrust the severely mangled newspaper into his outstretched hand.

"Thank you," he said with a pained expression and held out his other hand.

She stared at it for a minute. What did he want? She looked down, assessed the situation, and realized he hadn't wanted the paper, but had given her his hand to help her up. The heat rose to her face once more.

"Oh. Yes, of course.  I'm sorry," she said, hesitantly placing her hand in his.  When his skin touched hers, a tingle started in her fingertips and moved up her arm to her chest where it took her breath away.  As soon as she was on her feet, she snatched her hand away and looked up at her husband with wide, wondering eyes.

She watched in surprise and took a step back as his eyes hardened.  "I'll have Mrs. Hutchinson send up a maid to clean this up," he snapped before turning and walking briskly out the door.

Caroline stood staring after him her mind a jumble of emotions. Not sure which was stranger, her fear of the feelings raging through her, or confusion of not understanding what made her husband so angry.

# Chapter 7

*And for the future - (but I write this reeling
having got drunk exceedingly today
so that I seem to stand upon the ceiling)
I say – the future is a serious matter –
And so – for Godsake – Hock and Sodawater.*
-Lord Byron

Edward sat back in his chair and ran his finger around the edge of his half empty brandy glass and smiled. All of this silliness with his wife would end tonight. He didn't know why he hadn't thought of it before. His title was only one part of what women wanted. There were also all the jewels, clothes, and a place in the inner circles of society. He had taken care of one of those things today. He had the jeweler come by with the best of his wares and had purchased a sapphire necklace that would turn any woman's head. As he gave it to her, he would tell her she could go to the modiste of her choice on the morrow and soon enough he would be able to introduce her to those "inner circles" she was so desirous to move in.

Though it hurt his ego a bit to know she would only capitulate to him because of the things he would give her and not just because of him, the point was that it would get him what he wanted. He needed an heir and a spare, and after that he and his wife could each live their own lives. There were plenty of women who found him attractive and would like to share a bed with him. If his wife was occasionally one of them, all the better, but he didn't expect it. It was not the way he had pictured his marriage to be, but it was no different than most. His parents' marriage had been the exception rather than the rule.

He reached down into the bottom drawer of his desk and pulled out a long flat box. He opened it and laid it on the desk in front of him. Yes, it was a beauty, elegant in its simpleness. He was sure she would like it. It was still a bit early in the day, but why not present it to her now? It could make for a pleasant evening...or afternoon. He closed the box, stood, and slipped it into his jacket pocket. Yes, he was sure to have her in his been this evening. A smile spread across his face.

He headed for the morning room, as that was where she seemed to spend most of her time. She was there just as he had supposed. Just inside the door he paused and watched her for a moment. She looked like a picture standing there in front of the window gazing out at the greenery below. She shivered slightly as if becoming aware of his presence, then turned her glance toward the door. Her eyes widened a bit and she ran her hands up her arms crossing them in front of her breasts to rub the chill from the top of her arms.

"Do you need anything?"

"No," he answered walking further into the room. As he did, she backed up slightly and looked at him warily. "You come in here a lot," he said to break the silence.

Caroline relaxed slightly and smiled. "Yes, I love to look at the garden and I find the color soothing. It's a beautiful room."

"My mother decorated it. She spent a lot of time in here also," he said, remembering. He quickly shut the door on those thoughts. It wouldn't do to compare his wife with his mother. She was nothing like her. No one was like her, besides he was here for a purpose.

"I like green," she said interrupting his thoughts. He quickly turned them back to the mission at hand.

"I thought you might," he said, slipping his hand into his pocket. "But, tell me, how do you feel about blue?" He pulled out the case and handed it to her.

She opened the case and gasped in surprise. "It's beautiful," she breathed.

"As are you," he said slipping into a more familiar territory. "Here let me help you."

Removing the necklace from the box she held, he stepped closer to her and wrapped his arms around her neck to fasten the clasp. He could feel her quiver from his touch and noticed her breathing accelerate. Yes, nothing made a woman feel amorous like jewels. He made sure to brush her neck with his fingers as he withdrew his hands and stepped back. Eyes wide, she clumsily set the box on the small table beside her. Things were going perfectly. His eyes never left hers as one side of his mouth raised in a crooked smile.

"Yes, Beautiful."

He bent his head toward hers. She looked like a mouse caught in the stare of a cobra. This was different than any woman he'd been with in the past, but she was young. She was new to the ways of the world, but like any woman, she knew what she wanted, and like any man, he would give it to her so he could get what he desired. Slowly, he moved closer as she stood immobile. When his lips touched hers, he felt the sharp intake of breath before her body leaned slightly into his.

He lifted his lips from hers and began running a burning path of kisses across her cheek and down her neck.  His hands roamed over her back. He felt her tremble at his touch. When he reached her ear he murmured, "I should have known better."

"What?"

"I should have known that was what you wanted," he said in a voice that had enticed many women to his bed, as he continued to caress her. "I know that a woman wants her baubles.  I shouldn't have waited so long.  I should have done this the first night we were married.  It would have prevented a lot of unpleasantness. Forgive me for being so thoughtless."

Edward congratulated himself on the addition of an apology. Second to gifts, there was nothing women loved more than an apology, even if one hadn't done anything wrong. He worked his way back up his wife's neck and took her lips once more.

He felt the difference at once.  When he had explored her lips the first time, his wife's kisses had been inexperienced, but tinged with a hint of hunger.  Now it felt as if he were kissing the dead. As that thought began registering in his cloudy brain, he began to feel that she was shaking. Not the quiver of passion, but a violent, jerky motion. He pulled back in confusion and looked at his wife, amazed to see tears coursing down her face.

"What the hell?"

Edward dropped his hands to his sides, and, as

he did, Caroline stepped quickly back from him wiping her mouth with the back of her hand. Edward continued to stare at her in confusion as she took a deep breath, pulled her shoulders back and head held high gazed toward the heavens as she said in a wavering voice, "I understand my wifely duties and will fulfill them if I must, but I refuse to be paid for them like a common whore."

Edward stood with his mouth slightly open and his forehead creased with confusion. He looked at his wife and her slightly melodramatic pose and felt as if he were a participant in a bad play. It was almost comical. He would have laughed if he weren't so angry. He felt his anger and frustration continue to grow.

"I try to give you what you want and you act as if you're Joan of Arc preparing to be burned at the stake. I don't know what you are playing at, but there is a limit to my patience. I was going to tell you to order an entirely new wardrobe and that I will introduce you to the cream of society. I give you a sapphire necklace that will make you the envy of many women, but you say you don't want it!" He huffed in exasperation. "What do you want?"

"Don't you know?"

"No! What more could you want?"

Caroline looked at him with tear filled eyes, slowly removed the necklace from around her neck, and held it out to him at arm's length.

"Please, take it," she said.

"No, it's yours. It's a gift."

"No, it isn't. It's a payment. I don't want it."

He looked at the necklace that she was holding in front of her between two fingers as if she were holding a dead rat by the tail. "Keep the damn necklace," he said and stalked toward the door.

When he reached it, he turned and looked back at her in time to see her drop it back into its box resting on the table and turn her back on it. He huffed a sound of incredulity, shook his head, and stormed out.

Edward headed straight for his study, threw himself into the chair behind his desk, and ran his hand down his face. He leaned forward, propped his elbows on top of his desk, and cradled his head in his hands. Frustration continued to build in him until he thought he would explode. He ran his fingers through his hair and grabbed a handful. It was no use. He could not find peace.

His eyes roamed over the top of his desk and landed on a pile of unopened mail. There on top was a letter from his father. He groaned in frustration, swept the pile of letters to the floor, jumped up out of his chair and began to pace the room. He had to get out of here or he would go insane. He needed a drink.

He wondered what Lydford was doing. It would be a good time to get in touch with his old friend. Perhaps a game of cards would take his mind off his troubles. Who was he trying to fool, himself? He needed to talk, and Lydford was the only one he knew who might understand. He headed for his rooms and called for his valet. He was going out for the first time since the night of his wedding.

When Edward walked through the door of White's it was five o' clock in the evening, more a fashionable time for a drive in the park than a visit to one's club, but he wanted a drink, and he couldn't stay one more minute in his house. Lord, he'd been married less than a month and he was already forced to leave his own home to preserve his sanity.

He scanned the room as he walked in but found no one he really wanted to spend time with. Most of the men present were older married men, how telling. He ordered a bottle of brandy and sat at the table in the furthest corner from the door. The first glass he poured, he drank down in seconds, then he poured another and sat back to drink it slowly.

He really needed to talk to Lydford. Lydford had always been the level-headed one of the two of them. When they were in school, it was only Lydford who could talk sense into him when his blood was boiling, which, he was ashamed to admit, had happened with some regularity. He saved him from many a situation which could have escalated into something violent, perhaps even lethal. Lord knew his blood was boiling now, and it wouldn't take much to push him into something stupid.

Why did he let that woman get under his skin? She had no purpose to him except to breed. Of course, that was a bit difficult when she reacted to his touch the way she did. He was not like some men who found pleasure in taking a woman who resisted him. He had expected a timid wife, as she had never before known the pleasures of the marriage bed, but the looks of total aversion she cast at him when he just touched her hand were infuriating.

He probably just needed a new mistress. He had lost interest in Camille, what a ridiculous name, months before his wedding. Any man who went months without a woman would probably feel the same frustration. Perhaps, if his needs were being met, he could stand to be in the same room with his wife. There was still the matter of producing an heir, but as she certainly did not seem to be in a hurry to take a lover, he could put that off to a future date when she finally became resigned to the idea. He felt his anger grow at the thought. Who wanted a wife who was resigned to his touch? He knew half the ton lived that way, but couldn't help expecting more from his marriage. Why, he didn't know.   It was an arranged marriage after all.

He lifted his glass to his lips and found it to be empty. He poured himself another. He would have to pay attention this time and drink this one more slowly or he would be three sheets to the wind before Lydford graced the door of White's.

Now, back to the mistress... He racked his brain trying to think of anyone who might interest him. No one came to mind. Maybe he should go out, perhaps to the opera. Yes, there were always some opera dancers who were real lookers. Maybe one would be looking for a protector like him. But somehow the idea did not seem appealing.

He looked down at his glass, empty again. He picked up the bottle to fill it again and noticed how light it felt. His brow furrowed in thought. Perhaps he did have a couple of glasses as he racked his brain for an attractive woman to become his mistress. Thinking that hard is a lot of work, it requires plenty of fortification. In fact, he'd like to fortify himself a little more just now. He'd have himself another drink and then perhaps he'd take himself off to the opera.

At eleven o'clock, Lord Lydford, entered White's. His eyes roamed the room. He passed a few acquaintances, exchanged pleasantries, and then spotted his friend Edward in the far back corner. He worked his way back to his table.

"Montgomery, it's good to see you. You haven't been in for a while. Getting to know the new wife better, eh?"

Edward lifted his head drunkenly and scowled at him. It was apparent that he had been here for a while, and from the looks of him, the half empty bottle of brandy in front of him wasn't his first.

"No, been sick," he slurred.

Lydford sat in the chair next to him. "Bad, was it?"

"Almost died."

Lydford's face showed his shock. "My God Montgomery, I had no idea. I really did just think you were getting acquainted with your new wife. I didn't want to bother you with a call, honeymoon and all that."

Edward snorted, "Oh yes, the honeymoon."

"I imagine that did not go as expected if you were ill."

"It wouldn't have gone as expected if I weren't. Lydford, I have married a woman with the mind of a peahen, the voice of a shrew, and the grace of an elephant. Not to mention the libido of a dead slug."

"I'm sure she cannot be *that* bad. She seemed perfectly normal at the wedding. A little shy perhaps."

Edward propped his elbow on the table, rested his chin in his hand, and looked at his friend. "Lydford, you have no idea. My life has become a living hell. There are times I wonder if I would have been better off succumbing to my illness. I'm just glad I finally have enough strength to get out of there!"

"I'm sorry I wasn't there for you."

"Don't matter, couldn't have done anything anyway. I wouldn't have died, too stubborn. I wouldn't let that bitch get what she wanted without paying for it." He leaned back in his chair and took another drink.

Lydford's eyes widened. "Excuse me?"

"You know all the things women want, social position, jewels, dresses... *things*!" he almost yelled, gesturing wildly with the hand that was holding his drink, sloshing some over the side. Then he set his drink down on the table and hunched over it. "I tried to give her a necklace today. Cost me a pretty penny too, but it wasn't good enough. Practically threw it in my face. Well, if she doesn't want the necklace, fine! But I want an heir and by God, she's going to give me one!"

Lydford glanced around and noticed a few of the patrons at nearby tables looking their way. He laid his hand on his friend's arm. "Montgomery, calm down. What are you talking about? Your wife is refusing to give you an heir?"

"She refuses to give me anything!" He said, his face flushing with anger. "She won't even let me touch her hand! By God, I'll make her though, I'll make her give me an heir!"

Lydford glanced around once again at the other patrons of the club and then back at his friend with a puzzled expression as if unsure of what to say. Edward bowed his head for a moment and then lifted anguish filled eyes to him and said forlornly, "I really don't want to make her, Lydford. I want her to want to. I want her to choose me. I want it to be alright, just like the angel said. What is wrong with me, Richard?" Edward said returning to their childhood names. "Why is my own wife repulsed by my touch?"

Lydford glanced around again. "Let's go to my place, Montgomery. This is no place for a personal discussion. Come on, I'll get a carriage, you are in no shape for walking."

Lydford helped his friend up and guided him toward the door, then had the doorman acquire a carriage and help him assist Edward into it.

"I knew you'd know what to do, y'always do. You're the best friend I've ever had. You know that, Lydford?" Edward kept saying repeatedly as they helped him into the cab. Once inside he sagged into the corner, eyes closed, mumbling about friends. They had to stop twice before they reached Lydford's townhouse for him to cast up his accounts in the gutter. Finally, blessed sleep overtook him.

Edward awoke with his tongue stuck to the roof

of his mouth, and his head pounding.  This was becoming a much too familiar feeling.  He had thought himself accustomed to drinking, but apparently the illness had affected that aspect of his life too.  He opened his mouth a few times and ran his tongue over his teeth. His mouth felt and tasted like someone had stuffed their dirty socks in his mouth last night.

"Like a drink of water?"  Lydford's voice penetrated his sluggish brain.  "There's some in the pitcher on the table by your elbow.

Edward pushed himself into a sitting position and cracked open his eyes.  He found himself on the settee in Lydford's study.  He poured himself some water and took a couple of gulps, then filled his mouth with water and swished it around to moisten his whole mouth, and hopefully get rid of the terrible taste, before swallowing it.

"What time is it?" he croaked, putting his elbow on his knee, and holding his forehead.

"Half past two.  You've been sleeping about three hours, but I figured you needed it after the amount of brandy you poured down your throat. I have some coffee if you'd like some after your water."

"Thank you."  Edward ran his hand down his face. "How did I get here?

"I brought you here before you could spill all your secrets, along with the contents of your stomach, in front of the patrons of White's"

Edward closed his eyes and groaned. "That bad, was it? What did I say?"

"Something about your life being a living hell and your wife refusing to give you an heir or something to that effect, but I'd rather hear the whole story from the beginning."

So, Edward told him. He started with his disastrous wedding night. How he had left and remembered little of what happened until he woke in his room. How his wife had never come to see him while he was recovering. He told him of the confrontation in the library, of how after that he had tried, and failed, to converse with his wife, and ended with this afternoon's incident.

Lydford sat quietly listening until his friend had finished. "I know what you can do to help the situation. Just one simple thing and your marriage will improve dramatically."

"What is it?" Edward asked leaning forward and giving his friend all his attention.

"Stop behaving like an ass."

Edward sat back and sighed, "I'm serious, Lydford. I admit I haven't behaved the best, but she makes me so angry. I try to give her all those things women want and she just looks at me in disgust. It's like I'm some horrible ogre and she's some precious princess."

"I'm serious too. Look, I have known you since we were boys. Since your mother passed, I've watched you throw everything away. First, you gave your heart to a girl who didn't deserve it. Then gave away your life to drink and women you didn't even pretend to give your heart to. Now, you're throwing away your marriage. Have you ever stopped to realize how lucky you are to have those things to throw away?"

"Oh, yes, amazingly lucky," Edward said sarcastically.

Lydford shook his head. "You don't see it, do you? You have a father who cares about you enough to find a wife for you. I'm sure he would not saddle you with a shrew. Have you ever considered the fact that the poor girl is probably terrified of you?"

"Terrified of me! What reason would I have given her to be terrified of me?"

Lydford snorted. "Your wedding night was a pretty good start, then your behavior in the library. And what possessed you to try and gain her favors with a necklace? She must think you a horrible lecher who believes her only purpose is to breed. This is a lady you are dealing with Montgomery, your wife, not a mistress. Even mistresses deserve to be treated better than that."

Edward grimaced and ran his hand over his face. "I know. If only she didn't make me so angry. She actually wiped her mouth after I kissed her and stood there with this look like you would imagine on the face of a martyr about to be fed to the lions."

"She is eighteen.  You are twenty-eight. Think of how things must appear to her. I should think you would have the maturity to behave as a gentleman ought."

"I've tried, Lydford, I've tried.  I think I have been extremely patient so far.  I can't imagine living the rest of my life like this.  I had to leave my own house last night just to try to maintain my sanity.  I don't expect to love the girl, but there are expectations to be met."

"Perhaps that is the problem."

"What?"

Lydford sat back in his chair and rubbed his chin. "Expectations. You seem too focused on the need for an heir.  If it seems that way to me, imagine what it must seem like to your wife. Have you ever taken the time to get to know her?"

"I've tried to talk to her.  Believe me she had nothing to say."

"Good Lord, Edward, I know it's been a long time, but don't you even remember how to court a girl?"

"I suppose I never did, considering the way things turned out the last time."

Lydford ignored his comment and continued. "Don't you think it might improve matters if you tried to treat her like she was special?  Every woman, no matter how dull, likes to be courted. Honey does attract more bees than vinegar."

"I've never had to worry about those things. As

you said, I haven't really spent time in the more respectable circles for quite a while. How do I court her? She's impossible! I don't even know what she likes. It apparently isn't jewels, and every woman likes jewelry. This is ridiculous, I don't even know the girl."

"Exactly. You unfortunately had a rather unusual beginning to your marriage. Most men get to know their wives before marrying them. You chose not to do that. Why, I'll never know, but here you are, a married man, who has no idea of who his wife really is. Perhaps you should take time to find out."

"Why? I know she just married me for my title." Edward got up swiftly from the setee then pushed his fingers up through his hair rubbing his palm across his forehead to try and quell the pain and dizziness before walking over to the fireplace and leaning his elbow on the mantel.

"Do you?"

"What other reason would she have? She never met me. Didn't even set her eyes on me."

"Why don't you spend some time with her and find out? Even if she did marry you for your title, does that necessarily rule out love in the future?" Lydford smiled, "Let her see some of that Montgomery charm. Maybe she'll surprise you."

"So, you're saying I have to try to court my own wife?"

"That is precisely what I am saying."

# Chapter 8


*Wishing each other, not divorced, but dead,*
*They lived respectably as man and wife.*
*-Lord Byron*

Caroline locked her door again that night, but she still did not sleep waiting for the inevitable knock. She was sure her husband would come for what he said she promised him. She supposed it was true, she was his property now. He had the right to do whatever he wanted with her, but the thought of a complete stranger touching her made her want to retch and cry at the same time.

It was dawn before Caroline finally heard her husband enter the chambers next to hers. Not that she  cared, but she pressed her lips together tightly as her stomach heaved at the thought of what he had been doing all night. Apparently, his strength was back. It wouldn't be long before he came for her. Why did she have to be married to this libertine?  Why couldn't he be more like the man in the sickroom?  Oh God, she had begun to fall in love with him!  But it wasn't really her husband she cared for. It was the man she had nursed back to health.  Unfortunately, that man did not exist.

When enough time had passed that she felt sure her husband had fallen asleep, she unlocked her door and rang for her morning chocolate.  It was much earlier than usual, but she knew she could never sleep now.  Sally came to dress her as she was finishing up her chocolate, her expression grim.

"Sally is something wrong?" she asked, and shivered as she remembered saying much the same thing the morning of her wedding.

Sally took a deep breath. "Oh, my lady, I just think you deserve better.   I  know Lord Montgomery was out all night last night, and you know as well as I what he was out doing. I thought after this illness... well, after all the nursing you did and all, I thought things would have changed. How could he be so ungrateful?"

"I had hoped things would be different too, but I'm not sure he is even aware of the fact that I nursed him at all. Even if he were, I don't know if it would have made any difference. I guess it's best that I admit that all I will ever be to him is a vessel for his heir. Once I perform my duty, his pleasures will be found elsewhere. I will get used to that fact, most women do." Caroline sat up straighter and threw her legs over the side of the bed. "At least when he goes out, he leaves me alone. I have plenty of other things to concern myself with besides my husband's indiscretions. In fact, I'm glad I've risen early today. I need to go over the accounts with Mrs. Hutchinson and I am having my first at home since Lord Montgomery became sick. Come, help me get ready, I really have no time to dawdle."

Caroline kept her mind busy all morning. As she was preparing for visitors after luncheon, she worried a bit about her husband embarrassing her as he had with Lady Stahlwood and Lady Wharton. She couldn't really blame him for that day though, he had been incredibly ill, not drunk. It only appeared that way. It is just that he was so unpredictable. After last night's activities, whatever they were, she was fairly certain he would sleep until evening.

At four o'clock she was in the ground floor drawing room, with her needlework, awaiting her guests. When Edward had become sick, she had the knocker taken down. She had done it for her own comfort. She did not think she could handle any visitors, as tired as she was.  Most people assumed they had gone on a wedding trip. She thought it best to encourage that train of thought, it warded off questions. She had the footman leave her card at her acquaintance's houses yesterday, She hoped to see most of them today.

The next hour passed pleasantly, many of her acquaintances stopped by, but she was sad that Emily had not stopped by. She did not have many friends, but felt that, despite just meeting her this spring, she had found a true one. She was surprised Emily did not come, but she knew that the season was busy. Perhaps her friend was much too busy to think of her.

It was almost five o'clock when Danvers came in to announce two more visitors.  "Lady Owen and Miss Whithers are here, my lady," he said. Caroline had the feeling that he disapproved of something, but wasn't saying it, but she was too happy to hear her friends name to pay him much attention. "Oh, show them up, Danvers."

"Yes, my lady," he said stiffly.

Caroline smiled. Emily had come. She hadn't forgotten her. It would have been nice if they could have had a nice chat alone. She had never met Lady Owen, but if she were a friend of Emily's she was sure to like her.

"Please, have a seat," Caroline said gesturing to the chairs beside her.

"Thank you."  Emily gestured to the woman

with her, "May I present my cousin, Lady Owen."

"Pleased to meet you, Lady Owen."

"Oh, you must call me Sarah.  Anyone who is a friend of Emily's is a friend of mine," the woman said making herself at home quickly.

Caroline felt her guest was behaving quite forward at first meeting her, but she smiled and said, "Certainly."  She was not about to invite this woman to call her by her first name in return. Instead, she turned to her friend who sat across from her.  "Emily, it is so good to see you, you must tell me how you have been since my marriage.  I apologize for being out of touch.  Have you enjoyed the season so far?"

Her friend grimaced, "As well as could be expected."

Lady Owen's tinkling laugh floated through the air as she patted the girl's arm.  "Oh, don't let my little cousin fool you, things are absolutely wonderful.  In the short while I've been in London, she is well on her way to making a wonderful match.  Aren't you my dear?"

Oh, yes, this was the cousin Emily had told her about, the one who was trying to find her a match.

Emily nodded and gave a fleeting smile, but didn't raise her eyes from her hands that were clenched tightly in her lap.

"You needn't act so modest, my dear," she said to her cousin and then turned to Caroline.  "Yes, we couldn't be more pleased. Lord Mutton should be talking to her father any day now."

Caroline found it hard to hide her shock, Lord Mutton!  Why he must be thirty-five at least and that was being generous.  He was balding, had a prominent overbite and a laugh like a donkey's bray.  She wouldn't even mention his taste in clothes. Worst of all, he hadn't a brain in his head. She had no idea how he made it through university, unless it was by way of generous gifts to the school from his father.  It was not possible that her intelligent friend would consider spending the rest of her life with him.

She looked closely at Emily as she said slowly, "That's wonderful, Emily.  I'm so glad you have found someone you want to spend your life with."

Emily looked up at her and her eyes confirmed Caroline's suspicions.  She hadn't chosen him, but for some reason felt as if she couldn't refuse.

Her cousin chattered on.  "Wonderful isn't it. She will be a viscountess.  If it weren't for me, he never would have considered her at all.  She has always been so backward.  I keep telling her you have to go after what you want... in a ladylike way of course," she added.  "Anyway, he wouldn't have even noticed her if I hadn't pointed out her positive attributes and let it slip that her dowry was extensive.  It is a good thing I came to town when I did, the poor thing might have never landed a gentleman, certainly not one with a title."

As Emily's cousin continued on about the

failings of her cousin and the merits of being a viscountess, Caroline found herself liking her less and less. She sat, letting Lady Owen's words flow past her, nodding her head and studying the miserable expression on her friend's face. Suddenly something Lady Owen said claimed her attention.

"Excuse me, what were you saying?" Caroline asked keeping a polite smile on her face.

Lady Owen smiled an innocent smile which didn't match the expression in her eyes. "Oh, I was just mentioning the fact that Emily is not the only friend we have in common. Edward and I grew up together and have been friends practically ever since we could walk."

*Edward? Had this woman just called her husband Edward? She didn't even call him Edward! How close was this friendship?* Suddenly she remembered. She felt her stomach drop. Sarah. Her husband had called to Sarah in the throes of his fever. Sarah wasn't dead. She was alive and sitting right in front of her.

After a few moments of awkward silence Lady Owen continued, "Yes, it was even thought we would marry once." She looked at Caroline. "Of course, we couldn't as he was already promised to you and so I married Lord Owen." Lady Owen gave an exaggerated sigh, "Yes, no one ever suspected that Edward would inherit the Earldom. After all, he had two brothers before him. It is strange the way fate steps in, but, of course, sad that he had to lose his brothers to gain a title. Of course, you probably considered it quite a windfall when that happened. Being only the daughter of a baronet, I imagine you only supposed to be married to Mr. Montgomery, not an Earl." She turned her smile back on Caroline.

"He isn't an earl. His father is the earl," Caroline said.

Lady Owen tilted her head a bit. "Yes, but it is only a matter of time," she said her smile bright.

Caroline couldn't help but stare. *Was this woman actually saying such things? Whatever could Edward have seen in her? Of course, he probably never saw this side of her. She was beautiful. There was no question about that. Dark hair, almost black, was piled on her head, little curls surrounding her delicately featured face. Maybe that's all it took to attract a man. All the talk about presenting yourself as a lady was untrue. All it took was a pretty face.*

She looked at her guest's dark eyes which were tilted slightly up at the edges, rather French-like in appearance. *They had to be enhanced by kohl, no one could have lashes that long and dark.* She found herself studying her eyes for evidence of the help of cosmetics. As they gazed back at her, she realized she was staring.

Caroline blinked and shook her head a bit. "I'm sorry," she said rising. "I just noticed the time. I hate to end our visit, but I have some things I must get ready for this evening."

"Oh, I understand," Lady Owen said with a rather smug smile. "It *is* the height of the season. We had better be on our way ourselves. I'm afraid we have dreadfully overstayed our call. I did want to extend an invitation to you and Edward to a small dinner party I'm having Wednesday next. I would so love to see Edward again." She gushed then paused and added, "Oh, and to get to know you better too, of course. Emily and her beau will be there. It should prove to be an interesting evening."

"I'm sure it will. I will have to consult my calendar, but I am sure Lord Montgomery and I would love to spend the evening in the company of you and your husband."

"Oh, there is no Lord Owen, my husband died last year. Riding accident, you know. He always thought he could ride better than he actually did. No, it will just be me and a few select gentleman and ladies. I do hope you will be one of them."

"I shall have to let you know," Caroline said non-committedly, and then turned her attention to her friend who was standing mutely beside her animated cousin. "Emily it was good to see you. Please don't let it be so long before we see each other again. Come by any time. I would love to talk." She squeezed her friend's hand to convey her sympathy and walked with them to the sitting room door.

"Yes, we must do this again soon. It was so nice to meet you." As she went out the door, Lady Owen turned and said "Oh, and give my love to Edward. Tell him it will be a joy to see him again and talk over old times."

"Yes, of course," Caroline said stiffly and closed the door behind them. She stood there a moment staring at the closed door, her mouth slack. Did that woman just give her love to *her* husband?

That night Caroline ate with her husband for the first time since the debacle of their wedding breakfast. She had been taking her meals on a tray in the morning room, but her husband had requested her presence, so tonight she was seated at the other end of the long dining room table. It was not conducive to conversation so it was a rather quiet affair. Caroline wondered why he had subjected them both to it. They were near the end of the second course before more than a greeting was uttered.

"How was your day?" he asked.

"Fine."

"That's nice."

Silence again.

She sat thinking, as she had all evening, about the conversation with Lady Owen. The woman had made it fairly clear what her feelings were for her husband, just what were his for her? She looked up to the end of the table where he sat calmly eating his supper.

"I had an at home today."

"That's nice."

That seemed to be his standard reply. *What did he invite me to dinner for if not for conversation? Perhaps a mention of his old friend could elicit a different one.*

"Yes, it was nice to see my friends again." After a pause she added, "Oh, I had almost forgotten, Emily Whithers brought her cousin with her. I had never met her before, but she said she was an old friend of yours."

"A friend of mine?" Edward looked puzzled. "Who would that be?"

"Let me see," she said feigning innocence. "What was her name? Lady...Gowen? No... Oh yes, it was Owen. Lady Sarah Owen."

She watched her husband's strained face as he choked on his supper. His Adam's apple bobbed in the effort to swallow the mouthful of food which seemed to have turned to dust in his mouth. He reached for his wine and took a rather large swallow before saying, "Ah yes, she was a neighbor of ours at Kendleston Hall," and returning his attention to his plate.

They ate a few moments in silence.

"She seemed to know you rather well," Caroline ventured, calmly cutting the beef on her plate while seething inside.

"As I said, she was a neighbor of ours. When my brothers and I were children, we spent quite a lot of time at our country home. My mother was more comfortable there. I guess she would have known me rather well." He paused a moment, then said defensively, "I couldn't very well *not* talk to her. She lived only a mile away."

"Of course not. Who else would there be to talk to?"

"Exactly."

They lapsed into silence once more.

"She invited us to a dinner party she is having. I thought that rather nice." She couldn't help saying studying his reaction from under her lashes while trying to appear as interested as possible in the food on her plate.

She couldn't decipher the look on his face as his head shot up. "Did you accept?"

"I told her I would let her know."

"Good, good," he said absently. She knew he was thinking of Lady Owen, but his expression didn't give his feelings away. Did he still care for her, or was he just surprised to hear her name? She had the overwhelming feeling she had to know, and the only way she knew how to gauge his feelings was to see them together. Perhaps she was playing with fire, but... "We don't have anything on Wednesday next, perhaps we should go. My friend Emily will be there, and I'm sure you'd love to talk with an old friend."

He paused with his fork halfway to his mouth and his mouth hanging open, until he seemed to realize he needed to reply. "Whatever you think," he said, not looking at her.

"Alright, I'll send our acceptance tomorrow."

Fine," was his absent-minded reply.

The rest of the meal passed in silence. When the dessert had been cleared and Edward was preparing to have his port Caroline rose and said, "I believe I will retire early tonight."

"Goodnight," he said while pouring his drink.

"Oh, I almost forgot," Caroline said as she reached the door. "Lady Owen sends her love." She swept out the door, leaving him in the company of his port and his thoughts.

Though his mind continually strayed to thoughts of Sarah, Edward tried over the next week to listen to Lydford's advice and court his wife. Every night he subjected himself to uncomfortable dinners with stilted conversation. He resigned himself to behaving like the perfect husband, but she still stubbornly shrank from his touch. When they went to Lady Westerham's musicale, she sat so rigidly beside him he swore if he touched her, she would shatter into a thousand pieces. He actually nudged her arm during Mozart's sonata just to test his theory. He found that he was wrong, but that his wife had a look that could freeze you until you were almost as rigid as she.

He dutifully accompanied her to all the engagements she had on her calendar as a proper husband should.  He brought her refreshments and made sure she was settled before he went to the card room at Lady Jersey's ball.  He fought his way through the crowd at Lord and Lady Wharton's rout only losing her once, and that was quite a feat considering what a crush it had been.  He even endured a dinner at Lord and Lady Henty's house where, for some reason unknown to him, Lady Henty kept glancing worriedly at him all evening long as if he were going to turn into a slavering fiend at any moment, but all his sacrifices seemed for naught.  She didn't jump as if she wanted to run away when he touched her arm, but the look in her eyes was far from amorous.  In fact, he couldn't even call it trusting.  His patience was wearing thin.

The days continued to pass.  Unaware that he was doing so, he counted down the days to Sarah's dinner party.  As it drew closer, her face began to intrude upon his thoughts more and more.  Then suddenly the day was upon him.  He would be seeing her face to face for the first time in eight years.  Anticipation mixed with dread as he prepared to have dinner with the girl who had shattered his heart all those years ago.

# Chapter 9



*Once a Man's Thirty, he's already old.*
*He is indeed as good as dead.*
*It's best to kill him right away.*
*-Goethe*

Edward was pleased with his wife's appearance as he watched her walk down the steps and into the hall on the night of the dinner party. Her rose dress brought color to her cheeks and accentuated the blue of her eyes. He might have been proud to take her anywhere, if only it weren't to the house of Sarah Preston. He could not think of her as Lady Owen.

The conversation on the way to the dinner party was even more stilted than usual, if that was possible. Edward could not stop thinking about seeing Sarah for the first time in years. Would she be much changed?  He knew he was.  He thought he had seen small lines at the corners of his eyes as he was preparing for the evening. Wasn't he too young for that?  He wasn't quite thirty. He had checked his hair for the inevitable trace of gray, but had been relieved to find that he had eluded it for the time being. Still there were the lines. What would Sarah think of him?  He hoped he didn't look old to her. What would it be like talking to her?    It  surely  couldn't  be  any  more uncomfortable than conversing with his wife.

At the reminder of his wife, he studied the profile of the girl sitting across from him gazing out the window.  She seemed so young to him, too young.  She really knew nothing of life.  Did she know about his past with Sarah?  No, how could she? If she did, what were her thoughts?  He would never know, for even if he had wanted to ask, he couldn't. They had arrived.

He got out of the carriage and turned back to help his wife down after him.  She didn't snatch her hand away as she usually did, but laid it on his arm for him to escort her in.  He looked down at her in surprise.  They locked gazes, and he tried to decipher the look in hers, but she turned away before he could identify it. As he walked with her toward the door, it struck him that it was almost as if she were searching his eyes for answers too.

The door was opened by a footman, and the

butler led them to the drawing room where the guests were gathering before going in to dinner. As they were announced, the woman on his arm was forgotten as he scanned the room. His friends Lydford and St. James were standing to his right talking to two young ladies with their usual charm. Lord Amberly and Lord Warren seemed to be in a heated discussion beside, appropriately enough, the fire. It was sure to be about politics if the bored faces of their wives were anything to go on. Lord Mutton was sitting on the settee with his usual idiotic grin on his face, which only exacerbated his overbite, chattering at a girl who looked as if she wanted to disappear. He wondered if this was his wife's friend Emily. He was about to ask her if she would like to go over and save her when Sarah stepped into view and all such thoughts fled from his mind.

My God, she was beautiful, even more beautiful than she had been all those years ago. His jaw went slack. Her crimson dress set off her dark hair perfectly, the sheer overdress doing more than just hinting at her curves, flowed around her sensually with every move she made. Her dress was unadorned except for a golden ribbon around the edge of her décolletage and another as a sash under her breasts. Her jewelry was subtle too, just a single gold bangle on her wrist and a golden pendant which hung between her breasts calling attention to their perfection. Edward did not think he had ever seen a woman so perfect in all his life. He watched her every move as she made her way over to him.

"Edward," she purred, a sensual smile lighting up her features. "It's so good to see you again."

Edward just stood and gazed at her. Eight years fell away in an instant, and he found himself overcome with the same feelings he had for her as a young man suffused with the mature passions of the more experienced man he was today. Sarah gazed back, but the message in her eyes was not the same as it had been when she was young. It was the gaze of an experienced woman, a woman who knew what she wanted. He was glad to see that it was him. She turned her eyes away from his and looked at someone beside him. "And how nice to see your wife again too."

Edward felt as if a cold glass of water had been thrown in his face. In the last few moments, it felt as if it were only him and Sarah just as it had been in the past. He had completely forgotten that he was married. There was an uncomfortable silence that seemed to stretch forever. He could think of nothing to say. In his confusion, he heard a voice beside him say, "Thank you for inviting us, Lady Owen. I had little time before my marriage to spend in society and am looking forward to meeting your other guests. I am afraid I'm not familiar with many of them."

"Oh," she said, "I was sure you would have met

everyone here. They are all Edward's friends." She looked at Edward, "I hope I haven't done anything wrong."

"Er, no." he stuttered. Until that moment, he hadn't realized that although he had accompanied his wife to social events and made sure she was comfortable before spending the evening playing cards or billiards, he had not danced a single dance with her and had made no introductions.

"Well, I certainly don't want to make you uncomfortable, I just thought --" She broke off and looked at Caroline.

Just then another gentleman entered the room. Sarah glanced in the direction of the door and then back. "I must see to my other guests, but I am sure we will have many opportunities to get to know one another better this evening." Her last statement was supposedly to Caroline, but was made while looking directly at Edward.

Edward watched her walk away, her dress clinging to her curves as she swayed across the room to greet her newest arrival.

Caroline watched the expression on her husband's face as Lady Owen walked away. When she had made the decision to accept Lady Owen's invitation, she had known she was playing with fire, she just hadn't realized how much. In the back of her mind, she had cherished the idea that the attraction would be one-sided, but it was apparent that her husband had been taken in by the widow's not so subtle charms. *How can he be so blind?  Can he not see the kind of woman she is?*

She followed the path of Edward's eyes and sighed.  Her husband was not blind, she knew what he saw.  She did not even compare to the beauty and sophistication of her hostess, though she was sure that Lady Owen had dampened her skirts to make them cling that way.  She could never wear something like that in public herself, but judging from the expression on at least half the men present, they certainly appreciated it. She had nothing to compare.  Next to Lady Owen she looked like a mousy little girl. Her only advantage was that Edward was her husband.  He may not be the Edward she had fallen in love with, but he was hers, and she was not about to give him up without a fight.  Though why she wanted to, and what ammunition she had to use against the enemy, she didn't know.

Edward stood gazing after their hostess until Caroline touched him lightly on the arm.  He jerked his attention back to her.  "Er, yes, um, shall we?" he said as he held out his arm for her.

She took his arm, and he led her over to the nearest group which contained two couples.

"Montgomery, I had no idea you'd be here," the shorter of the two men said with a smile.

"I don't spend all my time at the club, St. James. Caroline, this is Mr. St James, St. James, I'd like to present my wife, Lady Montgomery."

"Charmed, Lady Montgomery," he turned to the petite blond next to him, "and have you met Miss Brightmore?"

"I do believe we met earlier in the season. Did you attend Lady Roberts' soirée? "

"Yes, I did. My, you have a good memory. I've met so many new people I can't seem to keep them straight," Miss Brightmore said with a silly giggle that was tempered by a genuine smile.

Caroline smiled, "I'm afraid that my memory is not that good. I haven't spent as much time about since my marriage. I have a good deal fewer faces to remember."

"Perhaps you remember my friend, Miss Law. She was also at Lady Roberts'." Miss Brightmore said as she pulled forward a tall, thin brunette whose shoulders were slightly hunched as if she were embarrassed by her height. Caroline could understand why, as she was taller than everyone in the group except for the man beside her, but felt if only she had a little more confidence, she would make quite a dashing girl.

"Yes of course, how nice to see you again, Miss Law."

"Good evening, Lady Montgomery, nice to see you too," the tall brunette said while studying the toe of her slipper.

The group slipped into silence waiting for Edward to complete his introductions. He seemed unaware of their presence. His eyes were glued to the brunette in the red dress across the room. Finally, St. James took the initiative, "Lady Montgomery, Lord Lydford. He can tell you just about everything you would possibly want to know about your husband, and probably quite a few things that you would rather not." He said with a grin. "He's known him forever. Lord Lydford, Lady Montgomery."

"Yes, actually we met once, at the party for... the party at your parents' home. I'm sorry I was not able to stay long."

"That is forgivable, Lord Lydford, as I heard you had to help a friend. Good friends are important."

Lord Lydford studied her and gave a small smile. "Yes, they are."

They slipped back into an awkward silence once more. Edward was still watching their hostess. St. James began a conversation with Miss Brightmore once again and Caroline hoped that Lord Lydford would follow suit with Miss Law, but he seemed to be busy assessing her. His gaze made her uncomfortable. Finally, she felt she could take his scrutiny and the silence no more. She laid her hand on her husband's arm, but she had to shake it before she could get his attention.

"Hmmm. Oh yes, and this is Lydford," he said

offhandedly.

"We've already been introduced by Mr. St. James." Caroline said.

Edward gave a sheepish look at his friend. "Well, that's good."

"I was wondering if you would mind terribly if I visited a while with my friend Emily."

His face cleared. "No, no, feel free to visit as long as you like."

She gave a self-conscious nod in Lord Lydford's direction and made her way over to Emily who was seated by Lord Mutton. She wasn't sure if the conversation would be much better here, but she couldn't just stand there and watch her husband salivating over another woman. Perhaps she could be of some relief to her friend, if only by suffering with her.

It was as bad as she had feared, but only lasted about five minutes before the butler came to announce dinner. Caroline rose and looked around for her husband to escort her in. She was horrified to see him escorting Lady Owen. That honor should have gone to Lord Lydford as he was a marquess and her husband only a viscount. She looked around in confusion for a moment unsure of who her escort would be until she was surprised to find Lord Lydford at her side offering his arm.

"My lady," he said with a reassuring smile. Caroline gratefully took his arm and smiled back as he escorted her into the dining room.

Once there, she found that her hostess's lack of decorum had carried into the dining room. She was seated halfway down the table between Lord Mutton and Lord Lydford both of whom should have been sitting near the head of the table. Her husband was seated in the seat to Lady Owen's right. Undoubtedly, the whole company, except of course for her husband who only had eyes for their hostess, would notice her total lack of protocol. Mrs. Whithers, who had allowed Lady Owen to hold this party at her house, looked as if she were going to suffer an apoplexy. One thing was certain, they were bound to be a favorite topic of gossip tomorrow.

The first ten minutes of dinner were tortuous as she spent her time trying to hold a conversation with Lord Mutton. There must be inbreeding in the family, for she was certain the man was a half-wit. He babbled on as if she were not even there and then turned to her as if waiting for a comment. She would barely get through half a sentence before he would interrupt her to begin talking about something completely unrelated to the subject at hand. Then he would pause and bray a laugh for no apparent reason, as if enjoying some private joke. By the end of her obligatory ten minutes, she pitied Emily even more than she had before.

She turned toward Lord Lydford hoping that he would not unnerve her as badly as he had in the drawing room.

"So, Lady Montgomery, I know that you have not seen much of the season, but have you been to Almack's yet?"

"Yes, I was there a few times before I married."

"And what did you think of it."

"Actually, I was rather disappointed. I had heard that it was *the* place to be seen in London society. I thought that I would find a richly decorated room with a marvelous dance floor and sumptuous delicacies to nibble on. Imagine my surprise when I walked into a bare room with a bad floor. I shall not even comment on the refreshments."

Lord Lydford chuckled, putting her at ease. "I am afraid everyone is slightly disillusioned after their first excursion to Almack's, but it is frequented by the cream of society, so everyone feels privileged to partake of their dry cakes and watered down punch."

"It is amazing what we will subject ourselves to just to impress others. Of course there are those who don't seem to care at all. Even for the most basic forms of etiquette." She said as she glanced toward the head of the table. There was Lady Owen with her hand on Edward's arm, his hand covering it. Their heads were bent towards each other as if engrossed in an intimate discussion. She laughed, a light tinkling sound. Edward smiled and patted her hand. They were behaving as if they were the only two people in the room.

"They grew up together," said a voice beside her.

She turned her eyes away from her husband to look at Lord Lydford. "I know," she said.

"He's been down that road before. He knows where it will take him. Don't worry he wouldn't be foolish enough to go there again."

She glanced back at her husband who was staring at their hostess like a starving man would gaze at a piece of bread. "I'm not so sure of that."

Lydford turned to follow her gaze and set his lips in a thin line. Then he turned back to Caroline and smiled reassuringly. "I'm sure he is just trying to make the best of his situation for he knows that I have the privilege of being seated by the most entertaining lady present."

"I am afraid, my lord, you are nothing but a hardened flirt. I will soon think I cannot believe a single word you say." She bantered back with a smile, appreciating his effort to distract her from the shameful behavior of her husband.

His expression was serious as he looked deep into her eyes. "Lady Montgomery, you have my word, I would never lie to you." Then, in a heartbeat, he resumed his playful air and began regaling her with the newest story about the Prince Regent.

Caroline was thankful that Lord Lydford provided a distraction during the rest of the meal.

She tried to direct all her attention to his outrageous stories and studiously avoided looking at the couple at the head of the table, but she was aware of almost every move her husband made. It seemed that some strange tie had been forged between her and her husband, one that she found incredibly hard to break.

Finally, Lady Owen felt they had lingered over the dinner table long enough. She rose, which was the signal to the ladies to do the same and follow her to the drawing room while the men took their port.    Lydford joined in with the general discussion, but he was just biding his time until he could have a private word with Edward. That time came when they had finished their drinks and cigars and were going to join the ladies once again. Edward would have been one of the first out of the room, but Lydford put his hand on his arm to restrain him.

"What are you doing?" he asked his friend as the last man left the room.

"Trying to join the ladies as everyone else already has."

"You know what I mean. I just spent dinner talking with your wife, one of the most delightful dinner partners it had been my fortune to sup with. She was quite contrary to the peahen you had led me to believe she was.  I was surprised to find her quite a good conversationalist. How this could have escaped your notice is beyond me, but perhaps it was because you were spending your time staring at your hostess like you wanted to eat her rather than the dessert."

"I did no such thing," Edward snapped, his face reddening with anger. "I was just reminiscing with an old friend."

"Remind me to never reminisce with you, old friend. I'm afraid I would feel terribly uncomfortable if you gazed at me like that. I wasn't the only one who noticed your behavior, you know, I'm sure the gossips will be out in full force tomorrow."

Edward snorted, "Let them talk."

"What about your wife, she seemed very disturbed by it also."

Edward said nothing, just leaned against the doorjamb with a rather sulky expression on his face.

"Your wife is charming. It is a shame you are so blind you cannot see it yourself. You should've taken my advice and gotten to know her better."

"I *have* been trying to get to know her better. Getting her to talk is like trying to break down a wall with a feather."

"She is not nearly as hard as the woman you spent the evening with. As for her conversation, it seemed rather free and easy to me."

"Then you should have married her," Edward

blustered. "I've carted her all around London this week and practically all the conversation I get from her is 'Yes, Lord Montgomery' or 'No, Lord Montgomery'. Good Lord, we've been married over a month, and she has never even called me by my given name!"

"Calm down, Montgomery." Lydford said gripping his friend by the upper arm and glancing into the hall. "You have to admit you have a lot to make up for in your past behavior. It will take more than just 'carting her around.' Show an interest in her, find out what she likes to do. The way you are acting, I would swear you had never tried to please a lady before. I know if you could gain your wife's affections you would find it well worth your effort."

Edward took a deep breath and ran his fingers through his hair.

"Now," said Lydford like a nurse placating a sullen charge, "why not start by spending the rest of the evening in your wife's company." He led him down the hall and to the doors of the drawing room.

As they opened the doors and walked into the drawing room, Sarah began to move in their direction. Lydford firmly steered his friend toward his wife who was sitting on the settee with a young lady with light brown hair wearing a serious expression. When he reached the ladies he asked, and was given permission, to join them.

He sat in one of the chairs opposite the ladies and Edward, with a final longing glance in the direction of their hostess, followed suit.

"So, ladies, what shall we discuss?  The weather, or..." he leaned forward smiling conspiratorially, 'the latest on-dit I just heard about Lady Elphinstone's musicale?"

Caroline took up the bantering tone they had conversed with during dinner. "Knowing the tendencies of both, I find myself in a quandary. Would it be preferable to converse about incessant rain or hours of ear pain? I am uncertain as to which would be the least disagreeable."

Lydford chuckled.  "Well, perhaps we would be safer with a subject like art.  Have you seen any of the exhibits in town?"

"Actually, that would be an extremely safe topic as I have not seen any of the exhibits."

"Ah, but it would make for a very boring topic, as I would have to prose on about the wonders of the London Museum of Art myself.  What about books?  This is an art that can be appreciated in your own sitting room."

"Oh yes, I love to read."

"And what, my lady, do you enjoy reading. Novels?  Poetry? Farming journals?"

"Oh, I read all of them, but I must admit that my favorites are farming journals.  Back at our home in the country I was known for my expertise in lambing."

Caroline laughed when she saw the expression on the faces of the two men across from her. "I was only joking Lord Lydford. I don't know a thing about lambs. I don't believe my parents even own any. I do enjoy novels, though they tend to be exhausting. There is so much running through dimly lit halls and dark woods, not to mention hanging off the sides of cliffs or old towers. The women in them tend to have strong constitutions aside from fainting a lot. I have just recently begun a new book called 'Phillip Stanley'. Have you read it?"

"No, I'm sorry I haven't."

"The author is American. I do hope it is not too moralizing. I have heard that Americans tend to be rather puritanical in their views. I don't mind a good message, but when the writer keeps driving it into you it makes me uncomfortable."

"Yes, rather like the books I had to read when I was young, the ones about the ungrateful boy who wouldn't listen to his tutor and do his schoolwork, but instead ran off to play with the children from the village. After all kinds of horrible things, reminiscent of your novels, Lady Montgomery, only from a child's perspective, he ends up at last in the gutter covered in filth and regretting his disobedience all those years ago."

Caroline laughed, "Weren't they horrible?"

"Ah, but they must have served their purpose, I never left my schoolwork undone. Though that may have had less to do with the stories I read and more with the birch rod that my tutor carried."

The conversation swirled around Edward. At first, he only had eyes for Sarah, who was flitting among her guests, but slowly the light tenor of the conversation drew him in. As he listened to their talk, he found that he had to agree with his friend's opinion that his wife was a good conversationalist. Her comments were intelligent and rather witty. He noticed that when her interest was sparked her eyes lit up and her face became alive with emotion. Though she could never compare to Sarah's dark beauty, there was something appealing in the way she looked tonight.

As the conversation continued, he began to get irritated with Lydford. Why did he cause this change in her? He should be the one to animate her so. He was her husband after all. Suddenly he was overcome by the desire to remove his wife from his friend's presence.

He jumped up from his chair. "I think it is time we went home."

Three pairs of eyes stared up at him in silence. His face reddened. He had spoken without thinking and interrupted the conversation.

"Oh, yes," Caroline said trying to save the situation. "It has been a long day." She turned to Emily. "Miss Whithers I'm afraid we have not had enough time to visit, you will come tomorrow, won't you? Perhaps around eleven o'clock?"

"I would love to, Lady Montgomery."

"Until tomorrow then," she rose and turned toward Lydford. "Lord Lydford," she said with a nod.

"Lady Montgomery." Lydford nodded in return.

Caroline put her hand on Edward's arm. They said their goodbyes to their hostess, whose eyes flashed in dislike when they rested on Caroline even as she tried to convince them to stay. Edward seemed rather distracted as he brushed off her objections and asked for their carriage to be brought around.

The carriage ride home was silent as usual for the first few minutes.

"You appeared to enjoy your visit with my friend Lydford."

Caroline hesitated for a moment surprised that anything she did interested him. Though he had escorted her many places the last two weeks, he had never seemed to notice her much. "Yes, very much, I found him very pleasant."

Edward seemed to think on that for a moment. "I have heard that he is considered attractive by many of the ladies."

Caroline drew her brows down and pursed her lips. Why ever was he mentioning that? "Yes, I can see how he could be thought so."

"Hmm," he grunted and leaned back in his seat. He was silent a few minutes more and then abruptly asked, "Would you like to go for a drive in the park tomorrow?"

Caroline looked up in surprise. This was the first time he had asked her if she wanted anything. He usually just told her he would accompany her. "Yes," she said slowly, "that would be nice."

"Good. Shall we say five o' clock?"

She nodded, "I will be ready then."

They lapsed into silence once more and Caroline couldn't help but wonder what was making her husband act so peculiar.

# Chapter 10

*Through all the drama*
*-whether damned or not*
*-Love guilds the scene*
*And women guide the plot.*
                    *-Richard Sheridan*

The next morning found Edward riding in the park, an unusual thing for him as he usually spent this time sleeping off the effects of the night before.  He was surprised to find anyone there at this time, though it was not anywhere near the crowd one would find at five o'clock that evening.  Only five minutes into his ride, he had nodded his head in greeting to over a dozen acquaintances.  His neck was beginning to get sore.  Now he knew why he had avoided the park.

He would not be here at all if it weren't for the plans made over dinner last night to meet Sarah here.  When he went to bed last night, he had changed his mind and was determined not to go, but he woke early and began to feel it was not proper to go back on his word.  As the minutes ticked past, he grew more agitated.  It was only a ride in the park with an old friend, he reasoned with himself, unable to resist the temptation to see her once more.

Just before leaving the house, he had gone to his study, opened the bottom drawer of his desk, and removed a long thin box. He opened it, glancing at the contents before snapping it shut. As he closed the desk drawer, his eyes fell on his father's letter that called from the corner of his desk. At the sight of it, guilt and doubt began to creep in about what he was about to do. He quickly turned away, shut the drawer, and left the study, closing the door firmly between him and his conscience. He slipped the box in his coat pocket. It was just a necklace. If his wife didn't appreciate it, it wasn't wrong to give it to someone who would.

It seemed to take forever to get to the copse where they had planned to meet.  He had to take a leisurely pace, or he was sure to draw attention to himself, so he rode at the speed of all the other riders in the park, clenching his jaw in impatience.

At last, he saw the trees ahead and there was Sarah, more stunning than ever in a green riding habit. He resisted the urge to pick up speed as he approached her.

"Good morning, Lady Owen," he said as he stopped beside her.

"Good morning, Lord Montgomery. What a surprise to see you here. I was just about to ask my groom to accompany me on a walk down the alee, perhaps I could persuade you to accompany me instead?"

"Certainly, Lady Owen, I would be happy to accompany you," Edward said dismounting and handing the reins to her groom, he turned to help her dismount.

"Thank you, Lord Montgomery," she said with a nod and a flirtatious smile.

"My pleasure, Lady Owen," he said smiling back.

She placed her hand on his arm and they began walking down the gravel path. The trees seemed to welcome them into a world set apart from the rest of the park.

"Please, call me Sarah. I would rather not be reminded of unpleasant things." Her voice trembled slightly.

He looked down at her bowed head and felt pity for her. It couldn't have been easy for her being married to that old lecher, Owen, for all those years. "Certainly, Sarah," he said patting the small hand on his arm.

They walked along the path in companionable silence until they turned a bend and could no longer be seen from the riding path.

Sarah stopped and turned toward him. 'Oh Edward, you know I have never stopped regretting letting you go, never in all these years. I was such a stupid, silly girl."

Edward stood looking at her.

Sarah laid her hand on his arm. "I didn't understand what I was doing. I had no idea what it meant to live each day in a loveless marriage dreaming of what you had lost."

"I'm sorry," he said slowly, "but it was your choice, Sarah."

She hung her head. "I know, I know, but I hadn't thought of..." she paused, and then looked up at him from the corner of her eyes, "the physical side."

A mixture of pity, anger, and jealousy filled his heart at the thought of pretty Sarah with portly, balding, Lord Owen.

"Edward?"

He looked down at the woman before him and shook his head slightly to clear his thoughts. "I'm sorry?"

"Do you ever think you can forgive me?"

"Sarah, it's been a long time."

"Long enough to have forgotten?" He saw the hope shining in her eyes.

"No, I don't think I'll ever forget," he said truthfully, "but it is past time to forgive. We can't be held forever by the mistakes we made in our youth."

Sarah threw her arms around him, her smile more beautiful than ever. "I knew you would forgive me. You always have." She pressed herself closer to him and then pulled back a bit, looking up at him from beneath her lashes, "Why Edward, is there something in your pocket?

Edward smiled, reached into his jacket pocket and pulled a long, thin box from it. It was the necklace his wife had so callously discarded. It had sat untouched on the table for three days until finally he picked it up and put it in his desk. He meant to have Roth take it back to the jeweler, but never managed to get around to asking him. He was glad he hadn't. He knew Sarah would appreciate the value of such a gift.

He opened the box and held it out to her. He watched her face as it took on an almost mesmerized look and her eyes glistened in a strange way. The look was gone so quickly he was unsure if he had really seen it and was replaced with a look of unabashed pleasure like a child at Christmas.

"Oh Edward, its exquisite," she reverently touched the exquisite stone. Plucking it out of the box, she let it dangle from the gold chain watching the way it glowed in the sunlight. Then she put the chain around her neck and fumbled with the clasp.

"Edward, would you please help me?"

She turned around and with shaking fingers he did as he was told, comparing the way Sarah had welcomed his gift to his wife's reaction. This was a woman who understood and appreciated things. This was a woman he could understand. She knew what his gift meant and welcomed it. A small voice inside his head whispered that the kinds of women he understood were mostly ladies of the night and that perhaps it was not such an admirable thing to sell one's body for jewels, but he censored it immediately. Sarah knew him. They understood each other. That made it different.

They continued their walk down the path, Sarah reaching her fingers up to touch the pendant and chattering like a magpie with something shiny. Edward walked in silence letting her words flow around him, an undulating brook of sound. Suddenly the flow stopped. He looked down at the beautiful woman on his arm.

"Edward, what are you thinking?"

He looked at her, mind blank, then smiled.

"Just how badly I would like to kiss you now."

"Why Edward, that happens to be exactly what I was thinking," she purred.

She began to lean into him and he met her halfway, covering her lips with his own. After they pulled apart, she teased his lips with her tongue and nibbled a bit on his lower lip. The thought came to him that hers was a practiced kiss, quite unlike the few he had shared with his wife. Quickly, he shoved the unwanted thought away. He clasped Sarah's face between his hands and deepened the kiss until they were both breathless and she broke away.

"Soon," she said, before gently kissing him. She pushed away and slipped her arm through his continuing down the path walking much closer than was proper. "Remember the time I put eggs in your boots when we went wading? If you could have seen your face when you put them back on," she laughed her tinkling laugh, "I'll never forget it."

He remembered. It had been incredibly uncomfortable walking all the way back home with eggs squishing between his toes. Not to mention the tongue lashing he received from his tutor when he arrived there. It was not a memory he liked to relive.

"It just feels so good to be with you again," she continued. "You don't know how much I've missed you. Now that I have found you again, I don't think I ever want to leave you."

"I was not that hard to find. I spent most of my time in London."

"Yes, but I was married then."

"And now I am."

"But it is different for a man. Most men are not faithful to their wives. I know Bertram was not. As long as you are discreet people generally look the other way."

Edward studied her for a long time before saying, "Yes, that is the general rule."

"Is it your rule?"

"I imagine that would depend."

"Upon what?"

"Upon why you are asking."

Sarah straightened her spine and looked him straight in the eye. "I want to be with you, Edward. Is there anything wrong with that?"

His heart surged in his chest and there was a buzzing sound in his ears. "No, no I imagine not," he answered, continuing to stare at her. He had imagined this scenario over and over the last eight years, Sarah coming to him and asking forgiveness, telling him of her undying love for him. Now that it was actually happening it felt as unreal as his dreams. The only difference was that in his dreams she accepted his proposal of marriage, now it seemed that she was the one proposing something else.

"Edward?"

He looked down at the girl he had spent most of his life desiring. She stood there with trembling lips and eyes shining with unshed tears. His head bent toward hers. Slowly he touched his lips reverently to hers. As soon as their lips made contact all the pent-up frustrations of the past month came to the surface. He crushed her to him, his mouth devouring hers. His hands caressed her back and moved up to her hair, her beautiful hair. How he longed to see it falling around her face. He began to move his hands through it knocking the pins loose. Suddenly she broke away.

"Edward, not here," she said backing away and pushing her hair back into place. "Anyone could see. We need someplace to go. You don't happen to have another holding in town, do you?"

Reality hit him. His Sarah was truly offering to be his mistress. He looked down at her once more. Her lips were slightly swollen from his assault. He watched as she ran her tongue over their fullness. There was nothing wrong with a man having a mistress, most did. He smiled and tucked a stray lock of her hair back into place.

"I had been thinking of acquiring some property, but it may take some time. I will need to get in touch with my solicitor."

She stepped back to his side, slipped her arm through his, and smiled up at him as he led her back the way they had come. "That's alright, I can wait." She gave him a smoky glance. "Just don't make me wait too long."

The riding path came into sight. "You know," she said thoughtfully. "It might be best if you put the house in my name. Everyone would think I purchased it. I could move there so that I could always be there for you. It is so hard to get away for extended periods of time when one is living with relatives."

What she was asking was not unusual. It was what most men did for their mistresses, but it still didn't seem real. It was all happening so fast. They were almost to their horses now. "I'll see what can be done," he said pulling away to a proper distance.

"When can we meet again," she murmured before releasing his arm.

"Here, Tuesday," he said under his breath.

"Thank you for the stroll, Lord Montgomery," she said as she mounted her horse once more. "I can't wait until we meet again." She turned her horse onto the path.

Edward mounted his horse and watched her ride away. At last, he had his Sarah. He smiled as he turned his horse toward home.

Sarah smiled as she rode away. He had never stopped loving her. She saw it in his eyes. She had heard tales of his reckless behavior and had hoped that it had been because of her, but she had never known until the night of her party. Suddenly, her smile fell. If only it weren't for that silly chit he had married. She would be the one living in his townhouse.

She should have pursued him as soon after her husband's death as it was acceptable in polite society, but she had been enjoying her freedom too much. She thought Edward would be there when she needed him. He had not made a move toward marriage in all these years what would one more matter. She had no idea how foolish her thoughts were until she read of his marriage in the paper.

She had missed her chance at marriage with him, but that wasn't the only option open to her. She had given her body to Lord Owen, the thought of which still unsettled her stomach, for a title. It would certainly be much more pleasant to give it to Edward for security. Infinitely better than entering into marriage with another aging roué like Lord Grimley who had been sniffing around her door.

His marriage was not necessarily a permanent situation. People died all the time. There was sickness, childbirth, who knew what could befall Lady Montgomery. She would not miss her chance if it came again. She would place herself in the perfect position to become the next Lady Montgomery. She would keep Edward's love burning. She would become his mistress.

She looked down at her hands holding the reins and was annoyed to notice a small rip in her right glove. She cursed her late husband for leaving her in such a financial state. When she found out, after his death, the extent of what he owed she began to wonder if his death was indeed an accident.  Whether it was or not didn't matter. She was still left with nothing. She was quickly becoming the poor relation, going from family member to family member with no home of her own, mending and remending her gloves. No, she could not live like that. She needed a home of her own. Edward had to come through.

At precisely eleven o'clock Emily Whithers was shown into the morning room where Caroline was working on her needlework in a chair next to the window.

"What a lovely room," she said upon entering.

"Thank you, it's my favorite.  Please sit down.  I thought it would be more enjoyable to visit in here since it overlooks the garden.  Would you care for some tea?"

"Yes, that would be nice," Emily said sitting on the chair across from her friend.

Caroline turned to the butler who was still standing by the door.  "Please have Mary bring us some tea, Danvers."

"Yes, my lady."  He said and left the room leaving the ladies alone.

"Emily, I am so glad you came unaccompanied. I felt you needed to talk and knew you would not feel free to do so in certain company."

Emily smiled.  "Luckily Cousin Sarah went riding this morning, so I brought my abigail.  I feel as if I have been let out of prison.  It seems my cousin has decided to take me under her wing. Mother is no help at all.  She claims she is sick and tired all the time and that Cousin Sarah is being such a help, especially because of her knowledge of how to get along in society, although she is beginning to wonder after her seating arrangements at the dinner party.  And her behavior! I could not say anything the night of the party, but Caroline I am so sorry."

Caroline shook her head, "You have nothing to apologize for."

"Mother and I should have paid attention to her plans. We should have made the seating arrangements ourselves instead of leaving everything up to Sarah. I know she said *she* was having a party, but it was really supposed to be for me. At least I got to invite a few friends, though I did not get to talk to them much. Lord Mutton monopolized most of my time and whenever he would go visit with someone else Sarah would lead him back to me."

Mary came in with the tea service. They discussed her mother's health and other subjects of general interest until the maid set the tea on the table between them and left the room. As soon as they were once again alone, Emily gave vent to the frustrations which had been plaguing her since the appearance of her cousin. "Oh Caroline, I don't know what to do. Lord Mutton is going to offer for me soon, I just know it. Sarah has mama and papa so blinded by his money and title I'm sure they will accept his offer. I cannot bear to think how horrible marriage to him would be. I can barely tolerate sitting next to him." She looked at Caroline in horror, "What about wifely duties? Oh Caroline, the thought makes me ill. That awful Sarah, how could she do this to me? Why does she hate me so much?"

Caroline reached over and grabbed her friend's hand in both of hers. "I don't think Lady Owen hates you. The sad thing is I think she feels as if she's doing you a favor. All she sees is a title, not the man himself. Just look at her own marriage, she married Lord Owen after all and considered it quite a conquest."

"But why can't she see that I don't want to marry that awful man? I care nothing for titles. I only want a man who loves me and I love back. He could be a groom for all I care."

"Actually, if you are a member of society reciprocal love can be a rare thing," Caroline said thinking of her own situation.

Emily sighed. "So, you think I should marry Lord Mutton too?"

"No! I never said that. I wouldn't wish him on my worst enemy let alone a good friend like you. Is there anyone you are interested in?"

"Not a single man in London. Certainly not Lord Mutton," she said with a shudder.

"Have you ever told Lady Owen this?"

"I tried, but she doesn't hear a single thing I have said. She has her mind set on this match, and you have to admit she can be rather overbearing at times."

Caroline grimaced slightly, thinking of Lady Owen's behavior the night before toward her husband. "I had noticed that. Surely your parents would be easier to talk to."

Emily frowned. "I doubt anything I would say would change their minds. Mama would probably pat my hand and say something like 'many people fall in love with their husbands after they are married, dear', as if that could ever happen with Lord Mutton. I am certain papa already sees his eldest daughter as the wife of an Earl. He can envision all my younger sisters coming out with the advantages of both money and a title in their family."

"But your father has a title."

"Yes, but only a baronet, just as your father. Do not tell me that your parents were not overjoyed to welcome a future Earl into their family."

"I can't deny that, but I do know, if I had had an objection, they would not have forced the marriage on me."

"I don't think mine would *think* they were forcing it on me. They would just suppose that I don't know my own mind and would do what they thought best."

"Sometimes, I think that people who think they know what is best for you can hurt you worse than those who are trying to do you harm," Caroline sighed.  Both ladies were silent for a while, each deep in thought.  Suddenly, Caroline sat up straighter. "Wait," she said with a conspiratorial grin. "I think I have an idea. Your family is eager for you to attain a title, correct?"

"It certainly seems so," Emily said hesitantly.

"Then you shall give them one, the bigger the better.  What would they say if instead of an earl you landed a marquess?"

"A marquess!  That's impossible!  I don't even know any marquesses.  Well, I know some of course, but only from a distance, and certainly not enough to marry."

"You don't have to marry one, just be engaged to one until you find the real man you want to marry.  Pretend to be engaged, or at least courted by, a marquess until you've gotten rid of Lord Mutton and found the gentleman of your choice. Then you can break it off and marry your man and be happy."

Emily looked at her friend as if she had lost her mind. "Caroline, you forget, in order for your plan to work I must produce a flesh and blood man.  I do not think a packet of letters would suffice. Thank you for trying, but it would never work."

"Oh yes it can.  I'll have to ask him first, but I think I know the perfect flesh and blood man for the job.  In fact, you do too.  We were speaking with him just last night."

Emily looked at her friend in confusion.

"Lord Lydford," Caroline said triumphantly.

"Lord Lydford!  But I never spoke more than a few words to him.  Why would he agree to do this?"

"Because he's a good man, that's why.  I felt it as soon as we began conversing the other night at dinner.  He enjoys putting others at ease, and you have to admit if he helped you, it would certainly ease your mind.  Also, to our benefit, is the fact that he is a very good friend of my husband, though I can't see why.  They are so different. Lord Lydford seems so much more...stable than my husband."

"Oh Caroline, here I have been talking about my problems without thinking of yours. I thought there was something troubling you, but I never dreamed –"

"No, no," Caroline interrupted, "That was a poor choice of words.  His mind is completely sound, believe me.  It is just that I feel as if I am walking on shifting sand around him, not on solid ground.   I'm never sure which way our conversations will turn, most of the time I come away from them feeling either puzzled or furious. Lord  Lydford  just  seems  steadier,  more predictable perhaps."

"I imagine learning to live with anyone takes some time, but you would let me know if anything was really wrong, wouldn't you?  I've been concerned about you, especially after I heard the rumours."

"Rumours?"

Emily colored slightly.  "Please don't think badly of me, I wasn't gossiping, but I hadn't heard anything from you for such a long while that I paid attention whenever I heard the names Lord or Lady Montgomery mentioned in discussions.  I know that things are seldom what they say anyway, but I was hungry for information."

"So, what are the gossips saying about Lord and Lady Montgomery?"

Emily looked uncomfortable as she said, "Only that Lord Montgomery was a terrible rake and was almost disinherited by his father because of his behavior."

"I have a hard time believing that one small comment would cause you such concern. There is more isn't there?"  Caroline knew that her friend would have at least heard the story about Lady Stahlwood and Lady Wharton's infamous tea. She had even heard the whispers herself when she was out.

Emily pressed her lips together and her brow puckered.  Her face seemed to squeeze together until it seemed as if would explode.  "Alright, I'll tell all," she burst out. "It was said that he walked out on you on the night of your wedding and went on a drinking binge. He was seen all around town doing things that should not even be spoken of in polite society. Then, later in the week, when you had a roomful of ladies in to tea, he entered the room falling down drunk and had to be removed. After that, he disappeared for at least a month before starting anew." Emily looked at Caroline's pinched face and her eyes widened. "There isn't any truth to the stories is there Caroline?"

Caroline took a deep breath. "As with any gossip there is a small grain of truth. It is true that he was gone for a few days and that he could barely stand up when he arrived back home, but that was because of illness, not drink. Only two ladies were here when he arrived home and they never actually saw him, only heard the commotion as the servants were helping him upstairs. He was very ill. The month of his so-called disappearance, he spent in bed with a fever and then recovering."

"What a horrible start to your marriage, but at least it is better than I had heard. So, then things are going well?"

Caroline thought a moment before answering. "I suppose so. Except for my parent's marriage, I really don't have anything to compare. I can't say we are friends, but we are not enemies. I'm not completely certain what I feel."

Which was certainly true. One minute, she

thought him despicable and the next her heart surged inside her when he touched her hand. She knew one thing, he was her husband, and there was a strange possessiveness that filled her when he looked at Lady Owen.

She hadn't realized how much time had passed lost in her own thoughts until Emily broke the silence. "I can't imagine marrying a man I didn't know."

Caroline laughed. "This is coming from the one who is trying to avoid marriage to the one she does know. Honestly, how much do people know each other? I have heard horrible stories of the way men treat their wives, men who were extremely charming when they were courting them. I imagine you never really know anyone until you are married. I knew that Edward was kind, my father told me. He knew him when he was young. I trusted his judgment. Besides, I had grown up knowing that I would marry him. It was like he was a part of my life all along. I hadn't even considered anyone else."

"I still can't imagine feeling as you do about marriage, but I suppose if I had my whole childhood to become used to the idea I would think differently. As it is, I could never marry anyone I didn't care for deeply."

"Which is exactly what we're trying to prevent. So, you agree with my plan?"

"Your plan?" Emily wrinkled her brow and

pursed her lips as she tried to remember. Her eyes widened as she realized what plan her friend was speaking of.  "Oh Caroline, I'm certain Lord Lydford wouldn't care about the troubles of a girl he barely met."

"Don't you know you should never jump to conclusions about someone you have admittedly 'barely met'? Trust me. I think he would be game. I just need to find a way to talk to him.  He'll probably be at Lady Ramsey's ball this evening.  It isn't the best place for a private conversation, but I will try to approach him about it there.  You need to try to hold off Lord Mutton's advances as long as possible."

"It is not his advances toward me I fear. Sometimes I wonder if he even notices when I am gone.  It is his conversations with my parents.  I cannot stop him from offering for me."

"Then I definitely will have to find a way to talk to Lord Lydford tonight.  Don't worry.  Even if Lord Lydford doesn't help, we will think of something."

The mantle clock began to chime the hour.

"Oh my, I had no idea it was so late.  I am supposed to go shopping with Cousin Sarah this afternoon.  I must be going," Emily said rising.

Caroline stood also and walked with her to the door.  As they walked down the stairs to the front hall, she said, "I'm very glad you came today, Emily.  I want you to feel free to call at any time.

There is no need to hold to conventions. Even though we never met before this season, I consider you one of my most intimate friends, very much like the sister I never had, and would be glad to see you at any hour of the day."

"Thank you, Caroline, I feel the same about you. Unfortunately, my mother can be extremely conventional."

Caroline chuckled, "That's alright, I'm sure I could confine myself to visiting you during late afternoon hours."

Emily waited in the hall for her abigail to put on her wrap.

"Will you be at Lady Ramsey's ball tonight?" Caroline asked.

"Of course, as I'm certain anybody who is anybody will be."

"Then I shall see you there."

After Emily had gone, Caroline climbed the stairs to her room to prepare for her drive with her husband, but her mind was swirling with plans. Would her idea work?  How could she get Lord Lydford in a place they could talk, and once they were there how would she persuade him to agree to her plan?

# Chapter 11



*Alas! It is delusion all*
*The future cheats us from afar:*
*Nor can we be what we recall*
*Nor dare we think on what we are.*
*-Lord Byron*

Caroline put on her favorite cream day dress overlaid with lace with a lavender sash. A lavender shawl and lavender bonnet with a chip brim completed her ensemble.  She took one last look in the mirror as she was pulling on her gloves, adjusted a few curls, and hurried out the door.

Today was the first day of her campaign. She knew that her looks could not compare to the seductive Lady Owen. The only thing she could use to win her husband was herself. She had to stop being so unsure, seeming like a simple girl around him. She had to be strong and let her real self out, hoping that who she was would win her husband. It was all the ammunition she possessed. She thought about what she said to Emily about not really knowing the person you marry and decided she wanted to change that now. She needed to know more about Edward, too.

She was smiling to herself as she stepped off the bottom stair and into the hall. Edward was standing there looking incredibly handsome in his buff breeches and green coat. His beaver hat was in one hand and gloves in the other.

Truly looking at him for the first time in weeks she realized he looked much better than he had on their wedding day. During his illness, he had lost weight, so the paunch was gone. His complexion despite his recent illness was not as haggard, and his eyes as they swept over her were definitely not as cold. She walked with him out to the waiting curricle. When she put her hand in his as he helped her into it, she felt that strange flutter in her stomach, but the moment was quickly gone as he released her hand and strolled over to the other side of the curricle to get in.

The tiger let go of the horses' heads and as Edward snapped the reins, ran to the back of the curricle to jump on. Their ride had begun, but

Caroline was barely conscious of it. She was too busy wondering when the curricle seat had become so narrow. It seemed like every bump in the road caused his leg to brush hers. She was so absorbed with the sensations this contact caused that by the time her husband's words penetrated her foggy mind they had almost arrived at Hyde Park.

"The other night you mentioned that you hadn't gone to the art museum. Would you like to go?"

Caroline looked at her husband in surprise. She hadn't thought he heard a thing said last night his attention was so intent on their hostess.

"Oh yes, that would be wonderful."

"I'm surprised you haven't been there. This surely isn't the first trip you have made to London?"

"Actually, it is. Well, I did visit when I was twelve, but that was because my father had legal matters to attend to. I can't say I partook much in amusements, though my governess did take me to see the menagerie."

"And have you had your fill of amusements this season?"

"I have been to a number of routs and balls, but I would like to see a play."

"You have never seen one?"

Caroline felt incredibly gauche. "No."

"Everyone should have the experience of a play in London. Although I warn you, it may be much different than you think.  So, what play would you like to see?"

"I really couldn't say.  It just sounds so wonderful.  I have heard some excellent readers, but aside from the players who came to the fair I have never seen an actual performance.  I'm sure the acting must be superb and the story much better than 'The Maidservant's Mistake'."

He chuckled.  "With expectations like that I had better take you to see one of Siddons plays.  She is known for her good performances and because of that the crowd is usually less boisterous.  It may almost live up to your expectations."

"I'm certain it will, but what do you mean the crowd is less boisterous?"

"Let's just say if they don't consider the acting to be of excellent quality they will let the actors know they are not happy."

"I can understand that.  Although, I should think they would not have to say anything.  If it is not a good performance people would not go."

Edward smiled.  "Oh, they come up with much more colorful ways of showing their displeasure," he said thinking of the near brawl that had taken place on the floor of the last show he had been at.

One of the young bucks present had found the acting of Mr. Marlowe, who played the romantic lead, not convincing enough and thought to give him lessons.  He had jumped on the stage and grabbed the young woman playing his fiancé and proceeded to show him how kissing was supposed to be done to the hoots and hollers of the audience. Mr. Marlowe, understandably, did not appreciate his thunder being stolen and so cuffed him from behind. He, of course, was promptly set upon by the young man's friends, who were in turn assaulted by angry actors. Through it all, the fellow who started the fracas continued his lessons in romance much to the satisfaction of the pretty young actress. He chuckled. It was not a performance one would forget, but probably not one his young wife would enjoy.

"I do believe you are laughing at me, Lord Montgomery," Caroline said looking at him through slightly narrowed eyes belied by the humor behind them.

"No, I am only thinking of the farce I saw the last time I went to the theatre," he replied. He seemed about to say more when Lord St. James and a young woman came up alongside them in his carriage

"Ho, Montgomery, lovely day, isn't it? I see that you were of the same opinion as me and thought it a perfect day to take a lovely lady for a drive."

He cast Miss Brightmore a look of decided affection and the subject of his attentions colored a pretty pink.

"Yes, it is rather pleasant," Edward said looking rather uncomfortable.

Miss Brightmore chimed in, "I was very pleased

when Lord St. James asked my mother if I could go driving today. It was much too lovely to sit inside and do needlework."

"Oh, so I am only to be used as a way to get away from the daily drudgery of a society lady," St. James teased with mock distress.

"Oh, no," Miss Brightmore said in alarm, "I didn't mean that."

St. James chuckled. "It is perfectly fine. I'll save you from wearisome duties whenever you wish." He turned back to his friend. "Montgomery, you must find it especially fine. I heard you were out for a ride this morning. Rather unusual for you, I never thought you rose before one."

Edward shot his friend a look that could kill. St. James' eyes widened and he glanced at Caroline before stuttering, "Uh, yes, an exceptionally fine day. Yes. Are you planning on attending Lady Ramsey's ball tonight?"

"Oh, please say you are going. It will be such fun," Miss Brightmore said clapping her hands in an excited way.

Edward was silent so Caroline answered, "Of course, we wouldn't think of not going. The cream of society will be there."

She glanced at her husband whose expression had grown even grimmer and wondered what it was that angered her husband so much.

"Well then, I guess we shall see you there," said

St. James sensing the tension emanating from his friend and eager to be off.

"Yes, I so look forward to seeing you tonight," Miss Brightmore said smiling at Caroline.

Caroline smiled and nodded to her friend as Edward said, "Yes, Good day," and urged their horses forward.

They continued in silence for a while until Caroline felt her husband's tension recede a bit.

"Your friend seems to be quite taken with Miss Brightmore," she ventured.

"Who? St. James?" Edward laughed. "Oh, I'm sure it is nothing serious.   St. James is a determined bachelor."

"As I'm sure you were, Lord Montgomery," she said with a smile.

Edward said nothing, his face serious as he continued driving.  The smile faded on Caroline's face.  He didn't seem angry, but she had no idea what he was thinking. She wished she had not tried to flirt with her husband.

Finally, he began to speak, studying the horse's back as he did so, "Caroline, do you think you could call me by my given name?"  He turned to look at her.

His question caught her completely by surprise. She dropped her gaze.  "I...I imagine I could."

"Why not try it now?"

Caroline snapped her head back up. "Try what now?"

He grinned. "Try calling me by my given name."

Caroline felt her face heat up and knew that she had become an unbecoming shade of red. "Alright...Edward." She looked back down at the hands on her lap with a shy smile.

Edward turned his attention back to the path, grinning. "Much better."

They continued on in companionable silence for a while. Caroline was beginning to enjoy herself more than she imagined. She didn't want their ride to come to an end. Suddenly she saw a pretty path leading through some trees down to a small pond.

"Oh, look at that pretty path. Would you mind if we stopped and walked for a while? It looks like it leads to that pond. Could we secure the horses and stroll around it?"

Edward turned in the direction she indicated and the smile fell from his face.

"No." he snapped.

Caroline looked at him in surprise. His jaw was clenched and there was no remnant of the congenial man he was just moments earlier. "Alright." She said slowly wondering what she did wrong.

"I'm sorry," he snapped, not sounding sorry at all. "I have some things I need to attend to before we go to the ball tonight."

"Yes, I probably have things to attend to

myself," she said slowly, still wondering at the change in him.

The silent ride back home seemed to stretch on forever.  Caroline found herself wanting to end it with as much passion as she had earlier wanted it to continue.  When at last they pulled up to the house, he jumped down and walked briskly around the curricle to help her down.  As he reached up to support her, she flashed him a tentative smile, but he didn't notice. He quickly finished his task and turned away

Once inside he promptly excused himself. "Thank you for accompanying me for a drive today, Caroline.  I most likely will not see you before it is time to leave, but I should be ready to accompany you by ten o'clock."  Then he turned on his heel and quickly walked to is study.

Caroline stood in the hall gaping after him. What had she done to make him so angry?  She had thoroughly enjoyed herself during the first half of their drive and she had been almost certain he had too.  She thought that they were beginning to forge a connection.  He had even asked her to call him by his given name. Then suddenly, he changed. What had she done wrong?

She heard the slam of his study door. She didn't feel like she had done much to further her campaign. She took a deep breath and stiffened her spine. A war isn't won with one battle. She had to prepare herself for a long fight. She marched up the steps to her room in retreat to re-strategize.

Edward strode into his study cursing as he slammed the door behind him. He threw himself down in his chair, ran his hand over his face and swore again. Propping his elbows on his desk, he pinched the bridge of his nose between the fingers of his left hand, and took a deep breath.

Things were getting way too complicated. Just when he had gotten what he had dreamed of for so long his wife had to make him feel like a naughty child. When she had asked him to walk down the very path he had walked with Sarah just hours before, he felt just as he had when he was a boy and his nanny had asked him if he had stolen any of his mother's chocolates.

He had vehemently denied it of course. Nanny had just looked at him sadly and told him to run along, his mother was waiting for him in the garden. He had run down the stairs feeling lucky to have gotten away with his wrongdoing, and thinking he must have really grown if he could fool nanny so easily. As he ran through the hall, he caught sight of himself in the mirror. He stopped in horror, for there smeared all over his face was the evidence of his crime.

He thought he would never feel the shame he had felt then, but today felt a hundred times worse. Who would have thought she would have picked that particular path for a stroll?  It was if it had been marked somehow, just like the smudges of chocolate had marked his face.

He ran his hand down his face and dropped his arm to his desk.  He had been enjoying himself in his wife's company, more than he had ever supposed he would.  When she had said his given name, she had blushed so prettily.  He liked the way it had sounded on her lips.

He threw himself back in his chair.  She had made him think of things he hadn't thought of for a long time.  Things like his mother.

A lot of those memories had faded, but he remembered how his parents had looked at each other.  His mother was always smiling, and his father always seemed to be touching her in some way, a hand on her shoulder, his thigh resting against hers as they sat on the settee.  Even as a young boy he could see the connection between them.  After her death, his father had never remarried, but had raised his young sons on his own.  He had remained faithful to her even through death.

He looked down at his desk and the first thing he saw was the still unopened letter his father had sent weeks ago. He lifted his eyes to the ceiling and shook his head. He didn't have to read it to know what it said. That he hoped his son would change his ways. That he should learn to love the wife he provided for him.

He leaned forward and slammed his fist onto his desk. It was silly to think of such things. His wife had one purpose, to furnish him with an heir. He didn't love her like his father had loved his mother. It was just a marriage of convenience. All this so-called courting was just a ploy to soften her towards his advances. She had her own little place in his life, a little box he had neatly put her into and now she threatened to spill out. Well, he would not let that happen. If he wanted to maintain his sanity, he could not let that happen.

He needed a drink.

He pushed back his chair and walked over to the brandy decanter. He poured himself a drink and downed it, then turned and walked back to his seat while pouring himself another. He sat back in his chair staring at the ceiling and trying to forget everything that happened this afternoon. After a few drinks he began to see things from a better perspective.

It was surely unnatural the way his father felt about his mother. Everyone had a mistress these days. There was nothing wrong with what he was doing. For God's sake, he had wanted Sarah since he had noticed the difference between boys and girls. Was he going to give up all his dreams because of a silly drive? No! By God, he was a man, and he was going to act like one. He poured himself another drink and proceeded to lock his wife back into her box with an alcoholic key.

# Chapter 12

*Not drunk is he who from the floor*
*Can rise alone and still drink more;*
*But drunk is he who prostate lies,*
*Without the power to drink or rise.*
                    *-Thomas Love Peacock*

Sally was arranging Caroline's hair, but had a hard time keeping her mind on it.  She was too busy thinking about what she had heard earlier.  She had been out taking air for a few minutes this afternoon while Caroline was out riding with Lord Montgomery when she heard Jem, their footman, gossiping with the neighbor's footman.

"You'll never guess what I heard today, I was at The White Hart this afternoon having meself a pint when who walks in but that jessamy footman of Lady Owen's, Luke.  Guess what he had to say."

"I'm sure I don't care what that popinjay 'ad to say.  'e'll be trying to get your job soon, I bet.  I 'eard Lady Owen was going to have to let 'im go," Jem bit back.

"That's just what you may find interesting.  He said that he wasn't going to lose his job, but that someone else was going to be paying his salary."

"I guess she found 'erself some swell who'll take care of 'er.  Why would I care oo's paying some tart's footman?"

"Because it's your master, that's why."

"No, 'e'd never," Jem said, but he didn't sound very sure.

"Luke heard it straight from her groom what held their horses while they went for a walk through some trees in the park.  He said that he nearly had her right there, and that Lady Owen wore a brand new, fancy necklace home."

Sally had not stayed to hear any more, but it had troubled her all day.  She knew it was commonplace for the gentry to have mistresses, and Caroline herself had said she would get used to it, but it just didn't seem right somehow.  She felt guilty not sharing her knowledge, yet she was sure it would hurt her mistress.  Suddenly the acrid smell of scorched hair reached her nose.

"Sally!"  Caroline said sharply.

Sally jumped and unwrapped the frizzed curl.

"I'm ever so sorry, milady. My mind was not where it should be. I won't let it happen again."

"Please don't, I'm trying to look my best tonight," Caroline said

The anticipation shining in her eyes made Sally's heart sink even lower. She sincerely hoped they were not shining for Lord Montgomery. He didn't deserve it.

Caroline had dressed with care that evening, hoping that it would bring back the closeness that she had shared with her husband during their drive earlier. She had chosen her blue silk. A key figure was embroidered in gold around the square neckline and was repeated around the hem and edges of her skirt which was split in the front to reveal a thin white muslin underskirt. When she had worn it to her first ball, she had been told by a hardened flirt that it matched her eyes. She hoped her husband noticed the same thing tonight.

She was hoping to make an entrance and so she was a few minutes late coming down. Her plan succeeded. Her husband was waiting at the bottom of the stairs putting on his gloves. As she walked down toward him, she thought she saw the return of the light she had seen so briefly during their ride, but when she reached the bottom, it was to find she had been mistaken. She looked into his eyes to find a gaze as cold as the one she had seen on their wedding day. She shivered slightly, as she had on that day, and put her hand on his proffered arm.

"You look very nice, my dear," he said with a tight smile. When he spoke, she caught the smell of brandy on his breath. As they walked out to the waiting carriage, she sent up a prayer that he would not drink any more at Lady Ramsey's ball.

Caroline's hopes fell even further on the drive. The much-anticipated evening was not going as she had hoped. Her husband sat in the same tense silence that he had on the drive home this afternoon, leaning back against the seat and staring out the window, ignoring her completely. Caroline could not understand how everything could have gone so wrong.

Edward escorted her into the ball, but as soon as they were announced he excused himself and headed for the refreshment table. From there he went straight to the card room.

Caroline tried to forget her disappointment and focus on her mission this evening, trying to catch a few words with Lord Lydford. A dance, of course, would be the best remedy, but it would be best if it were to be a waltz or the supper dance and she was disappointed to find her hostess was one who did not approve of the waltz. Her dance card was getting perilously full, but she could not save a dance for him without causing speculation. She kept combing the crowd for his face. Perhaps he would not come. It could be days before the chance to see him could come again. She closed her eyes for a second and concentrated all her will on the unsuspecting marquess. He had to come, she needed to help Emily and time was short.

"Enjoying the ball, Lady Montgomery?" came a familiar voice from over her shoulder. Her eyes flew open and she turned to find that the man of her thoughts had actually appeared.

She smiled, "Yes, the twenty minutes I have been here have been exceedingly enjoyable."

"Do you dance tonight?"
"With more enjoyment than style, but yes."

"Then you must be enjoying yourself immensely. I can't imagine your dancing to be anything but enchanting. May I ask the privilege of a dance?"

"Of course, Lord Lydford, I should be happy to dance with you," she said offering him her dance card.

He scanned it. "I see that my opinion must be correct. You must be a tolerably good dancer as you seem to be a popular dance partner. Not much to pick from I'm afraid. I'm sure you are saving the supper dance for Montgomery, so I'll claim the dance before that."

Caroline thought frantically. She had actually been saving the supper dance for him. She thought that would be an excellent opportunity to engage him in conversation. A country dance offered plenty of time for a light flirtation, but little chance for private discussion.

"I'm sure Lord Montgomery would not mind if you claimed the supper dance, you are a close friend and he does not care to dance."

"Edward, not care to dance!" He laughed. Then he looked Caroline and became serious. He scribbled his name on the line for the dance before the supper dance, then scanned the floor for his friend. "Where is Edward?"

"I am not certain. The last time I saw him he was heading for the refreshment table"

Just then Lord Amberly came to collect her for his dance.

"Until later then, Lady Montgomery," Lord Lydford said bowing. She nodded and went off with Lord Amberly to join a set.

Caroline had always enjoyed herself at balls in the past, but this one seemed interminable. Her dance with Lord Lydford seemed like it would never arrive. Every time she caught a glimpse of Edward, he had a glass in his hand which she was quite certain did not contain lemonade. This did not bode well for her.

She danced and chatted with her partners, seeming as if she had not a care in the world, but her mind was preoccupied. Would Lord Lydford refuse her request? Would he think her a fool? What about Edward? He was unpredictable enough, but when liquor was added into the mix, she was afraid of what he might do. She felt the strain of not knowing how either man would act tonight, as if she were walking a tightrope and one step to either side could be devastating.

Just as her anxiety had reached its limit, Lord Lydford appeared at her side.

"I believe this is our dance, Lady Montgomery."

"And about time too," Caroline said before she thought. She looked up wide-eyed at Lord Lydford, but he just chuckled as he led her onto the floor.

"I wish all my partners were so enthusiastic."

"I'm sure they are, Lord Lydford, just a bit more discreet."

Caroline glanced around the room as they prepared for the set. She wondered where Emily was. Every time she had seen her that evening she had been accompanied by Lord Mutton. The only time she had danced that evening had been with him, and his dancing appeared to be painful in the extreme. In addition to his other faults, Lord Mutton had no sense of rhythm. As she caught sight of Emily being led onto the floor by him once more, she winced. Lord Lydford caught her expression and chuckled.

"It seems your enthusiasm has waned. I promise not to step too heavily on your toes, Lady Montgomery."

"It is not *my* toes I fear for, but my friend's,

Miss Whithers.  She is the one opposite Lord Mutton.  It is the second dance she has had with him this evening."

"A brave soul indeed, it's a wonder she can walk at all after the first."

The dance began and they moved forward to start the first figure.

"The reason I was impatient for our dance is that I have a favor to ask of you," Caroline said, deciding to broach the subject immediately rather than suffer any longer.

As they took a turn to the right he replied, "Anything, Lady Montgomery."

"It is rather personal.  I am afraid the middle of a country dance is not the place to discuss it," she said as they broke apart and went back to their beginning positions.

When they walked forward once more Lord Lydford said, "Do you see that alcove near the palms over there?"

She glanced in the direction he indicated with his eyes.  "Yes," she said as they took a turn to the left.

"There is a seat there which is in plain sight, but enough removed that we can talk without being heard.  Meet me there after the dance."

"Thank you," she said as they broke apart once more, a grateful smile on her face.

She enjoyed the rest of the dance immensely. After talking to him, she felt fairly certain that he would not completely dismiss her idea, so felt herself relax a bit. The only thing that dimmed her enjoyment was the occasional glimpse of Emily and her incompetent partner.  Edward was nowhere to be seen.

After the dance Lord Lydford bowed over her hand and led her from the dance floor.  "Five minutes," he murmured in a low voice before he left her.

Caroline immediately began to make her way around the edges of the room to the alcove Lord Lydford had indicated.  Upon arriving there she found that it was already occupied by two intimidating dowagers.  She avoided their stony glares as she continued past and stopped on the other side of the palms to wait for Lydford.

"It's occupied," she said to Lydford as he approached.

"So I see."  He eyed the dowagers, one of which actually blushed at his attentions.  "We are in luck though," he continued quietly.  "I believe those doors just ten feet away will take us to a balcony. If we are quick, no one will notice our exit."

They slipped quickly through the doors and onto the balcony. The night was cool, but not cool enough to drive her back indoors. She gave a little giggle of relief.

Lord Lydford smiled. "Well, we have made it past the dragons which guard the doors," he said.

"Yes," she said playing along, "and now I must

complete my quest. I must find a knight in shining armor to rescue a damsel in distress."

Caroline saw the look on Lydford's face and read it well. She knew he was thinking of her and Edward and didn't want to get involved. She quickly spoke to ease his mind. "Oh, the damsel is not me, Lord Lydford, but my friend, Miss Whithers."

Relief flooded his face and he smiled. "Miss Whithers of the tortured feet?"

Caroline laughed. "Yes, you met her once before at Lady Owen's dinner."

"Ah yes, quiet girl." He assumed what he considered a knightly stance. "I would be delighted to polish my armor for any friend of yours, Lady Montgomery. Just tell me what dragons must be slain."

Caroline told him about her friend's plight.

"I see, and you would like me to save Miss Whithers by banishing this dragon or in this situation this...er...donkey."

"Yes," laughed Caroline. "I thought that if someone with a higher title were to come along and appear to be interested in her, her parents would not be in such a hurry to marry her off. This would give her time to find a man she really cares for."

"An admirable idea, milady, Richard Morgan Alexander Blakemoor, fourth Marquess of Lydford, second Earl of Sutherleigh, is at your service," he said executing a low, courtly bow.

"Truly, can I count on you?"

"Anything for you, milady."

Lydford raised her hand to his lips and kissed the back of it.

Suddenly a voice came out of the darkness, "Excuse me, but I believe that is my wife you were just kissing."

They turned to find Edward standing against the light of the door, fury emanating from his rigid pose.

"It was just the back of my hand, Lord Montgomery," Caroline stuttered, "it was only meant as a joke."

"I did not find it funny, *Lady* Montgomery," he spat out, swaying a bit as he did so, "though I suppose you may find it humorous to make a cuckold of me."

Lydford sighed. He walked over to him rather like one trying to put a lead on an angry dog, he placed his hand carefully on Edwards arm. Then in his most ingratiating manner he said, "I know this might look bad to some people, but you know better Montgomery. You know me."

Edward looked pointedly down at Lydford's hand on his arm, shook it off and said coldly, "I thought I did. Apparently, I was mistaken." Then he turned to Caroline with a light burning in his eyes that chilled her soul. "Come wife," he said his voice like ice. "It is time to leave."

She stood frozen to the spot, staring at him.  He let out a strangled growl as he grabbed her by the hand, dragged her through the doors, through the crowded ballroom and out to the hall.  Caroline tripped behind him, trying to keep up with his angry strides.  She kept her eyes focused on her husband's back not wanting to see the expressions on the faces of the guests he rushed her past.  She had apparently fallen off the tightrope she had been walking all evening and she wasn't sure which emotion was stronger fear or embarrassment.

As they waited in the hall for their carriage to be brought around, Edward paced back and forth angrily.  Caroline began to hope that he would become too impatient and decide to walk home.  She had no such luck and within five minutes found herself trapped in an enclosed carriage with a simmering husband.

He had not said a word to her since he had confronted her with Lydford.  The entire trip home he stared out the window with a clenched jaw.  Her fear grew into anger.  He had made a spectacle of them.  The tale of their dramatic exit was bound to be bandied about the drawing rooms of the ton tomorrow.  Just before they reached their townhouse Caroline broke the silence.

"There was no need to behave the way you did back there.  I do not appreciate being the subject of gossip.  I was only out on the balcony to converse with Lord Lydford.  I needed to ask him to do me a favor."

He turned to her at last and she saw from his eyes that not a modicum of his temper had cooled. In fact, she may have just thrown fuel on the fire. She pressed back against the seat as her husband fixed her with an icy glare.

"And did he ask one of you too? You don't seem to find the idea of granting favors to your husband as appealing as granting them to his friends."

Caroline gasped. "I wasn't granting anyone favors, I just —"

She was cut off as the carriage came to a stop and Edward threw open the door.  He pulled her out of the carriage, up the steps and through the front door.  He did not pause in the hall to remove his outside garments, but began pulling her up the stairs.  When he reached the third floor, he threw open the door to his chamber, thrust her inside, stepped in after her and slammed the door behind him.

"Now," he said, "it is time for your husband to collect his favors.  I'm sorry that you do not find it as appealing to bed a future earl as much as a present marquess."

"Lord Montgomery!" Caroline gasped.

"Oh please, call me Edward. We shall be on very familiar terms after tonight."  He advanced toward her with an unholy gleam in his eyes.  "I understand that most women would feel the way you do, a marquess is quite a catch, but unfortunately you are wed to me and you must present me with an heir before you indulge in your own affairs."

Caroline's eyes locked with his and she could not break away from his gaze. The predatory look in his eyes made her feel like a rabbit caught in the gaze of a hawk. She began to slowly back up. "Now, Lord Montgomery, don't do something we will both regret when you are sober."

"Oh, my lady," he said ominously, "I won't regret a thing."

Suddenly he dove at her just like the hawk she had envisioned him to be. She backed up quickly. He had not anticipated her move and fell to the floor. He started to scramble up to go after her once more, but fell back to his hands and knees and became violently ill.

"You, my lord, are disgusting," she said when he had finished retching and was trying to recover. He remained on his hands and knees, head hanging, spitting the remaining bile from his mouth as she raised the hem of her dress and stepped gingerly around his mess. "I'll call for Roth to clean you up," she finished disdainfully.

She rang for Roth as she watched Edward try to pull himself up and not succeeding. As Roth entered the room, he got sick for the second time, "Please take care of His Lordship, he seems to be unwell," she said trying to keep the contents of her own stomach down. Roth bent down to help Edward up as she hurried out of the room and locked her door behind her.

After Caroline turned the lock, effectively barring her husband from her room, she kicked off her ruined slippers, threw herself face down on the bed and let out a sob. He looked as if he hated her tonight. She shivered thinking what would have happened to her if he had not gotten ill.

If only she could go back to that day in the carriage and tell her father she did not want to marry him. He had said Edward had a good heart, but Caroline was beginning to wonder if her husband had one at all. She was being crushed by him. Her heart was being pulled in two opposite directions. She almost felt it would be easier if he was always cruel, then she would know to always have her guard up, but to give her hope and then rip it away was crushing her soul. It was silly to think that she could win him by being her true self. It was accomplishing nothing, but hurting her. She needed to put up a wall of defense. She needed to be as cold as him. She sat up and dried her eyes. It was time for her to grow up. Tomorrow Lord Montgomery would awake to a new Lady Montgomery.

# Chapter 13



*A sadder and wiser man*
*He rose the morrow morn.*
*-Samuel Coleridge*

Edward awoke around noon with the usual dry mouth and pounding head. This had to stop. He had been drinking rather heavily since his early twenties. It was just part of life. Funny how much worse one felt when one was near thirty. How could a mere eight years make such a difference?

He ran his hand over his face and groaned as he began to remember the night before. Had he really behaved so? He had put on a pretty display in front of at least half the ton and he knew the other half would hear about it before the day was done. In the light of day, his reaction to Lydford seemed ridiculous. He wasn't sure what came over him. His behavior to his wife was even worse. Overall, it had been a banner of an evening. He had acted more immature than his wife who was ten years younger than him and had topped it off with the ultimate humiliation of emptying the contents of his stomach on her dancing slippers while in the process of forcing himself upon her. Now that had to make an impression. Unfortunately, it was not the impression he wanted to give, not to anyone, especially his wife.

He groaned once more and threw his arm across his eyes. He lay there for a minute wishing it would all just go away, then sighed threw his arm back down on the bed and opened his eyes only to wince and shut them again at the first stab of light. He sighed once more and then slowly cracked them open one at a time. Finally, they were both open, if slightly squinted. He sat up slowly and once his head could take the change of altitude, swung his legs one at a time over the edge of the bed.

He sat there with his hands on his knees inhaling long breaths through his nose and trying to calm his roiling stomach. At last, he felt able to rise and ring for Roth. After some of his lifesaving restorative and a small breakfast he should be much more himself. He had a lot of apologizing to do this afternoon. Maybe he'd better tell Roth to make a double dose of his hangover cure. He needed all the strength he could get.

Two hours later he presented himself freshly scrubbed and shaved to his wife in the morning room. Most of his headache was gone, as long as he didn't move his eyes too much, and his stomach had settled enough that he didn't fear a repeat performance of last night.

She was sitting in a chair with a cup of tea beside her, seemingly engrossed in a novel. She calmly looked up as he walked into the room and sat across from her. Once sitting, he closed his eyes against the bright sun, then pinched the bridge of his nose between his thumb and forefinger and sighed. He dropped his hand to his lap and looked straight at his wife saying, "I'm afraid I owe you an apology."

Caroline just looked at him.

After a moment of uncomfortable silence, he tried again. "I have no excuse for my behavior last night. I know I behaved abominably. For some reason I have had trouble holding my liquor as of late. That has not been a problem in the past."

She continued to stare at him. He shifted in his seat. His head began to pound once again. What did she want from him? "Honestly, I have not behaved this badly in years. "

Caroline's eyebrows rose.

"At least not in public. I know you may find that difficult to believe considering the way I behaved around you, but it is true. You may ask Lydford if you like."

"Should I?" she said spearing him with her look, "It could be misconstrued."

Edward winced. She wasn't making this easy. "I guess I deserved that. It is not that I don't want you to speak with Lydford, or any of my other friends. It was everything yesterday, the ride, your dress, the way you laughed as you danced. When I found you with Lydford and he was kissing your hand I lost control and did some tremendously foolish things."

"You certainly did. I have never been so humiliated in my life. I do not like being the subject of gossip Lord Montgomery, and it seems that since I have married you, I have become a favored topic." She paused a moment. "I think there is someone else you owe an apology to."

Edward ran his hand over his face and took a deep breath. "I know, I was going to pay him a visit after I spoke with you." He looked her straight in the eye. "Can you forgive me?"

She stood frozen in his gaze for a few seconds then turned her eyes away, but not before he saw the softening in them. "I can," she said, "but it will be hard to forget when I am certain half of London will remind me of it constantly. You have a way of being very public with your indiscretions. Please try to refrain from that in the future. You may be used to such attentions, but I most certainly am not. I do not find them comfortable at all."

Edward smiled at the picture his wife made. She sat avoiding his eyes and fiddling with her book as a child, while speaking the sharp words of a disappointed governess. He was filled with the desire to do better for her. He at least owed her that. "I promise to avoid such behavior in the future," he said quietly.

"That is all I can ask," she said looking down at the book in her lap.

Edward rose from his chair. "Well, I guess I had better take myself over to Lydford's where I can grovel at his feet now." He looked back just before leaving the room. His wife was still sitting there staring at her hands clasped in her lap, her brow furrowed in thought. As he watched a slow smile spread over her face. He wondered what she was thinking and realized with a jolt that he hoped it was about him.

The apology to Lydford was not nearly as hard. Lydford brushed it off as behavior typical for a man in his cups.

"Who knows, I may have acted the very same way had I been in your shoes."

Edward rather doubted that.

"I am more concerned that, from what I have seen, this behavior has become commonplace as of late. What has happened Montgomery? I have not seen you in such a state since you were twenty. You spent so many years drinking yourself into a stupor and doing things that affect your reputation to this day. The last few years you may have imbibed a little too much, a little too often, but you seemed to have control over your actions. Now that control has slipped away once more. What has happened? Is it her? I should think you would have learned your lesson the last time."

"I know. I need to handle things better. I shouldn't push things. It's just that I feel like a fool being married for weeks and never having bedded my wife."

"I don't mean your wife."

"Then who?"

"The woman who started all of this."

"Sarah?" Edward sighed. "We are both quite a bit older now. I think she is really sorry for what happened all those years ago. We all make mistakes when we are young."

"Yes, and most are unfortunate, although in this case I'm not sure. I never did think she was the one for you."

"Why?"

"You lose yourself around her. I think a wife should help a man become a better version of himself, not another person entirely. Honestly, I don't like the man you are around her."

It struck Edward that he didn't either.

"I just feel restless, and unfortunately when I

feel restless, I find myself doing rash things. I am a little confused, that's all."

Lydford studied him for a moment. "This is something you'll have to work out on your own, but perhaps the bottom of a bottle is not the best place to sort out things."

"You are right about that, Lydford. I had pretty much determined to give up excess drinking the minute I opened my eyes." He gave a weak grin and passed his hand over his aching eyes. "You could say the problem came to a head this morning."

Lydford snorted. "It's no more than you deserve."

"I am sorry for ruining your evening last night."

"Well, if it makes you feel any better, last night was not a total loss for me. Before you so rudely interrupted, your lovely wife was enlisting my help in saving a damsel in distress. The poor girl is being hounded by Lord Mutton."

Edward grinned. "Old Muttonhead, that is distress indeed!"

"My thoughts exactly. Anyway, I was more than happy to assist. I enjoyed two dances with the young woman last night and asked and gained permission to pay a call today. Which I need to prepare for, so, although I am enjoying your groveling immensely, I must unfortunately put an end to it and ready myself to pay a call on Miss Whithers. I plan on beginning my campaign in earnest today."

"Far be it from me to prevent a man from rescuing his lady." Turning serious he said, "Thank you, Lydford, for putting up with me. I don't know what I'd do without a friend like you."

Lydford put his arm around his shoulders as they walked to the door of his study. "Montgomery, if it weren't for me, you wouldn't have any of the problems you have today." At the questioning look in his friend's eyes he continued with a grin, "You would have been run through years ago."

After Edward left, Caroline sat thinking. She felt the walls, so carefully constructed last night, beginning to crumble already. Her husband had seemed different this morning. Perhaps the unfortunate episode at the ball last night was for good. This was the first apology she had ever received from him.

She wondered what he meant about his actions being brought about by her behavior. She couldn't find anything wrong with any of the things he listed. She had found the ride enjoyable. The neckline on her dress was slightly lower than some she owned, but no lower than any other of the ladies wore. In fact, it was considerably higher than some. She didn't even remember laughing during a dance, unless it was the one she shared with Lord Lydford.  She had been much too keyed up earlier.

What could she have done wrong? Her heart jumped. Wait a minute! Perhaps she did nothing wrong.  Perhaps she had done everything right. She had out ruled jealousy as the reason for her husband's behavior because he never showed her any kind of affection until yesterday's ride, but now she began to wonder.  Could he have been jealous? What did that mean? She began to smile, her walls wavering precariously.  Perhaps her Edward wasn't dead.

She was still pondering the idea when Danvers came into the room to announce the arrival of Emily.  As soon as she entered the room Caroline noticed the difference in her friend.  Her movements were once again quick, not lethargic as they had grown of late, and her eyes glowed with happiness.

Caroline rose from her seat and walked over to greet her friend.  "My, you are looking well today, Emily.  Did anything happen last night after we left the ball?" she asked with a smile.

Emily was about to speak when a shadow passed over her face.  "Oh Caroline, I was so excited I almost forgot what happened to you last night."

Caroline laughed, "Well, let's hope all of society forgets as easily you do."

Emily searched her friends face, "Are you

alright?"

Caroline smiled and led her to the chairs by the window. She sat in the one she had been sitting in as Emily sat in the one previously occupied by her husband.

"Perfectly alright, Lord Montgomery came to me with a very pretty apology this morning. He was really quite embarrassed himself. He knew he had too much to drink and behaved badly. He promised not to do so again."

"I'm so glad. I worried about you last night."

"That couldn't have been all you did last night from the look on your face when you entered the room. I'm dying to hear your good news."

The light came back into her friend's eyes. "Oh, it was wonderful, Caroline. I'm certain it was the best night of my life, and I'm sure it's all because of you. You talked to Lord Lydford, didn't you?"

Caroline nodded and Emily continued, "I knew it! Soon after you left, Lord Lydford asked me to dance. Lady Owen was actually speechless if you can imagine that!" she said with a giggle. "He was every bit as nice as you said he would be. He didn't just talk at me like Lord Mutton, but asked questions and really seemed to listen to my answers. He dances divinely. I felt as if I were dancing on air, especially as I am accustomed to dancing with Lord Mutton."

"I am not sure your description is very complimentary to Lord Lydford. Someone accustomed to Lord Mutton form of dance would probably find a one-legged drunken sailor a divine partner."

Emily's eyes danced in merriment and she let out a giggle. "Quite right, because the most frequent dancing partners I can claim in my short dancing experience are my little sister and Lord Mutton, I cannot claim to be a good judge of dancing, but I do think Lord Lydford may have surpassed a one- legged sailor."

It felt good to hear her friend laugh again. Caroline had almost forgotten how lighthearted Emily was before the advent of Lord Mutton. After seeing her this way once more she knew she could never let her marry that horrible man.

"The dance was only the beginning," she continued. "After he escorted me back to my mother, he asked if I would like a glass of lemonade. When he brought it back, he sat in the seat next to mine and talked to me for a whole fifteen minutes! You should have seen Lord Mutton's face. It fluctuated between crimson and puce. I wondered if he was going to burst. Later that evening Lord Lydford asked me for a second dance! I had to have been the talk of the ball having the only two men who danced with me all evening, stand up with me twice! When he escorted me back to my seat, he asked Mother if he could call on me today. The whole way home mother regaled father with the details of the night.

I do think your plan may work after all, for my parents seem to have forgotten all about Lord Mutton."

"And how did Lord Mutton take these new developments? He had to think he had at last found a bride."

Emily's smile dimmed a bit," Actually, he took it well, though he seemed quite sad sad. I felt bad for dismissing him so."

"Well," Caroline said with a mischievous smile, "If you feel bad about breaking things off with him, just let him know. I'm sure he's still available."

"I don't feel *that* bad. No, things are going wonderfully. Now, if only Lord Lydford can keep up his efforts, my parents will not pressure me any longer and I won't have to worry about marrying someone I don't love."

Caroline tapped her finger on her lips. "Hmm... this is really just the beginning of a plan. Lord Lydford can't pretend to court you for the entire season."

"Why not? He told me he is not looking for a wife. It seems a perfect situation."

Caroline shook her head, "No, no, that won't do. You said that you would only marry a man who you loved and loved you in return. If you appear to be courted by Lord Lydford, how will you find one? No, Lord Lydford is just a temporary situation." She pursed her lips and drew down her brows in thought. Then suddenly her face cleared and she smiled. "Why don't we start by making a list of suitable gentlemen we want to consider?"

Emily frowned. "That doesn't seem proper somehow."

Caroline got up and brought a sheet of paper, pen and ink to the table between her and Emily. "What could be wrong with it? We can't consider every single man available. We only have a limited time. We cannot waste it. As I said, Lord Lydford can't pretend to court you forever. This will help us channel our energies. Now, who can you think of who is looking for a wife?"

"I thought it might be nice to hold a dinner party," Caroline said that evening as she dined with an Edward whose behavior had turned cold once more.

"A dinner party?" Edward repeated looking up from his plate.

"Yes, a dinner party."

He did not seem enthusiastic about the idea, and she was afraid he might refuse, so she used the only weapon she could think of, "I thought it might quell some of the gossip." She looked at him pointedly.

"Ah, yes," he cleared his throat and looked embarrassed. "A dinner party would be fine. When were you thinking of holding it?"

"How is Tuesday next?"

"I can think of no other engagements we have that night. Tuesday next it is," he said and turned his attention back to his meal.

That was easy enough, thought Caroline to herself. She planned to invite all eight of the eligible gentlemen on their list. Hopefully it would not be too overwhelming for Emily. She hoped to give her friend the chance to spend time with each of them to see which ones could be considered real hopefuls. Perhaps they could pare the list by half.

Maybe she should have tried for an earlier date, it seemed so far away. Unfortunately, it took time to arrange such a thing. She didn't know how she'd get through the next week and a half. Oh, if only the party could be tomorrow.

# Chapter 14

*There are certain women of good fashion who*
*Practice irregularities*
*Not consistent with the strictness of virtue,*
*While their good sense and knowledge*
*Of the world makes them at the same time*
*Keenly alive to the value of reputation.*
*-Hannah More*

Tuesday morning Edward awoke with the dawn. He had not slept well that night knowing that the next morning he was to meet Sarah in the park. He lay on his back, his arms pillowing his head as he tried to sort out his life. It felt right when he was with Sarah, but the moment she was gone it felt somehow wrong. Even now, as he eagerly anticipated meeting her, he felt a heaviness in his chest. He sighed. *Life had been so much easier when he only dallied with women who had no expectations.* He grinned wryly. *And didn't have a wife.*

The sun was rising higher in the sky. He pushed himself up and swung his legs over the side of the bed. He might as well ring for Roth and get dressed.

The valet was there before he had even wiped the sleep from his eyes.

"Please lay out my riding clothes. I plan on taking a ride in the park this morning," he said as soon as his valet entered the room.

"Yes, my lord," he said throwing a surprised glance his way. Edward could understand his surprise. It was the only the second time since he had entered hiss employ that he had requested his services at this hour of the morning. The other being the first time he had met Sarah in the park. He dressed with care, having more than enough time to do so, and went downstairs to the dining room for breakfast only to find his wife sitting at the table perusing the newspaper.

He didn't know that Caroline had begun taking her breakfast in the dining room after realizing that her husband never rose before noon.

"You are awake already?" she said looking at the clock on the mantle as if accusing it of lying to her, then glanced at his clothes and smiled. "Are you going out riding this morning? I haven't been riding since we came to London at the end of February."

"Oh," he said trying to avoid her gaze by walking to the sideboard to help himself to some eggs and toast. Perhaps he could just let her hint go by without comment. It was not as if she actually asked to go.

He grabbed a plate and looked at the food before him. What kind of muck was this? Kippers and boiled eggs? Who would eat such things? He would have to have a word with the cook. He wrinkled up his nose and moved past. Putting a few pieces of toast on his plate, he turned back to the table.

"Could I go with you?"

Edward's heart fell as he sat in his seat. He felt the prickle of perspiration beginning. He focused all his attention on putting preserves on his toast. "It's not the fashionable hour for riding. There will be very few people in the park. I'm afraid you might find it dull."

"That doesn't matter," she said laughing lightly. "You forget, Lord Montgomery, I am a country girl and go riding for the joy of riding, not for who I meet along the way. I would just love to be on a horse again. I don't think I've ever gone this long without riding since I was lifted on to the back of my first pony."

Edward said nothing. The silence grew. Caroline played with the silver next to her plate.

"You haven't breakfasted yet."   He said motioning to the clean plate in front of her.

"I've already had my kippers and eggs."

Edward raised his eyes to the ceiling.  So that explained the kippers.

"I would love to go riding."  She paused and looked down at her empty plate.  "But, if you would rather I not go…"

Edward looked at the crestfallen expression on his wife's face and then closed his eyes and sighed. Women could surely drive a man insane.

"Not today.  I had planned on a solitary ride. Besides what would you ride?  You don't have a mount of your own."

"Yes, how silly," Caroline smiled weakly, "I am used to having an abundance of horses in the country. I'm afraid I still haven't accustomed myself to town life."

"Quite alright," he said smiling with relief, "I will look into acquiring one for you as soon as possible.  In the meantime, you could spend your time writing invitations for your dinner party."

Caroline's eyes widened. "Oh yes.  That had been my intent this morning.  I shall have plenty to occupy my time while you are riding, my lord."

Edward shook his head at Caroline's use of my lord again, but wasn't about to get into a discussion with his wife about it right now.  He rose and walked to the door.

"Montgomery?"

He stopped, closed his eyes, and sighed, before turning around.

"Thank you."

Edward felt a quick pang of guilt in his heart, which he quickly stifled, then nodded and quickly left the room.  He thought he would never escape his wife's attentions.  He certainly didn't want to be late.  He briskly walked across the hall, out the front door and down the steps to Tom, his groom, who was holding the bridle of his horse.

"Thank you, Tom.  I should be back in an hour," he said, patting the neck of Dionysus and hoisting himself up onto his back.  He was almost to the park before he recalled that he had forgotten to tell Tom to keep his ear to the ground about any mares for sale that might be nice for his wife. Oh well, he would have to get to that later, right now he had an appointment.

As he reached the trysting place, he felt a stab of guilt remembering the moment his wife had wanted to walk the path.  Soon he would not need to feel guilty.  Soon he would have a little place away from the park.  Somewhere he would never have to pass with his wife, somewhere for him and Sarah alone.  Until then, he had to be more careful where he took his wife for drives.

The park was a bit busier this morning and it put his nerves on edge.  He looked up along the riding path and caught sight of Sarah making her way towards him.  Even at a distance he knew it was her.  He was familiar with the way she sat her horse, and the hold of her proud head.  It was amazing how he remembered those details after all these years.    As she drew closer, he dismounted.

He tethered Dionysus to a nearby tree by the time she reached him, and approached her horse.

"Lady Owen," He said bowing slightly, "How nice to see you again.  I was just going for a stroll. It would be delightful if I were to have a companion for my walk."

Sarah smiled.   "I would be delighted to accompany you, Lord Montgomery."

She handed her reins to her groom and Edward helped her dismount.  She placed her hand on his arm and they started down the path they had traveled before.

"It's been such a long week without you, Edward.  I do wish we could see each other more often."

Edward smiled and pressed her hand on his arm.

"As to that, my dear, I have some news."

She turned to him, her eyes sparkling. "News? From your expression I believe it to be good news."

"I find it good news indeed.  By this time next week, I shall most probably be acquiring some real estate somewhere in London."

Sarah threw her head back and smiled.  "Ah.

Oh Edward, "I'm so happy.  Now we can truly be together whenever we want."  She laughed and squeezed his arm.  "I did not believe I could be this happy again."

They walked on, Sarah chattering about society gossip, the side of her body brushing his with every step, causing his heart to beat faster and his blood course through his veins, until he began to wish that it was not the fashion to wear such tight-fitting pants. When they reached a more secluded part of the path, he grabbed her by the waist turning her toward him and cutting off her chatter by covering her mouth with his.

He pulled her tight against him, pressing against her feminine areas. Sarah cupped his buttocks and pressed him even harder against her. His hands began to roam over her body and his lips left hers and began to trail kisses down her neck as her hands began an exploration of their own.

"Caroline," he said huskily.

Edwards eyes flew open as he felt Sarah hesitate a moment her body tensing. He thought desperately of something to say to hide the fact that he had just called his soon to be mistress, by his wife's name. The thought alone made his stomach turn. *What sounded like Caroline?*

"No, I can't lie," he said. *Can't lie sounds close to Caroline, even though that is precisely what I am doing.* "This is a dream come true."

And it was, in a way, the dream was just not ending like it usually did.

He felt Sarah's body relax against him, and she seemed to want to continue, but he grabbed her waist and set her away from him.

"We had best stop. It shouldn't be long, but it's best to be discreet.

Sarah placed her hand on his cheek and smiled, "Of course, Edward. But do hurry. I can't lie either. I am eager to fulfill all your dreams."

She turned and slipped her arm through his turning around to head back toward the main path. They walked back to their horses in silence. She mounted her horse and left, not uttering a word, but speaking volumes with her look.

Edward stood for a while after she left looking back down the path they had walked. Each time they had walked down the alee they had gone a bit further. Absently he wondered what lay at the end of the path. Would he feel fulfilled when he reached it? And why, when he was kissing Sarah, did he say his wife's name?

Though Caroline would not have believed you had you told her that morning, the next five days flew by quickly and without incident. Edward seemed to be busy with his own matters, so she put all of her energies into preparations for the dinner party. All of the people who had been invited had accepted.  Most were probably coming hoping to witness another scene between Lord and Lady Montgomery like the one at Lady Ramsey's ball, but they were coming, and that's all that mattered to Caroline.

In addition to the eight eligible men in their list, Caroline had invited nine young ladies including Miss Brightmore and Miss Law.  She had crossed Lady Owen's name off her list, even though it was bad manners, but added it back on when she decided it was a better revenge to invite Lord Grimley.  It was rumoured that he was looking for a new wife, and that Lady Owen was at the top of his list.  He should keep her uncomfortable enough the entire evening, she thought with a smile.  She also invited Mr. St. James whom she believed had formed a tendre for Miss Brightmore, and Lord Lydford, of course, to keep up the pretense.

Lord Lydford had done a wonderful job at pretending to court Emily.  He had called on her several times, even taking her for a drive once. Mrs. Whithers was in raptures.  He was playing his part to perfection.  Now all that remained was to find that perfect man for Emily out of their list of eligibles.

Edward decided to remove himself from the chaos the night before the party.  His wife was doing the finishing touches and making sure everything was in order. He decided the best place for the man of the house to be was at his club.

When he entered White's, St. James waved him over.

"Up for a game of cards?"

"Exactly what I came for. You don't know what it can be like when a woman is getting a dinner party ready."

"Oh, believe me, I do. If she's anything like my mother, I'm surprised I didn't see you here sooner," St. James replied with a chuckle. "Brandy?"

"Sounds good."

St. James retrieved a couple glasses and they both headed to the card room. A number of games were in progress so they waited until a spot opened up at one of the tables. Edward took a swallow of his drink.

"So, am I going to get a wedding invitation any time soon?"

St. James coloured a bit, "I'm sure I don't know what you are talking about."

"Oh, I think you do. Perhaps you could work on wooing your young lady at the dinner tomorrow. Miss Brightmore is coming"

"Yes, I know. When I spoke with her this afternoon..." St. James left his sentence hanging.

"No wedding bells, huh?"

"So, who else will be at your dinner?" St. James

asked trying to change the subject.

"Miss Brightmore's friend, Miss Law, Lydford, Sherrington, Dane, Miss Whithers, Miss Dalrimple, Lady Owen and Lord Grimley. I'm sure there a few others I have forgotten."

"Grimley seems a rather odd addition to the company, a bit older than the rest of us. How did he come about getting invited?"

Edward shrugged. "My wife issued the invitations. I'm not sure of her reasoning."

"Perhaps Lady Owen asked her to invite him. The old codger does have bags of money."

Edward bit down his irritation, "I don't know why that would persuade Lady Owen to solicit my wife for an invitation for him."

"Well, everyone knows that she needs to marry money this time. Last time she got the title, but Owen always was a bit loose with his money and a horrible gambler on top of it. Left her destitute I heard."

Edward felt his stomach drop. Did Sarah just want his money? Was that the only reason she had been so attentive to him? He had thought her to be a woman of independent means and that her interest in him was purely emotional. Suddenly he wasn't as keen on a game of cards. He downed his glass of Brandy.

"You know, I think I'll pass on the game of cards. I suppose I should try to be the supportive husband at a time like this. First dinner party and all."

St. James slapped him on the back, "You're a braver man than I am," he said and walked off to the seat that had just opened at one of the tables.

Edward made his way slowly home. Was Sarah playing him once again?

The night of the dinner party Caroline was half nervous, half relieved that the preparations were completed. When she sat down sat her dressing table and Sally began fixing her hair she sighed heavily and tried to let all the tension drain out of her body. She had done all she could, what happened from this point on was out of her control. Sally cleared her throat. Caroline closed her eyes and tried to empty her mind. She heard her maid clear her throat again.

"Did you need something, Sally?"

"No, Milady."

A minute later she heard her maid sigh.

"Sally, you might as well tell me."

"It's really just servant's gossip, Milady."

Caroline didn't reply.

Sally sighed again.

"Truly Sally, it would be much better if you would just get whatever it is off your chest, for it seems to be sitting heavily and restricting your breathing."

"Well, I did want to wait until after your party,

but I heard Lord Montgomery's footman talking with the Amherst's footman the other day.  They were saying that Lord Montgomery was taking Lady Owen under his protection.  Jem said he didn't believe it and I didn't want to either, but I just thought you should know so that you can decide for yourself if it were true or not."

Caroline gave a melancholy laugh.  "Sally, I have to say your timing is impeccable, but thank you.  Lady Owen will be here tonight.  I will keep what you have told me in mind."

The first to arrive was Lord Lydford.  Caroline thanked him effusively for helping Emily.

"Oh no, Lady Montgomery, it is I who should be thanking you. Your friend is delightful.  It is a pleasure to spend time with her."

"I am so glad you feel the way that I do, but we will try not to impose on you for too long."

"It is no imposition.  I will be available as long as you desire."

More guests began to arrive and Caroline excused herself to greet them.  As they continued to arrive Caroline made sure that those who were not acquainted with one another were introduced.  She tried to place people together who had the same interests, and as a result the conversation was flowing easily.

The decision of inviting Lord Grimley proved to be a good one.  Lady Owen's smile was quite brittle as she politely fended off his advances. The rest of the company avoided their corner as the smell of stale sweat mingling with perfume was overpowering. Lord Grimley was of the old school, those who eschewed bathing, considering it unhealthy.

Caroline almost felt sorry for her, until she caught one of the glances she flashed toward her husband. No, she decided, she deserved every stifling breath she took next to her aged suitor. Caroline did have the pleasure of noting that her husband did not return those glances. After a few uncomfortable moments when she first arrived, he turned all his attention to his other guests and avoided the attentions of Lady Owen with almost the same intensity that Lord Grimley pursued them.

The only thing that troubled her was that Emily had spent the entire evening thus far exclusively in the company of Lord Lydford. One would have thought that he would have insisted she talk to the other men present knowing their scheme. Perhaps he was sharing insights with her about the men present. That would be beneficial, but she needed to spend time with the men herself. Apparently, some intervention was needed. She walked over to the couple seated by the fire.

"Miss Whithers, I realized that I was neglecting my duties. I am sure you are not familiar with everyone in the room. I feel perhaps some introductions are in order, if you would please excuse us, Lord Lydford."

Lydford stood and bowed his head toward the ladies, "Of course."

Emily rose warily and joined Caroline who led her directly to Mr. Sherrington, the first gentleman on their list.

"Mr. Sherrington, I would like to introduce you to my good friend, Miss Whithers. Miss Whithers, Mr. Sherrington."

"Miss Whithers," The thin young man with cropped brown hair with a reddish tinge to it said with a small bow.

"Mr. Sherrington," Emily answered barely above a whisper.

Silence reigned as Emily stared at the floor and Mr. Sherrington began to look around the room. Caroline tried to save the situation. "Unusually dry weather we are having for this time of year, do you not think so, Mr. Sherrington?"

"Yes, yes, unusually dry," he replied absently still looking around the room with a rather desperate expression as if searching for someone to save him.

Emily said nothing.

Mr. Sherrington finally cleared his throat. "Well, if you ladies would not mind excusing me, I do need to talk to Burlington about...er...something and I see him over there." He inclined his head toward the depressed looking man on the other side of the room talking to her husband. "Pleasure to meet you, Miss Whithers," he said and hurried away as if being chased by the duns.

Caroline gave her friend a frustrated glare. "Emily, what are you doing? How will you ever know if you find a man interesting unless you talk to him?"

"I am very observant, Caroline," her friend replied patiently. "In fact, I learn much more about a person by just observing them rather than talking to them. When I try to talk to someone I don't know well, I get so nervous I can hardly think at all."

"That's strange, you seemed to hit it off with Lord Lydford and you didn't know him well."

"He's different," Emily said waving Caroline off. "I have actually accomplished quite a lot this evening. I have already crossed two men off the list."

"Two! In less than half an hour?"

"Yes, number one is Lord Dane. He is much too affected in his speech. I could not envision myself spending the rest of my life in the company of a man who gestures with every comment. I would feel as if I were watching a play every day. One with inferior actors I'm afraid. The second one is Mr. Burlington. I believe he is attempting to become the next Lord Byron. I simply could not tolerate his incessant brooding. And that curl which keeps falling down his forehead and into his eye, I swear I would have to sneak into his room in the middle of the night and cut it off!"

"You never know, if you are fortunate, with age he may begin balding," Caroline said with a giggle. "It seems I was wrong in thinking you were not accomplishing anything this evening.  Since you seem to have things well in hand, I shall return to tending to my other guests and let you continue."

As Caroline circled among her guests, she noticed that Emily drifted back to Lord Lydford's side.  She began to frown, thinking that his attentions might give someone the wrong idea. Then she laughed at herself realizing that's just what she wanted people to think, at least for a time. Why worry?  It seemed that Emily knew what she was doing.  Besides she had placed Lord Musgrave and Mr. Thorpe beside her at dinner, which would be starting soon, so she would be able to evaluate them later.

She persisted in her watch over Edward and Lady Owen.  Although the widow continued to send many languishing looks in her husband's direction, she did not see him return one. He continued to avoid her company. Whether that was a good sign she was not sure.  What man would pay special attention to another woman in his wife's presence? Of course, one never knew with Edward. There was no way she would know so she tried to put it from her mind, but her eyes continued to stray to one or the other periodically.

In spite of her preoccupation with her husband and Lady Owen, she did her best to see that all her guests were entertained, and was happy to see the entire dinner party went smoothly. The food was cooked to perfection. The seating was to everyone's liking, except of course Lady Owen who found herself once again paired with Lord Grimley. After dinner, the men were not overlong imbibing their port, by the time they joined the ladies in the drawing room tables had been set up for those who wished to play cards. No one left too early and everyone assured Caroline that it was one of the most delightful suppers of the season.

After the last guest had departed Caroline found herself alone in the hall with her husband.

"I think that went rather well."

"Yes, you plan a wonderful party." Edward said from directly behind her. He put his hand on her shoulder. His thumb brushed against her neck. Her heart skipped a beat, but she moved away and feigned a yawn. "Oh, my, it's been a busy day. I do think I'll turn in."

Edward breathed deeply and let his arm drop to his side. "I believe I'll have a nightcap first."

Caroline moved to the bottom of the staircase. "Goodnight then, Lord Montgomery," she said and began her ascent.

"Sweet dreams, Lady Montgomery." Caroline

felt her husband's eyes upon her until she reached the second floor.

Edward turned and walked down the hall to his study.  Once inside he shut the door and poured himself a drink.  He took a swallow and then stood staring into the amber liquid.  The corner of his mouth lifted in a smile.  He was proud of his wife.  She had really done a wonderful job tonight.  A more gracious hostess he doubted he had ever seen.  She saw to the comfort of all her guests and had an uncanny ability to know just who to pair together.  And to think it was her first dinner party.

He downed the rest of his drink and then poured himself another.  Sitting down in the chair behind his desk, he leaned over and toyed with his glass.  She was really not a bad person, his wife.  Perhaps he was just growing used to her ways, but she didn't seem nearly as annoying as she had when they had first wed.  Though he still could not understand her love of kippers, nasty things.

She was still young.  She had plenty of childbearing years left.  There was no need to be in a hurry.  Perhaps he should spend more time getting to know her, become almost friends.  It was not unheard of, and it would certainly be better than being at odds with her.

He nodded his head and then picked up his

glass and took a drink as if to seal the deal. He would start tomorrow. Yes, tomorrow he would begin his campaign to win the amity of his wife.

# Chapter 15



Caroline's' first call the next day was to the Withers'. She was shown into the drawing room and was displeased to find Emily's mother in attendance. She had gotten used to her own married state and had forgotten that as a young unmarried girl, Emily would not be accepting callers on her own. At least she was fortunate that it was not Lady Owen who was chaperoning today. As she was the one caller present, it would be terribly rude to ask if they could speak privately, not to mention the questions it would raise. This meant she would not be able to question Emily on her progress at the party last night.

After five minutes of meaningless conversation about the latest fashions and the fact that soon the season would be coming to an end, which did nothing to ease Caroline's frustrations, Lady Elphinstone was shown in. Caroline brightened seeing the possibility of the chance of a few private words with Emily greatly increase. Lady Elphinstone was a great friend of Mrs. Withers having gone to school with her. Caroline had never cared for the woman with her overbearing personality and lack of discretion, but she seemed to improve a hundredfold as she walked into the room. Lady Elphinstone sat down next to her friend on the settee and, after a quick acknowledgement of the two young ladies, began relating the latest on dit with such intensity that she and Emily were able to remove themselves to the other side of the room without either woman directing so much as a glance in their direction.

"So," said Caroline as they reached the windows and feigned an interest in the view of the street. "Which of our men have you decided upon?"

Emily frowned. "I'm afraid this isn't going to work."

"Don't worry, just give it time. At least you have

eliminated two of the men from the list. Six is not an overly large number of men to compare. I admit, after you had ruthlessly cut two men from the list in the first thirty minutes or so, I had hoped you would have reduced the number two or three more by the end of the night, but we will just have to work with what we have. Are there any on the remaining list that appeal to you more than others?"

"No, I'm afraid you don't understand," Emile said as she looked down at her hands which she was twisting together. "I have eliminated the entire list."

"What! You can't possibly mean that. Is there not one man on the list you could consider as a husband?"

"Which one would you have me have?" Emily asked in frustration. "The one who attacks his food like a lion and sucks on his teeth when finished, or the one who talks of nothing but the latest fashion, and is so concerned about the state of his clothing, he must fix all his attention on the miniscule bites of food he places in his mouth lest he permit a small morsel to fall on his attire."

"Surely there must be one man with admirable qualities on our list?"

"I am certain they all have admirable qualities. I merely have a hard time seeing past their annoying habits to discern them. Lord knows, any one of them is better than Lord Mutton, but when

I try to imagine myself spending the entirety of my life with one of them, it begins to appear a very long life indeed."

"In that case, we need to make a new list. Surely, we can come up with a few more names."

Emily made a face. "I don't know, Caroline. I have pretty well exhausted my knowledge of eligible men. I guess we will just have to give up. It was all mother's idea anyway. I was happy just staying home. Thankfully, in only a few months. I'll be back there."

"Nonsense, you don't want to just stay home, and you shall not settle. We shall find the perfect man for you. We just need access to a larger group of men, and a way to learn more about them." She stood for a while, lips pursed and brow furrowed deep in thought, then suddenly her face cleared. "I have it! Lord Lydford!"

"What!" cried Emily, her eyes widening in surprise.

"He's the perfect choice!" She said to Emily, whose mouth had fallen open. "He knows all the men of the ton. We shall have to prevail upon him to make a list. He knows things about the men in question that we couldn't possibly know. Men are much more open in their clubs and among their friends than they are when out in society. We could eliminate those who are extremely crass or free with their women. Those who are close to ruin from gambling would never make the list. I don't know why I had never considered this before. He is sure to find the perfect man for you. I will undertake to ask him as soon as possible."

"Lord Lydford could make a list of eligible men?" Emily repeated with a bewildered look.

"That's what I said, silly." Caroline smiled at her friend. "Now, we had better get back to your mother and Lady Elphinstone before they begin to wonder what we've been talking about. It would never do for Lady Elphinstone to discover our deception. She would have you married off to an eighty-year-old lord in a trice!"

They both were quiet and stood for a moment thinking about poor Lucinda, her daughter, who was married off to a viscount three times her age, then slowly walked over and joined the other women who were still gossiping with great fervor. They continued without pause and so never noticed the reticence of the two girls until finally Caroline felt that she had stayed long enough to politely leave. She said her goodbyes and would have liked to go directly home to think about her new plan, but she had a few more calls to make. These she accomplished in the quickest manner possible without causing offense.

As she sat in the carriage, finally heading towards home, she once again found herself with time to think about Emily's list. When could she get the chance to talk to Lord Lydford? She certainly could not make a habit of sneaking out of balls to speak with him, especially after her husband's reaction after the last time. She quickly tilted her head to the side. Edward. Perhaps he could help her gain an audience with Lord Lydford. He had seemed a bit more approachable lately. Maybe if she included him in her plans, it would be better than trying to see Lord Lydford on her own, and since they were friends, he could ask him to come by. No one could overhear their plans, and she could certainly see him faster than having to wait until an opportune time. She was now even more impatient to arrive home.

When she entered the hall, she handed her wrap to Danvers and asked, "Do you know where I could find Lord Montgomery?"

"I believe he is in his study, my lady."

"Thank you, Danvers," she said, handed him her gloves and then walked down the hall to Edward's study. When she reached the door, she knocked lightly and when she heard a muffled "yes?" from inside, opened the door. Edward was sitting at his desk looking at some papers before him. He looked up in surprise and rose as his wife entered.

"Hello my dear, to what do I owe this pleasure?"

"I came to ask your advice."

"My advice?" He stood silent for a moment as if surprised by her statement, then shook his head as if to clear it and realized they were both standing staring at each other. He cleared his throat. "Why of course, whatever for?" he said gesturing to a chair for her to sit down. She sat and hesitated for a moment.

"Well..." Then she took a deep breath and blurted out, "I need to talk to Lord Lydford privately and I don't know how to get him alone."

"You need to talk to Lydford alone?" he said slowly.

"Yes."

"And you want me to arrange this for you?" he said looking confused.

"If you would," she said and then noticed the look on his face. "I know it seems odd, but he's been helping me with something and I would like to see if he can help me with something else."

"May I ask what it is?"

"I would rather not say," she squirmed a bit in her chair, "It involves other people and is of an extremely delicate nature."

Edward began to look angry. Caroline was sure he would refuse her request. Then, suddenly, his face cleared. "Ah, the damsel in distress?"

"He told you?"

Edward nodded, "When I went to see him the day after the ball."

"I need to ask him if he could do another favor for me. Can you think of a way we could arrange to meet?"

"My dear, it's perfectly simple. I can arrange

for him to stop by here before we go to the club, but I must insist upon one stipulation before I will agree."

"What is that?"

"I wish to be present during the appointment. It gives a man strange feeling to be setting up a clandestine meeting between his wife and his closest friend."

Caroline smiled. "It's not exactly clandestine if you know of it, but since you know the situation already, I have no objection to you being present."

"And if I hadn't known the situations?"

Her eyes twinkled mischievously, "I suppose we'll never know. Thank you, Lord Montgomery, for your help."

"It was nothing, my dear. We can meet in here, shall we say, nine o'clock?"

Dinner that night was very pleasant. They seemed to have formed camaraderie after their meeting in Edward's study. Talk flowed easily. They were about to be served dessert when Caroline realized that the vision of Lady Owen in her husband's arms had not come once to her mind as it had haunted her the last week. It came back in that instant and she pushed it away. She would not let Lady Owen spoil her pleasant evening.

Ever since that day in the park, she felt things may have changed between them. For one thing, her husband had made no mention of an heir.

Perhaps he was content with her company. Perhaps he had resigned himself at last to marriage with a celibate wife. Perhaps they could just be friends. Though the thought of such a situation should have made her happy, she found herself feeling hollow. She pushed that thought away too.

At eight forty-five Edward suggested they withdraw to his study to await Lydford. They had just settled before the fire with their drinks, sherry for her, brandy for him, when Lydford was shown into the room.

"Come in, Lydford," Edward said rising and walking over to his friend, arm outstretched. The two men shook hands as they greeted each other. "Would you care for a drink?"

"Yes, I believe I would."

"Brandy?"

"The good stuff?

"You need to ask?"

Lydford smiled and said, "Perfect."

As Edward poured him a drink, Lydford greeted Caroline and sat on the chair next to hers. After he was handed his brandy, he leaned back in his chair crossed his legs and said, "Edward said you wished to speak with me, Lady Montgomery."

"Yes, it's about Miss Whithers."

A concerned look crossed Lydford's features. He uncrossed his legs and leaned forward in his chair. "Is something wrong?"

"Oh no…well, yes….in a way," Caroline replied.

"I don't understand," Lydford said frowning.

At this point Edward broke in, "You must remember, Lydford, we are talking with a woman here, and believe me, I know from experience, my wife is one of the hardest to understand."

Caroline flashed him a venomous look as Lydford laughed.

"This is serious," she said, fighting the urge to stomp her foot.

"I'm sorry, please continue," Lydford replied, immediately contrite.

With one last quelling look at her husband, she turned to Lydford and said, "Our plan is not working."

"What?" said Lydford, "I thought Miss Whithers' parents were pleased with my attentions. I was positive they had changed their minds about the suitability of Lord Mutton. Should I call on her more often? I thought it would seem too excessive if I called more than twice a week. I spent a considerable amount of time with her at the engagements we both attended, but I have no objection to increasing that time, if it would help."

"No, no, it's not that. You have played your part beautifully. It's the other part of the plan."

Lydford raised his eyebrows as he said, "Other part of the plan? I was not aware there *was* another part of the plan."

"Of course there is.  It is not enough that she fends off the bad matches, but that she makes a good one.  She must marry after all and would prefer it be a man of her choice, so we made a list of all the eligible men she might possibly be interested in and th-"

Lydford cut her off, "You made a list!"

Caroline looked innocently at him. "We needed to start somewhere.  I thought a list would help. So, we made the list, and I invited the men on it to our dinner party last night.  Unfortunately, after spending time with them she found that none of them would suit."

Lydford jumped out of his chair and sputtered, "None of them would suit!"  He paced across the floor. "Of all the—" he checked himself and turned to Caroline who was observing his behavior with wide eyes, "were all the men present on your list?"

"No, of course not," she said as if he should know better. "Some of the men who were present are married!"

"Who---who was on this list?" Lydford asked.

Caroline recited the eight names from the list they had compiled.  Lydford took a deep breath and sat back down in the chair he had vacated.

"I didn't think nice young ladies made lists of eligible men," he said in a teasing tone.

"Oh, Lord Lydford," she tilted her head and smiled, "you would be surprised."

"You seem to be as eager as Miss Whithers

parents to see her wed."

"I am not in a hurry to see her married," Caroline protested, "but if she has to, I want to see her married to someone who will not make her unhappy."

Lydford studied her face intently for a moment as if making a decision and then said, "What are your criteria?"

Caroline smiled. He seemed to be softening to her idea. "Preferably they would learn to love each other," she began. "Unfortunately, that is not always possible, so we need to find someone she could live with. No excessive drinking, no excessive gambling, no annoying habits, and someone who will treat her with respect and kindness."

"Tall order there," Lydford mused.

"Yes, I'm beginning to discover that myself. This is where your help can come in. We thought you would be the perfect person to make our new list."

Lydford choked on the brandy he was sipping. "Me?" He sputtered.

"Yes, it's perfect. You know so much more about the men of the ton than we ever possibly could. How could we know which ones to avoid? We only see the side of a man he shows to society. You, on the other hand, see the way he really is when he lets his guard down among friends. You also know many more men than we do. The perfect man for her may be out there and we haven't met him yet." Warming to her subject she continued, "Perhaps you could even have a dinner party of your own so that she could meet some of these men."

"I will not have a dinner party so that my friends could be paraded about like horses at Tattersall's" he said firmly.

"It was just an idea. I didn't mean it to sound so vulgar."

"I am certain you didn't, Lady Montgomery." Lydford paused a moment and rubbed his chin, "Hmm..." he slanted a mischievous look at Edward, "This could take some thought." He paused a moment longer as if in deep thought and then slapped his leg, "I'll do it, but only if you agree to *my* conditions."

"Name them," was Caroline's reply.

"I think the first part of our plan is working for now. It is preventing Miss Whithers' parents from marrying her off before she reaches her goal. So, my first condition is that we continue as we have been."

"Agreed," said Caroline with a brisk nod.

"Secondly, you must agree not to try to make a new list yourself. It may take me a considerable amount of time to complete my research, and I don't want you getting impatient and inadvertently marrying her off to a gambling drunkard. You must agree to wait for my list."

Caroline nodded a bit slower this time. "Alright," she said with a sigh, "agreed. Please try not to take overly long though."

Lydford smiled, "Only as long as it takes to reach my goal. I want to do my best. Then it is agreed. When I've finished my list, I will let Montgomery know and we can meet again."

"That sounds wonderful Lord Lydford," Caroline said almost clapping her hands in delight, "Thank you."

"As I said before, anything for you, Lady Montgomery." He turned to Edward. "Well old man, ready to go?"

"Uh, yes, of course," Edward said, still incredulous that his friend had agreed to his wife's outrageous plan.

"Research my dear lady, research," Lydford said with a smile, as he and Edward quit the room.

Caroline sat for a minute in her chair letting the outcome of the meeting sink in. She didn't think it would have been so easy to convince Lord Lydford. He must have thought her plan a good one. She couldn't wait to tell Emily.

Edward studied his friend in silence almost the entire trip to White's. Finally, he could take it no longer and asked, "What are you playing at Lydford? I know you could not possibly take any of this nonsense seriously. Why would you agree to help?  I'm not sure whether to be happy with you for indulging my wife's fancies or to be angry with you for gulling her into believing you would actually carry out such a task."

Lydford gazed benignly at him.  "Oh, but I do intend to carry it out.  In fact, I have a very good idea who would suit Miss Whithers perfectly.  I just need a little more time to be certain."

Edward's mouth fell open.  "Are you serious?"

"Of course.  I would never intentionally mislead a lady, especially the wife of my closest friend.  Actually, I welcome this opportunity to lead Miss Whithers to a man who would cherish her the way she deserves.  She is a very nice girl, you know."

"Yes, she seemed rather nice when we met, nothing special, but nice.  So, what gentleman do you have in mind?  Perhaps I could help with your research."

"Oh, no," Lydford said grinning, "I swear, you are as bad as the ladies. You will find out the name of the gentleman at the same time as everyone else.  I wouldn't want my quarry to be scared off."

The conversation ended as they had reached White's.  They went to the back room where there were already a few games of cards in progress. They spotted St. James and Fairweather and soon began a game of their own.

Edward found it hard to concentrate on the game.  He just could not believe that Lydford had agreed to his wife's ridiculous plan.  In fact, he seemed happy to do it. 'Anything for you, Lady Montgomery,' he had said. Well, he'd better remember that she *was* Lady Montgomery. She was *his* wife. He shook his head, Lydford would never do something like that to him. And truly, when he looked at it, he didn't seem to have any other thought but friendship toward his wife, and it didn't seem like Caroline was interested in that sort of relationship with Lydford. Of course, she didn't seem like she wanted a relationship with him that way either. Why did that bother him so much? *And why did I say her name when kissing Sarah?* He shoved the thought from his mind.

Perhaps he should try harder to gain her affections. Home life had been better of late. He had always loved Sarah, he couldn't see that changing, but his wife had many good qualities. They could be good friends. Yes, he nodded and smiled to himself, very good friends.

Since he had cut down on his late nights and drinking his health had improved. He felt years younger. There was no rush for an heir. He had plenty of time. He would continue his plan of trying to become friends with his wife. Having settled that in his mind he brought his attention back to the game. That was when he noticed he was about to lose the first hand.

# Chapter 16

*She is a winsome wee thing,*
*She is a handsome we thing,*
*She is a lo'some wee thing,*
*This sweet wee wife o' mine.*
*-Robert Burns*

When Caroline told Emily about her meeting with Lydford, she found that her friend was not quite as excited as she was.

"You actually asked Lord Lydford to make a list?" Emily asked incredulously.

"Why yes, that's what we had agreed upon," Caroline replied.

"I don't recall having the time to recover from the shock of such a bold proposal to voice any objections to the subject.  He must be appalled."

"Well, he has agreed to do it, so he must not be exceptionally appalled."

Emily's eyes widened.  "He agreed?"

Caroline nodded.    "He only had two stipulations."

"Stipulations?"

"Yes, though one may prove to be extremely difficult."

"What are they", Emily asked warily

"First of all, we had to promise to agree to his continuing to pretend to court you.  He feels that part of the plan is working admirably, and I must agree with him."

"And the second stipulation?"

"That one is much more difficult to adhere to. He made me promise not to make another list or try to bring you to any man's attention until he has finished his list.  He promised to research the men he considered thoroughly and said that could take quite a while and he didn't want me to marry you off to some gambling drunkard."

Emily relaxed beside her.  "That sounds like him.  I think I can agree to those stipulations," she said with a relieved smile on her face.

In the following days, Edward's campaign to win his wife's affections did not weaken. He began to rise earlier so that he could breakfast with her and her kippers, though he still could not abide the things, and discuss the morning paper.  He found through their discussions that she loved London, but she missed the country terribly.  One morning, she expressed once more how she missed riding. He felt a bit uncomfortable when he remembered he had promised to get her a mount and resolved to make good on that promise that very afternoon.

He had luncheon at White's and put word about that he was looking for a mare for his wife.  Before he was finished with his Welsh Rarebit, he was told that Lord Tenbury was losing heavily in the card room and was the owner of a seven-year-old chestnut mare.  He decided to seek him out and discuss a possible remedy to both their problems when the gentleman himself walked into the dining room.  He tried to wave him over to his table, but Tenbury was oblivious to his ministrations and threw himself down in a chair at a table across the room.

Edward got up and walked over to him.  He stood next to the table and looked down at the man holding his head in his hands.

"Bad morning, eh Tenbury."

Lord Tenbury turned his head, and leaning it on his hand gazed at him with blood shot eyes.

"Bad night too," he said wearily.

"Mind if I have a seat?" he asked. At the despondent man's shrug, Edward pulled a chair out and sat beside him. "I may be able to help with your problem."

Tenbury sighed. "Do you have the recipe for a good hangover remedy and a couple hundred pounds?"

"As a matter of fact, I do, but I need a bit of help too."

Tenbury straightened up and dropped his hand to the table. Edward saw a gleam of hope in his eye.

"I'm looking for a mare for my wife, gentle, but with a bit of spirit. Know of any?"

Tenbury smiled, "I've got the prettiest little chestnut you ever did see. Has a real nice personality. A woman's horse for sure. Nice blood lines. Thought I'd breed her. Originally got her for my sister, but she never rides. Always uses the carriage."

"What's her name?"

"My sister? Ann."

"The horse," Edward said with a smile.

"Oh, Ariadne."

Edward chuckled when he heard the name. He had a feeling this was just the horse for his wife.

"How about we go see this horse now, and if I like her, you'll have your money within the hour."

Tenbury smiled weakly, ran his hands through his hair and squinted up at Edward. "I'm still left in need of a remedy."

Edward signaled to the waiter and asked for a

pen and paper. He scribbled something down sanded it and handed it back to the man. "Could you ask the kitchen to prepare this?"

The waiter looked down, raised his eyebrows, "You want this mixed together?"

"Yes, and brought to me as soon as possible."

The waiter shook his head and walked away with the paper.

Edward turned back to Tenbury who watched the waiter walk away and then glanced over with an apprehensive look.

"In about an hour we should be able to go take a look at this horse of yours," Edward said with confidence to a doubting Tenbury.

It was indeed an hour later when a lively, smiling Tenbury drew up to his stables with Edward beside him. Within five minutes of meeting Tenbury's mare he knew she was indeed the perfect mount for his wife. He quickly made the deal and, by that afternoon, he was in possession of a beautiful mare and Tenbury was back at the gambling tables with a smile, a full pocket, and too much confidence.

After arriving home, Edward went in search of his wife. He found her sitting in the morning room staring out the window at the garden with an open book in her lap. He stood in the doorway a moment anticipating her reaction. She started and looked toward the door as if she suddenly perceived his presence.

"Did you want something?" she asked putting her book on the small table beside her and starting to rise.

An unbidden thought rose to his mind, but he quickly put it aside. He wanted to be friends, nothing more. Duties would have to be fulfilled, but that would merely be a business dealing between friends. There was no room for overly friendly thoughts. Putting those thoughts aside he smiled.

"Well, if you don't mind, I'd like your opinion on something."

"Certainly," she said as if surprised he would ask at all. "What is it?"

"Come, I'll show you," he said and waited to let her pass from the room. It's out front." He had to stop himself from grabbing her hand and pulling her to the front door like a boy impatient to get to a carnival. Finally, they reached the front door and he threw it open. Caroline gave him a questioning look, passed through the door, and stopped, eyes wide, at the top of the steps leading down to the street. Edward came up beside her and leaned close to her ear to ask quietly, "So, what do you think?"

Caroline turned to him with a bright smile and opened her mouth to say something but froze at the close proximity of the husband. Her eyes locked with his and her expression became serious. They stood for a moment staring into each other's eyes, then Caroline's tongue darted across her top lip. She drew it bit in and bit the bottom one. Edward began to lean toward her, their lips almost touching when suddenly she blinked and backed off smiling a too bright smile and giving a shaky laugh.

"She's so beautiful, Edward. Oh, please may we go for a ride...now?'

Edward straightened and backed up a step before smiling. "Well, perhaps a saddle would be needed."

She looked down and her smile faded a bit. "Oh, yes. How silly of me."

Edward looked at her indulgently. "It's a good thing I purchased one."

Caroline's head jerked up and her eyes sparkled with happiness. She opened her arms wide and looked as if she were going to throw herself into his arms before checking herself. Instead, she brought her hands together and clasped them in front of herself. "Thank you, oh thank you, Edward."

He smiled at her use of his given name. "Now, not a long ride, mind you. By your own admission it's been a while since you've been in the saddle, and you need to get used to each other."

Caroline nodded her head. "Yes, Edward, only a short one." She ran her hand down her new horse's neck.  "What is her name?"

"Ariadne," he said with a smile.

"Isn't that..."

"Yes, Dionysus' wife," he said with a grin.

Edward turned for a moment to talk to Tom the groom.

Caroline leaned in to the mare and whispered in her ear.  "You'll have to let me know if you have any advice on how to deal with a hedonistic husband."

The horse whinnied and nodded her head.

Caroline laughed and gave her one last pat as her husband led her away to saddle her up.

Fifteen minutes later Edward was riding in the park with his wife.  He listened as she spoke soothingly to her horse telling her how lovely she was. The sun shone down on her face and Edward thought to himself how fetching she looked.  He was glad he got the horse for her. He was glad they were becoming friends.

Edward dragged his eyes off his wife and the pretty picture she made.  His heart fell when he realized they were nearing the path where he and Sarah would meet.

"Perhaps we should think about heading back now, it's probably enough for one day."

Caroline looked disappointed, but turned her mount around and began heading home.

Edward realized that he had not had more than

a passing thought of Sarah since the dinner party. He had never met with his man of business to finalize the purchase of a house to set her up in and now he found himself glad that he hadn't. Somehow it didn't seem right anymore.

He was haunted by the fact that she may be using him again for her own purposes. He wasn't sure exactly how he felt about the whole situation anymore. He had always loved her, but it seemed rather dull and tarnished now. He knew most mistresses used their protectors. He'd had enough to know that it was a mutually parasitic relationship, but somehow it was as if he expected more from Sarah. He knew he expected more from himself.

The mistresses he'd had were before he married, now something had changed in him. Just the thought of obtaining a mistress made his heart heavy. It was not that he loved his wife, it was just that he had a wife, He found it hard to explain, even to himself.

He wasn't sure what he was going to do about Sarah, so he avoided her. It had been two weeks and he knew he needed to make decision and act on it, but today wasn't the day. Today he preferred to think of more pleasant things, such as taking his wife to Vauxhall to see the fireworks. He smiled to himself. Yes, she would like that.

It was July, and entertainments began to thin as people prepared for their move to the country. Many people had already left the heat of London for the sea breezes of places like Brighton. Edward had become much more attentive since their meeting in his study. Caroline felt a camaraderie growing between them. Besides their morning breakfasts and rides, he had escorted Caroline to two musicales, a breakfast, and assembly and three balls. Tonight, they were to go to the opera. She enjoyed the opera.  If the talent was good, there were generally few interruptions, and she found she could lose herself in the story. Tonight promised to be one of those nights, as tonight was the season's last show with Angelina Catalini.  She had not yet seen the famed soprano, and so, was looking forward to it greatly.

They made their way to the Montgomery box and as she sat down, she appreciated its location. The box faced the stage directly rather than being on the sides and facing the boxes across from it. Most people came to the opera to see and be seen. But, not Caroline, and she was glad she did not have to strain her neck to see the stage.

The opera was not yet starting, so Caroline used this time to observe the other patrons who were attending.  Lord and Lady Amberly were in the third box on the right side and next to them, Lord Dane danced attendance upon Lady Emmeline Durant.  Caroline giggled remembering Emily's assessment of him.  His dramatic gestures were clear from even this distance.  It *was* rather like watching the antics of a bad actor.

She spotted Emily and her family along with Lord Lydford in his box in the left-hand corner. She caught her eye and gave her a small wave. Emily smiled and waved back and then turned and said something to Lord Lydford, who looked up and nodded in her directions.

"Lydford seems to have formed a tendre for your friend," her husband said from beside her.

"Oh no, it's all just a ruse. You were there when the plans were made, for goodness sake."

"True, I guess I'm not used to Lydford appearing so attentive. He certainly is giving a good performance."

Caroline considered the two closely as they conversed in Lord Lydford's box. Just then Emily looked up at Lord Lydford and gave him a dazzling smile.  A look of dismay crossed Caroline's features.  She turned to her husband. "You don't think she is becoming too attached?  I can see how she could let her gratitude begin to color her feelings, but it will not do.  Lord Lydford is just assisting her in finding the right husband.  It would be disastrous for her to begin to direct her affections toward him.  She might never be able to love one of the men he chooses."

Edward smiled, "I don't foresee that being a problem."

"Oh, do you know who is on the list?" she asked, clapping her hands in excitement.

"No, I do not, but Lydford has a way of reading people. He's a very good judge of character.  I'm sure he would pick someone she would admire and could possibly grow to...care for." As he said this, his mind went to Lydford's opinion of Sarah, but like most thoughts of Sarah, it felt uncomfortable to dwell on, so he dismissed it as quickly as he could. "Also, he has never been a man who toys with a woman's affections. I'm sure everything is very clear between them."  He nodded towards the stage.  "I believe the show is about to begin."

She turned her head to watch and quickly became caught up in the story.  It was a delightful performance. Miss Catalini certainly lived up to her reputation.  It seemed to Caroline that the intermission came all too quickly.

During the intermission, Lord Lydford and Emily came to chat.  After discussing the performance and other pleasantries, Edward began to talk to Lydford about Mr. Thorpe's set of greys which were coming up at Tattersall's Monday.  Caroline took this occasion to draw Emily aside and ask, "Emily, you are not falling in love wit Lord Lydford, are you?"

Emily was quite taken aback at the abruptness of her friend's question.  "What? Of course not, what would make you ask such a thing?"

"You seem to be having a very good time tonight."

"Am I supposed to look like I am being forced to sit in Lord Lydford's box against my will?"

"No, don't be silly, I just don't want to see you get hurt."

Emily turned serious. "I know my place, Caroline. I am not setting my sights on something I can never have. I realize that Lord Lydford would never have looked at me twice if it hadn't been for you soliciting his aid. I enjoy his company, plain and simple. We seem to have a lot of the same interests and opinions and I have decided to enjoy his company for as long as it lasts. At least it makes the season more bearable."

"Well, I am sure I can find nothing wrong in that." Caroline said smiling. "I wouldn't have said anything at all, it is just that I care about you and don't want to see you get hurt."

"I understand," Emily said as the men turned to join them.

"Would you ladies care for a little refreshment?" Edward asked.

"Oh yes, that would be nice," Caroline said and began to get up.

"No, no, you ladies visit for a while. I'll get some and bring it back.

So, it was decided that Lydford would stay and attend to the ladies, and Edward would retrieve refreshments for them all.

As Edward began to leave the box to carry out his errand, Lydford turned to Caroline. "I have heard through the grapevine that Lord and Lady Montgomery have been seen around town in each other's company quite often lately. May I hope that you have seen some of the wonderful exhibits in London, and can now share your impressions of them with me as you couldn't earlier?"

Caroline laughed and began to share her opinions on the exhibition at the Royal Academy.

As Edward made his way down the corridor which led to the steps to take him to the refreshment hall, he thought of his wife's laughter. He loved when she laughed. He knew that when she laughed, she really meant it, not like some women who practiced their laugh until it sounded like bells running up and down the register. There were no affectations for his wife. If she found something funny, she laughed.

He had almost reached the stairs when he heard someone call his name, and turned to see Sarah, Lady Owen, walking towards him. His heart fell. He knew in that second that he was never going to go through with the purchase of the townhouse for her. He was never going to share her bed. He needed to cut it off with her definitively, but not tonight. It was not the place or time for it. Besides, his wife was waiting.

Sarah slowed her steps as she walked toward Edward. She shouldn't look too eager. He couldn't know just how desperate she was. She hadn't seen him for weeks. Not since the day in the park when he had promised to get a house for her. The day he called her by his wife's name. She acted as if she hadn't noticed, but she most definitely had. Still, she had expected a message from him that he had secured a place for her, but there had been none. She had even thought of sending a message to him, but was afraid that it would be beyond the pale and she had already caused quite a stir at her dinner party. She had received a number of snubs from some of the ladies in society. She needed to watch her step, but she also needed to secure Edward.

The Whithers' were getting weary of her presence. She could feel it. They had already made plans to go back to their house in the country, without her. She had procured an invitation to the Sutton's house party which was next week and was hoping she could extend her stay until cousin Emily had hers in September, but wasn't positive she could extend her stay quite that long. Even if she could, what would she do after her stay at the Whithers? She could not go back home. Her father had passed four years ago and her cousin John inherited. His wife was very much the Lady of the manor, and didn't hesitate in letting her know. She had gone there the first month after her husband's death and had vowed never to go back. Never had she felt so wretchedly poor in her life.

There was always Lord Grimley she thought with a shudder. With very little encouragement she believed he would offer for her hand, but she hesitated to enter an alliance with another depraved old man, one with even coarser tastes than her late husband if the rumours were true. No, she needed to work harder to secure Edward.

"Why Edward," she said as she reached him, giving him a smoky gaze and lying her hand on his arm. To her dismay she felt him stiffen. She would have to loosen him up. "It has been a while."

As she steered him to an alcove, she said quietly, "I thought I would have heard from you by now. The last I heard you were looking to buy a new property."

She looked at him steadily.

Edward's eyes darted around. "Yes, well that fell through."

Sarah felt her stomach lurch. She could not let him get away. She must use all her feminine wiles, proper or not. She slid behind the curtain of the alcove and pulled him with her. She laid her hand on his chest and leaned into him.

"Oh, Edward, I've missed you so much."

Edward looked decidedly uncomfortable. "I really must be going."

Sarah slid her hand up his chest to the curls at the nape of his neck.  She pressed herself closer and ran her fingers through them.  Her lips tickled his ear as she whispered." I've waited so long, so, so long.  I've dreamed of your hands on my body."  She moved her body slowly back and forth across his. "Oh Edward, when will you get a house for us. I just can't wait much longer.  Soon I will be offering myself to you here at the opera."  She nipped his neck and tilted her head back to look at his face.  It was as rigid as his body which had not relaxed a bit. Perhaps she needed to play the emotional card.  Remind him of their past.

"Do you not remember, Edward, the picnics under the tree?  We would lie back looking up at the leaves and hold hands, telling each other stories of our future lives together.  I have never forgotten.  Please say you haven't"

"Of course I haven't, Sarah." Edward said his eyes softening a bit.

"Then how can you hesitate when all you need to do is buy a paltry piece of property?  It is nothing to you, but it is everything to us. Can't you see that it is the only thing that is keeping us apart?"

Edward hesitated a moment then said, "There always seems to be something, doesn't there, Sarah? Perhaps we weren't meant to be together."

"How can you say that?  You know we were supposed to be together. They say the path of true love never runs smooth."

Edward grabbed Sarah's wrists, pulled her arms down, and pushed her slightly away. "This isn't the time or the place. I must go. The next act will be starting soon."

Annoyance flashed in Sarah's eyes before she quickly looked away. "Edward, I don't understand."

"I must go," he said moving past her and exiting the protection of the alcove. Sarah stood within its confines for a few moments longer. She wouldn't lose. She would find a way. She had a few weeks to figure out a plan. She would see him again at her Cousin Emily's house party and she would persuade him then. Yes, Edward would be hers. She would get what she wanted no matter what she had to do to secure her desires.

Edward started to make his way back to his box without the promised refreshments. His heart was so heavy in his chest he thought he would burst. The evening had been going so well. Admittedly, he had not watched much of the show, but rather the expressions on his wife's face as she watched her first opera. She was guarded most of the time when she was around him, but tonight her feelings were there for anyone to see. He liked that.

His heart tumbled once again as he thought of Sarah. He realized he had been avoiding her of late. He felt trapped when she came across him tonight. It was a trap of his own making. Just a few weeks ago, he would have welcomed her attentions, but now he knew he could never be with her. He shook his head to clear it. He couldn't think of all that right now. He had to go back to his box and sit next to his wife and try to act like his mind was not ruled by confusion and his throat was not filled with the bile of deception.

He entered the box, mumbled something about the refreshments being too hard to get to, and sat down beside Caroline. Lydford and Miss Whithers talked for only a few more minutes and then left for their own box. The second half of the show began. Edward tried to look as if he was absorbed in it, but the evening was ruined now. He could not stop the thoughts running through his mind.

The evening had been ruined for Caroline also, for as he sat next to her, she detected a scent that tickled her memory until suddenly it dawned on her where she had smelled it before. It was the scent that Lady Owen always wore.

Time continued to pass quickly and Lord Lydford was still not coming forth with his list. Caroline was beginning to despair of ever receiving it before the end of the season, but at least Lord Lydford's efforts at keeping Emily's parents from trying to marry Emily off to anyone else were succeeding.  Lately, she found that her friend's situation was not consuming her thoughts as much as it had before, instead her thoughts kept returning to her husband.

He had been treating her with the utmost care and respect, both in company and when they were alone.  They breakfasted and supped almost every day together, went for drives in the park, and exhibits around London.  He escorted her to balls, dinner parties and musicales.  He did not avoid her company, but still maintained a distance, even during a dance. It was only country dances for Lord and Lady Montgomery. Never once did they waltz.

The disturbing thing was that the more he seemed to eschew physical contact the more her desire for it grew.  The few times he had touched her, her breath caught and she felt light-headed. At first, she was alarmed, but that feeling was quickly replaced by an ache for his touch.

She knew that there was so much more to being man and wife and felt that she might want to discover just exactly what these marital relations entailed.  She was from the country and understood mating, but it seemed like there was so much more to it than that. If these feelings had anything to do with it, it must be wonderful indeed. But she didn't know how to approach her husband. She couldn't just walk into his bedroom, that was too bold. Her face reddened at the thought. What if he refused her?  Or worse, what if she gave herself fully to him and he returned to his old self after she had given him her soul, for she knew that's what would happen if she gave him her body. If only she felt some solid evidence that he had some tender feelings for her, but she didn't.  So, she continued to wait

## *Chapter 17*



Can you believe the season has almost come to an end?" Caroline asked as she and Edward sat in the morning room, he reading the paper, she sorting through mail.

"Yes, I can. Myself, I won't be sad to see the end of it. The city is getting quite warm, not conducive to dancing and the like. Will you miss all the entertainments? I'm afraid I haven't given any thought of what to do after the season ends. I used to go from house party to house party till the season started up again, but that doesn't seem quite the thing to do when one is married." He bent the newspaper down with his index finger and looked over it at her. "Would you mind staying in London for a while? It won't be the same."

Caroline sighed. "No, I don't suppose it will. Whatever you think is best." She sighed again and tossed a small stack of invitations onto the small table that sat between their chairs. "It's pointless for me to look through these."

"And why is that?"

"In the middle of the season, all everyone talked about is the next event you couldn't possibly miss. It made it simple to decide which invitations to accept. Now, it seems all everyone talks about is when they are leaving the city. I still don't know much about half the people who send us invitations. I'm at a loss when it comes to which to pick."

"Is that why you accepted the Balfour's invitation to their turtle supper?"

Caroline rolled her eyes. "Oh, please don't mention that debacle. I had no idea the youngest person there would be nearing seventy."

Edward's mouth turned up at one side. "Yes, well, you did learn to project your voice beautifully. Perhaps we could take a look at these together."

He folded his paper, set it to the side, picked up the stack and read the first invitation.

"No," he said and tossed it to the side.

"No...no...hmmm maybe...no...yes...no...aaah," he said and lifted the invitation high as if he had found a veritable artifact. "Here we are."

"What is it? "Caroline asked.

"An invitation to the Landry's end of the season party."

"Is that good?"

Edward looked at her as if she'd sprouted another eye. "You've not heard of the Landry's end of the season party?"

Caroline shook her head.

"Sir Phillip is just a baronet, but rich as Croceus. No one who is still in town misses their party. It's practically the formal end of the season. They have a different theme every year. They shoot fireworks off. It's the one event I managed to go to every year. We must go to this one."

Caroline smiled, her eyes bright. She jumped from her chair and grabbed the stack that Edward had recommended. "I'll send responses to these this morning. I'll get the rest later." She took the invitation from his hand eyes sparkling. "Thank you, Edward," she said before ducking her head and kissing him on the cheek.

When she brought her head up, she couldn't look him in the eye and her cheeks were very pink. Edward felt a little squeeze in his chest and smiled, as his wife ran from the room. He sat a few moments shaking his head and chuckling to himself. His wife was surely an original. Suddenly, he froze, struck by just how original she was. His wife was more impressed with the few minutes he spent helping her sort through invitations, than with a gift of gold and jewels. Yes, very original.

Caroline continued to spend the next few weeks in the company of her husband. They awoke around the same time, breakfasted, spent the morning in the morning room reading or other various pursuits. Every afternoon they went for a drive in the park, which Caroline enjoyed quite a bit more now that the crowds were thinner. When they arrived home, they readied themselves for the evening's entertainments.

The weeks passed quickly and before she knew it, it was the eve of the Landry's end of the season party. It was with mixed feelings that she prepared for the event. Part of her was glad to see the end of all the bustle, but another part was sad. She would miss all her newfound friends. What would she do with herself? She had been spending quite a bit of time with her husband, but soon he would be her only company. There was a tremor in her stomach at the thought, whether it was from anticipation or trepidation, she wasn't sure.

She wore the blue silk dress that she knew was her husband's favorite by the way his eyes lit up when he saw her in it. As she walked down the stairs to meet him, she wasn't disappointed. His eyes showed his appreciation and a smile crept across his face.

"You look lovely tonight," he said as he gently took her hand to lead her out to the waiting carriage.

"Thank you," she said feeling the heat flood her face and knew that it had turned an unbecoming shade of red.

Edward laughed. "I love when you blush."

Caroline felt her face heat even more and ducked her head.

"Don't try and hide. It's beautiful." He said putting his fingers under neath her chin and lifting it so he could look at her. His eyes roamed over her face and he said in a low voice, barely over a whisper, "beautiful."

Caroline's heart skipped a beat when she saw the look in his eyes. They stood for a moment, eyes locked. Time seemed to stand still and the room around ceased to hold its claim on her consciousness. His fingers were feather light under her chin and he lifted it even more as his other hand drew her closer. Her heart fluttered frantically in her chest, her lips parted slightly and her eyes widened in expectation.

Suddenly, Edward's eyes darted from hers to something behind her. He cleared his throat and took a step back. "Yes, Danvers."

Caroline looked down quickly. As the butler acted as if nothing was amiss, Caroline's face flamed again.

"The carriage is ready, my lord. If there is nothing else, I would like to go now. If you remember, I did ask for the evening off,"

"Certainly, Danvers, and if I recall Mrs. Hutchinson has the evening off too. How serendipitous."

The butler cleared his throat. "Yes, quite. Enjoy your evening, my lord, my lady." He said with a slight bow to each of them.

"You also, Danvers."

"Thank you, my lord, I'm certain I will." The butler said and cracked a small smile before exiting the room.

Caroline's mouth fell open. "Did Danvers just smile?" she asked as they walked toward the door.

"I believe he did. Anticipating the company of a good woman seems to do that to a man." Edward smiled as he opened the door for her to pass through.

She looked up at him her mouth hanging open in surprise. "Mrs. Hutchenson?"

"I believe they have enjoyed each other's company for years, though as far as I am aware they have never associated outside of work. I imagine they are nearing retirement and may be considering matrimony."

Edward helped her up into the carriage and followed behind. When he sat across from her, he saw confusion on her face. "What is it?"

She sat across from him, her eyes moving around the carriage as if looking for an answer. Finally, she blurted out, "But they are old!"

Edward barked a laugh. "I don't think they think of themselves in such a light. The passions may mellow with age, but they don't disappear."

Carolines mouth opened as if to say something, then closed and opened again, rather like a fish, before regaining composure and saying, "How sad to think they had to wait all those years before being able to consider marriage."

"Yes," said Edward smiling a gentle smile at his wife. "Aren't we lucky?"

The Landry's lived in a large estate just outside of London. It was the perfect place for an end of the season party because it was outside of London, but not far removed. It was like the first step in society's transition from London to the country. Edward watched his wife's face as they lined up behind the many carriages making their way down the long drive to the gala. He could tell from her reaction she had never seen something of this magnitude.

The drive was lit the entire way from the road to the house, which itself shone like a beacon in the night, calling all lucky enough to receive an invitation to its wonders. When they reached the house, the door to the carriage was opened by a footman. Edward exited and offered his hand to Caroline who accepted it and stepped down from their equipage.

Edward could tell his wife was trying to act the proper matron but could not disguise her wonder at the spectacle that surrounded her. They walked up the stairs to the stately home and were greeted by their hosts. There were hundreds of people milling around everywhere and they fell into the flow of the crowd.

"There is the ballroom." Edward pointed through a set of wide double doors. The room beyond was dimly lit, but one could still make out the chalked floor and mirrored walls. "It won't be fully lit until the ball begins around eleven o'clock. Since the night is so balmy I assume most are out in the gardens."

They walked down a wide hall and into a room that had large windows and a set of doors made of panes of glass which opened onto a veranda. When one stood on the veranda, they could see out into the gardens beyond which was filled with what seemed like thousands of little lights. Caroline looked out over the sea of humanity and back at her husband as if looking for guidance through the maze of persons before her.

"Come on," he said smiling encouragement before taking her hand and leading her down the steps. "One is bound to find someone one knows in this mob."

When they reached the bottom of the steps, he dropped her hand and tucked her arm through his. "You'd better stay close, if I lose you here it could be an hour before I find you again," he said with a chuckle.

"I don't doubt it. I did not think you could have such a crush in an outdoor venue. If I weren't witnessing it, I would never believe it." Edward smiled indulgently and patted his wife's hand as they began to make their way through the crowd stopping here and there to talk to someone.

"Oh, look, there's Emily!" his wife pointed the young lady who appeared to be speaking to an enormous urn of flowers. "I haven't seen her in quite some time. She hasn't been attending the same events as we have lately."

"No, she hasn't," Edward answered mundanely.

He was sorry that his wife had missed her friend, but glad that he had been correct in surmising what entertainments would appeal to her cousin, Sarah. Although he knew he had to quash any hopes she had of a liaison, he didn't like the thought of the discussion that needed to take place, so he avoided contact and lived in hope that she would find another man to interest her and eliminate the need for him to say anything. He scanned the area around Miss Whithers and took a deep breath in relief. Sarah did not seem to be in the vicinity. Instead, Miss Whithers was conversing, not with an urn as it appeared at first, but with his good friend Lydford.

"Would you mind if I spoke a while with her?"

"Not at all, I wouldn't mind talking a bit with Lydford myself."

Caroline smiled up at him and the two made their way through the crowd to their friends.

"Lydford," Edward said giving him a nod.

"Montgomery! Have you been here long?"

"Just arrived."

Edward looked over at his wife. She and Miss Whithers were talking as though they had not seen each other in years, not weeks.

"Have you seen Sarah—uh-- Lady Owens?" Edward asked in a lowered voice.

Lydford's pleasant smile did not leave his face, but his body did not seem as relaxed and his eyes sharpened. "She is here somewhere. She came with the Whithers'" he sighed and shook his head, "I thought you had learned, but I guess you haven't. Just know I won't cover for you."

"What! No! I'm trying to stay away from her. Things are...pleasant right now and I don't want anything to jeopardize that."

Lydford smiled, "I'm glad to hear that. The last time I saw her she was talking to Lady Daschel, not many people can get away from her in under twenty minutes. So you've got some time."

"Not nearly enough. I was hoping she would

not be here. I wish something would happen to make her leave. She's bound to come around Miss Whithers and I can't keep Caroline from her friend all night."

"She may not be around as much as you would think. It seems she has taken a dislike to me. I imagine it's because I see through her thin façade. Actually, I believe the Whithers' are beginning to tire of her too. I think she knows that and has kept to herself more lately. Miss Whithers seems relieved. I believe she has also been much less assertive about finding her a suitor."

"I'm sure that's due to your attentions. I suppose you are glad the season is ending. Soon you will not have to accompany Miss Whithers to every event."

"Oh, she is good company. It really is no bother."

"Well, you're a better man than I am. Good company or not, I would not like to be saddled for the whole season."

Edwards eyes suddenly widened and he moved a step to his left. Then he tipped his head slightly to his right to look over Lydford's shoulder.

"What is it?" Lydford said and began to turn to look.

"Don't move! It's her! We have to get out of here before she sees us!"

"Aren't you being a bit ridiculous? What could she do? I doubt she'll make her designs any more apparent than she already has."

"I don't want to find out." Edward said.

Lydford rolled his eyes, shook his head, and said, "Miss Whithers and I will distract her and you take Caroline to find some refreshments. They have servants walking around with punch and lemonade, but I think there is also a table set up somewhere near the house."

"Yes, I believe we passed it on our way out. Thank you, Lydford."

Edward threw one last glance in Sarah's direction and his eyes caught a sparkle of blue around Sarah's neck. *Oh God, the necklace! I had almost forgotten I'd given her the damn thing! I can't let Caroline see that! She would recognize it in a second!*

"Shit!"

"What now?"

Edward looked at his best friend. He knew all his secrets, but this was one secret he wasn't telling.

"Nothing," he said and turned to ask his wife if she would like a glass of lemonade as Lydford claimed Miss Withers. They bid each other goodbye, promising to try and make a set when the dancing began and Edward hurried his wife off in the direction of the house.

"This is a wonderful party! I can't imagine the expense the put forth to have such a magnificent event. And fireworks too! I've never seen fireworks, but I hear they are beautiful. I can't wait! When will they be set off?" Caroline asked.

"Hmm...oh, sometime tonight, I think around two." Edward mumbled, his mind trying to solve the problem of the necklace. He needed to get it from her, but how? He couldn't just go up to her and ask for it back. He had to take it somehow.

"Yes, probably after the ball. Do they put some of the lights out so we can see them better? Or do we go to a special area to watch them?"

"Uh, oh, usually both."  Maybe if he walked behind Sarah, he could pull on it and break the chain. It looked pretty delicate it shouldn't take much. He had to figure out how to get away from Caroline for a few minutes.

"Edward?"

"Hmm,yes?"

"Didn't you want some lemonade?" she said.

Edward focused on her and realized she was standing in front of the refreshment table.

"Oh, yes," he looked beyond her," Oh, but would you mind waiting a minute, I see someone I need to ask something."

Caroline stopped short of picking up a glass. "Certainly, I am not terribly thirsty. Who did you need to talk to?" she asked and began searching the crowd.

"Just a gentleman from the club."

"Oh, well let's go then before you lose him in this crush," she said taking his arm.

Edward took a deep breath and did his best to restrain himself from running his fingers through his hair. His wife knew him well enough now to know there was something bothering him if he did. He removed her arm from his.

"Why don't you stay here and sip some lemonade? I don't want to have to drag you through this crowd just to ask a question. Look I think that is Miss Brightmore coming our way, isn't it? Perhaps you could while away the minutes in good conversation."

"I admit I haven't seen much of her since our dinner party. I wonder how she and Mr. St. James are doing."

"You will have to ask," he said with a smile that didn't quite hide the panic in his eyes.

Caroline looked at him curiously for a moment and then turned to Miss Brightmore who called her name.

Edward left his wife in the company of the unusually sedate Miss Brightmore, taking just a moment to wonder what it was that St. James saw in her. She was not unpleasant, just silly. She was closer to him in age than his wife, but Caroline possessed a maturity he truly appreciated. But he had no time to think about the attributes of his wife, he needed to get that necklace before said wife saw it and never forgave him for making such an unforgivable blunder.

He spotted Sarah by an urn full of flowers near

the opening of the hedge maze, a place sure to be well used by amorous couples throughout the night. Her eyes roamed the garden as Lord Grimley paid her court. He circled around trying to avoid her gaze. Finally, he came up behind her a little to her left. He thought he could head toward the opening of the maze and somehow catch the chain of the necklace and pull. He took a deep breath and let it out to steel himself and proceeded with his plan.

When he came behind Sarah, he had to touch the skin on the back of her neck to loop his finger under the chain. Sarah raised her hand to swat away what she thought was a bug. Seconds before her hand reached his, Edward pulled hard and fast. Sarah's head jerked back, she gave a gurgling sound and clasped her hand to her throat.

"My dear lady, what is it? May I help in some way?" Grimley asked taking the opportunity to place his moist hands on Sarah's shoulders.

Edward, who was gratefully in the shadows, slipped off into the maze, cursing the jeweler for making such a delicate looking chain so strong. He hoped to get well away from the situation but stopped as he heard Sarah say, "Please unhand me Lord Grimley and sound the alarm! There is a thief about! Someone tried to steal my sapphire necklace!"

He had no choice. He had to get that necklace before the alarm was sounded, for then everyone would be exclaiming over it. Why had he not thought of that before? He turned around and prepared to face the one person he did not want to meet tonight. As Lord Grimley toddled off to find Sir Phillip, he pasted a look of concern on his face and walked over.

"Lady Owen, I heard you exclaim. What happened?"

"Oh Edward, it was horrible!" she began to throw herself in his arms, but he held her at arm's length, she seemed a bit offput, but quickly recovered. "Someone almost strangled me trying to pull the beautiful necklace you gave me right off my neck!""

Edward glanced around, but it didn't seem that anyone had heard. He sincerely hoped they didn't and continued his charade.

"But you are alright?"

"My neck hurts a little from the chain pulling against it. Do you see any marks?" She stretched her neck up and pushed her breasts forward for him to look...wherever he wanted.

There was a time when he would have welcomed this, but now he saw her in a different light. Funny he never saw how pushy she was before. He looked at her neck and felt a bit bad about the red welt she had starting on the side of it.

"It's a little red, but not too bad. What about the necklace? Maybe I should inspect it. The clasp may be damaged. You wouldn't want to lose such a lovely piece."

"Oh, yes, I wouldn't want to lose such a lovely gift." She looked at him, her eyes dewy. He wondered how she could do that so well. Then shook his head to clear it. No time to think about anything except getting that necklace from around her neck.

"Turn around. Let me check the clasp."

Sarah did as she was told and he inspected the necklace. It was unbelievably not damaged a whit! He picked up the chain in both hands, one hand on each side of the clasp, sent a quick prayer to Providence and gave a quick and powerful pull. Finally, the chain parted and dangled from his fingers. He pulled the necklace from around her neck.

"Yes, I was right. It was damaged. It is a good thing you did not keep wearing it. You would have lost it for certain."

"Oh, thank you Edward. I would have been devastated had I lost it. I cherish that necklace greatly." She gave him a look that would have put any man under her power. Any man who wasn't busy thinking about his wife.

"I will keep it safe for you" he said popping the necklace into his pocket. "And tomorrow I'll take it to the jewelers and have the clasp fixed."

"Thank you, Edward, I can always depend on you."

Edward tried to brush away the guilt. She couldn't depend on him and he had to let her know, but now obviously was not the time.

"I had best go, or we will have people talking. Here comes Lord Grimley with Sir Phillip. Tell them you must have been mistaken so we don't raise any alarm."

"But if there is a thief about trying to steal women's jewels –"

"I'm sure he is long gone by now. You don't want to ruin the party, do you?"

Sarah looked unsure, but Edward was happy to find that she decided being the woman who ruined the Landry's party was more alarming than being accosted by a thief.

"Oh, silly me," she said when Landry, huffing and puffing from the long walk across the garden, questioned her about it, "I must've caught my necklace on a branch of the shrubbery."

"But you said you were nearly strangled!" exclaimed Lord Grimley.

"It is amazing how strong your shrubbery is, Sir Phillip. You must have a very good gardener," Edward said.

Sir Phillip puffed his chest out. "The best money can buy."

"So, there was no reason for alarm?" Lord Grimley asked, looking quite put out.

"Well, the lady was injured," Edward said and Sarah tilted her neck so that the men could see the welt which had turned quite red in the last few minutes.

Both men tutted, Sir Phillip apologized for having such strong bushes and Lord Grimley's eyes gleamed and his hands shook as he stroked the skin of Lady Owen's neck, while she tried not to shudder.

"But where is your necklace?" Grimley asked, suddenly noticing that the expanse of soft flesh was no longer broken by a golden chain.

"Lord Montgomery graciously offered to keep it safe for me and take it to the jewelers for repair tomorrow," Sarah said smiling up at him

"Well, I could do that," Lord Grimley grumbled.

"It is quite alright. I was going there anyway. Lady Owen, Lord Grimley, Sir Phillip," Edward gave a bow of his head to each. "I hope the rest of your evening goes well"

He quickly turned and headed back to the refreshment table. He was gone longer than he had liked and hoped Miss Brightmore had a lot to say and kept his wife busy in his absence. No such luck. He found his wife standing alone looking rather lost when he came upon her. She gave him an unreadable look, rather serious, like she could see into his soul, before she smiled and said, "Everything settled?"

"Yes, I think it's all settled now," he said giving his pocket an unconscious pat.

He realized what he was doing when her eyes

moved to his hand, neither mentioned it.

Just then music began to pour out of the doors and onto the lawn. "Would you like to dance? I think I hear the musicians starting up," he asked and offered her his arm.

"I would love to dance Lord Montgomery," she said smiling again, this time a real smile, and took his arm. And Edward would have sworn the Landry's had started the fireworks early.

# Chapter 18



The session of Parliament ended and the exodus of England's peerage had begun. It was as if on August twelfth, someone came with a snuffer and put out the flame on the wick of fashionable London. Gone were the dinner parties, assemblies at Almack's, and nights at the opera. The Landry's final celebration was no longer looked forward to in anticipation, but just another thing filed in the memory. Households were packed up and knockers taken down. The streets of Mayfair took on a deserted look.

Edward was at a loss of what to do. He had mentioned staying in London to Caroline earlier, but he really didn't want to do that. Actually, he found that he wanted to spend some time alone with his wife. He wanted to get her away from the hustle of London for a honeymoon of sorts, just someplace where they could spend time in each other's company. He found that he enjoyed her company. Her conversation was stimulating, but that was not the only thing stimulating about her.

Since the party, his feelings had grown more than he ever expected. He ached to touch her, but knew he had to control his desires, or he would scare her away, as he seemed destined to every time he made physical contact with her. If he wanted to win her affections, he had to progress slowly. But the way she looked at him the other day when he helped her down from the carriage made him think she might be starting to feel something for him. He just needed to give her more time, as difficult as that may be.

He could go to Kendleston Hall. He seldom went to his family's country home except for the holidays. The memories there haunted him. He thought of Sarah for many years. Then when his mother was gone, he felt her loss incredibly. This was followed by the loss of his brothers. Everything reminded him of someone he had lost.

His father was there, the only family, besides Caroline, he had left. Except for the wedding he had not seen his father for years. Whenever he had seen him before that, his father had spent the entire time condemning his son's completely debauched life, as he liked to call it. Although, he imagined his father would have nothing to say this time.  He had not had anything more than a social drink, or done anything to feed the gossips, in at least a month.  He found mornings much more pleasant, and he felt his old zest for life returning after all those miserable years.  He imagined his father would be happy at the change in him.

Still, the thought of returning to his ancestral home did not sit well with him. Someday he could visit it again, but it was too early yet. He needed to know the family he was starting was secure before confronting the ghosts of the old one. He needed to spend time alone with his wife, getting to know her better.

He sat at his desk spinning his letter opener thinking of where to spend the next few months. Suddenly his eyes fell upon the letter from his father, still unopened. He smiled to himself. How silly of him to put off opening his own father's letter. He picked up the letter opener and reached for the letter. He slid the blade through the top, and found that there was a piece of paper and another envelope inside.

He unfolded the paper. It was a short letter from his father notifying him that when he arrived home from the wedding, he found that this letter had been delivered to Kendleston Hall for him, and sending his hopes that all was going well with his marriage.

He laughed. All those months of feeling the condemnation of his father, and it wasn't even there. Then he turned his attention to the envelope. It was from a solicitor he had never heard of before. He opened it and began reading. as he read a plan began forming in his mind. When he finished a smile crossed his face. Though the circumstances that brought it about were not the happiest, he now knew where they would spend their winter.

He removed a paper and pen from the drawer, dipped the pen in the inkwell and began writing the solicitor to ask details and lay out his plan to him. When he finished, he leaned back in his seat, closed his eyes, and smiled. It was perfect, and not to far from the Whithers' home. They could go there after the house party. He wouldn't tell her now. He'd wait till the party was over to tell her. He smiled wider imagining her surprise. He could spend the winter with his new wife. Perhaps, if he was patient, she might begin to feel something for him.

The smile fell from his face as an unwanted thought came to mind – Sarah. He sighed. Before he could make plans with his wife, he had to do something about Sarah. Now, on top of that, there was another thing that bothered him. Since the night of the party, he had not seen the necklace. When he had awakened the next morning, his coat had already been taken away by Roth to be brushed. His watch and wallet were on his bureau, but not the necklace. Now he had another reason to avoid Sarah. It was all turning into a huge millstone wrapped around his neck, dragging him further into the deep.

Caroline resigned herself to stay in town after most of the hoards had left for the country. It was hot and sticky and there were no more social events or friends to spend the long afternoons with. Emily had gone to the country with her parents to prepare for the house party they were to have at the end of September. Miss Law had returned home also, to spend her time with her horses, which she seemed to be more comfortable with then people, but saddest of all was Miss Brightmore. She had gone home with a broken heart, as Mr. St. James had left town just before the Landry's party without making an offer for her.

Caroline was surprised, for she could have sworn Miss Brightmore had made quite an impression on him. Both she and Miss Law were supposed to be at the Whithers' in September. She was uncertain about Mr. St. James. Though after his behavior toward Miss Brightmore, she rather hoped not. But September seemed a long way away, and she had only her husband's company for the interval.

Edward was as mercurial as ever. He would be congenial, then suddenly turn morose and spend the afternoon in his study. She knew the cause of his moods, it had been confirmed at the Landry's party, but she also saw that he seemed to enjoy their time together. It was as if he were engaged in a dance with her, coming together then pulling away, confusing her about what he thought or felt. Then she realized that she was dancing just as well with him.

With an unpredictable husband and no friends to help while the hours away, Caroline kept herself busy by preparing to leave London. There *were* a lot of decisions to make. What to pack up, what to leave, what was to happen to the servants, all the where's and how's that needed to be answered when closing a house.

Caroline had never done any of this before, and so by the time the last thing was packed and she stepped into the carriage to take her to Emily's house, she felt completely drained. She leaned back in her seat, closed her eyes, and sighed, trying to will herself to relax. If she had forgotten to make sure Sally packed her favorite chip bonnet, the sun would still rise the next morning.

She opened her eyes to see her husband sitting on the seat across from her with a bemused smile on his face. She smiled back.

"It seems the only time I have seen you in the

past week you were rushing by me with an armful of something," he said.

"Yes," she said with a sigh, "but I am trying to put all that behind me now. If something has been forgotten, I would prefer it remain that way. I am intent on enjoying myself for the next two weeks."

"Only the next two weeks? That's a shame. I did have a bit of an idea which I had put into motion. I had thought it might be enjoyable, but if you have set your enjoyment limit at two weeks, I guess we shall have to do it another time," he teased.

Caroline smiled. This is what she had been missing the last few weeks, a certain camaraderie that had been forming since they had gone to the opera. The feeling that, even on opposite sides of a crowded room, they were bound by a friendship she'd never known before. She liked that feeling. They were coming together in the dance again and it made her heart sing. If only one day, they would learn to waltz.

"Montgomery," she said, her eyes twinkling, "you know I meant no such thing! I only meant that after the strain of the last week, the one thing I do hope to leave in London, are my worries. Oh, by the way, have you heard anything from Lord Lydford about the list?"

"That sounds suspiciously like a worry, my dear." Edward said, and then laughed at the expression on his wife's face. "As a matter of fact, before he left town, he informed me that his list was complete.  He was going to reveal its contents to us at the house party."

Caroline squealed and almost jumped out of her seat and into her husband's arms, but contented herself with saying, "Now I can truly let all my worries go," and leaned back in her seat with a smile to enjoy the remainder of her journey.

The Whithers' home was about a six-hour drive from London.  They stopped midway through their journey for a light luncheon and arrived shortly before dusk.  The party was still dining on town hours, so she had sufficient time for a short rest before dressing for dinner.

She was shown to her room by the housekeeper who asked if she would like a bath drawn.

"Yes, in about three quarters of an hour please," she answered.

"Very good, my lady," she said and quit the room.  Caroline looked around.  It was beautiful. The walls were rose with dark woodwork, but the thing that caught her eye was the large mahogany bed.  It had an emerald green coverlet with tiny rosebuds embroidered in pink ribbon on it and large fluffy rose pillows which called to her from across the room.   She made her way like a sleepwalker towards it and was almost asleep before her head hit those wonderful pillows.

# *Chapter 19*

*Ay me! For aught that I could ever read,*
*Could ever hear by tale or history*
*The course of true love never did run smooth.*
*-William Shakespear*

It seemed to Caroline that she had been asleep only seconds before Sally was waking her to dress for dinner.

Your bath is ready, my lady," she said shaking her gently. "I'm sure you'll feel much more the thing after you have washed."

Sally was right. By the time she had finished bathing and dressed, she found she was looking forward to the evening ahead. She made her way downstairs to the hall and asked the footman where the rest of the party could be found. He led her to the drawing room which was just off the hall to the left of the stairs.

As she entered the room, her eyes immediately fell upon her husband who was standing to the right of the fireplace having a discussion with three other men.  He looked up and paused for a moment gazing at her with a look in his eye that made her stomach flutter, then gave her a smile and nod of acknowledgement. She smiled back and their gazes held a moment, until the spell was broken when the man next to Edward put his hand on his arm and asked a question.  He shot her another smile, then turned back to the man and went back to his discussion. She was still looking at him, thinking how handsome he looked in his evening dress, when Emily came up on her left and put her hand on her arm. Caroline had barely turned in her direction when Emily began talking, her tone desperate.

"Caroline, I'm glad you're here.  Lady Elphinstone has been here since yesterday, and if I hear one more time about some fifty-year-old widowed lord who has children older than me and what a perfect match he would be for me, I think I shall scream! What is it about a single woman that makes married ones so eager to marry them off?"

Caroline laughed. "I haven't. In fact, I have helped you evade marriage, at least until you find the right person.  Lord Lydford has surely been a help to you. Where is Lord Lydford?""

A shadow passed across her friend's face.  "He has not come," she said bleakly.

"I should not worry, he will. In the meantime, has there been no one else present to save you from this fate?" Caroline asked with a laugh.

"No.  Miss Law hasn't arrived yet. I received a letter from her today. It seems there was some kind of horse emergency. Whoever heard of a lady missing a house party because of a horse emergency?  Apparently, her whole family is obsessed with them. Miss Brightmore is here, but she's been unusually quiet. She's out in the garden now. I imagine it's because of Mr. St. James. I invited him and he said he was coming, but near the beginning of September he sent his regrets."

Caroline sighed, "Poor Miss Brightmore. Soon after you departed from London, Mr. St. James abruptly left. No one knows why, but they do know that he did not ask for her hand as it was supposed he would."

"I thought they were as good as engaged. That is why I invited him. Perhaps he just had some business at home to take care of."

Carolyn smiled. "As did Lydford. I happen to be the bearer of good news.  Lord Montgomery told me on the way here that Lord Lydford informed him that he has finished the list and he intends to give it to us during your party."

The expression on Emily's face seemed to fold in on itself.  "Caroline," she said slowly, "I know

I've mentioned this before, but I really don't want to marry. I think I would be much happier if I didn't."

"Nonsense," said Caroline, "you haven't even seen the list yet. It could contain the perfect man for you. Lord Lydford certainly must have put a lot of thought into it if it took this long. You couldn't possibly want to be an old maid. I am certain you would like children of you own someday."

Emily looked down avoiding Caroline's eyes. "I really have my mind made up. I do have sisters who will marry someday. I think it would be preferable to be an aunt rather than a mother. You can have every advantage, the ability to travel and do what you like and then have the nieces and nephews to visit when you would like the company of a child. It sounds perfect to me."

"Well, we'll see. You may change your mind when you see his list." Caroline said and then fell silent and studied her friend rather intently for a moment, wondering if it were her imagination or if she had been crying earlier. She decided the best thing for Emily was a change of subject. "The ride here was unmercifully warm. I was exhausted by the time I arrived and was very happy with the accommodations you arranged for me. The bed was so comfortable I admit I slept quite a while before preparing for dinner."

She kept on in this vein until it was almost time

for dinner, when she noticed a small rip in her dress. She knew that a small rip could become a large one rather quickly, so she excused herself to go to her room and repair it. The repair was rather quick as she had supposed, and she was soon ready to go back down to join the party. She opened the door to the hallway and walked out to find herself colliding with a decidedly masculine chest. She titled her head back and looked directly into the eyes of her husband.

"I came to check on you," he said without moving.

Caroline's breath began to quicken along with the beat of her heart as she said, "I had a rip in my dress."

Suddenly he let out a groan and his lips were upon hers. He pressed her body against his so tightly she felt like they would meld together and become one. She found herself overcome by a desire to make exactly that happen. She put her arms around his neck and wound her fingers through the curls she found there. He tenderly eased open her lips and deepened their kiss, his hand coming up to her hair running through it and knocking the pins loose.

She pressed her body closer straining to touch him deep within. His hands began moving up and down her body and hers began to move of their own volition, caressing his neck and shoulders.

Then just as suddenly as he brought them

together, he pulled apart. Caroline felt cold where his body was no longer touching hers.

"Oh God," he rasped in a voice full of passion, "I want you so much it hurts."

Caroline opened her eyes and stared at him. She had never seen him this way. His breathing was uneven and the look in his eyes, she had never seen anything like it, but it made her heart flip. She longed to touch his cheek, but he held both of her hands in his.

"I promised myself I wouldn't scare you by doing things you were not prepared for. I have been holding myself back for so long.'" He looked deep into her eyes. "Dare I hope, from your reaction, that you might feel the same as I?"

Caroline smiled and nodded her head slightly as her eyes remained locked with his. He let out an unsteady breath.

"I needed to know that. I needed you to come to me. Will you? Will you come to me tonight?" he asked, his eyes continually searching hers.

"Yes," she breathed, and then they both laughed.

Edward took a deep breath and backed away further. "Here, I think you need help repairing your hair now. We can't have you going downstairs looking like that, even if we are married," Edward said and dropped her hands, bending to begin picking pins off the floor, while she walked to the mirror to inspect the damage.

Ten minutes later, Lord and Lady Montgomery walked into the drawing room where everyone was waiting to go into dinner, and much was said about what the causes might be that brought such felicity to the couple.

Supper that night was indescribable. There was a myriad of emotions swirling around the table. The ones who were not experiencing them, felt rather confused, as if they had walked into a theater during the last act of a play they had never seen.

The host and hostess seemed distracted and slightly dismayed. Their daughter had an expression which reminded one of someone awaiting their execution the following day. Lord and Lady Montgomery were so happily oblivious to anything outside of each other that they could have been eating raw pheasant and uncooked turnips and smiled through every bite. Lady Owen was looking daggers at the two, especially Lady Montgomery, and making comments of how unpredictable newly married couples could be through clenched teeth. And the help seemed terribly inept, as if they were all newly hired and this was the first time they had ever served a large party.

The atmosphere was incredibly charged and everyone felt that something was bound to happen. They were not going to be let down.

# Chapter 20



*Oh, how many torments lie in the small circle*
*Of a wedding ring.*
              *-William Congreve*

After the tension felt during dinner, no one was up to socializing much. The women breathed a sigh of relief when the men joined them after port, but it didn't seem to alleviate the awkwardness of the mood. After an hour of stilted conversation, Mrs. Whithers began to discreetly suggest that it was time to retire.

Before Caroline quit the drawing room, she stole one last glance at her husband. As their eyes locked, she was rendered motionless by the look there. It was a look filled with promise of pleasures to come. Tonight, she would at last give herself fully to her husband. The country dance they had been preforming as of late would at long last become a waltz as she had hoped. Caroline's heart flipped in her chest. She smiled a brilliant smile and left the room to prepare for what would truly be her wedding night.

When she reached her room, she could not stop smiling. Sally, who was waiting to prepare her for bed, wondered at her mistress's happiness and the excitement emanating from her.

"I think I would like to wear the night rail with the pink ribbons," Caroline said with sparkling eyes.

Sally shot a curious look at her mistress. She had never worn that particular night rail before. It was supposed to be for her wedding night. She told Sally that she would never wear it. In fact, Sally was surprised she packed it at all.

Sally was still unsure of Lord Montgomery. Over the time spent in his household, she learned that his servants were extremely loyal, which was a good sign. She had also noticed that lately he had changed in his behavior toward her mistress, but she had a hard time forgiving him for the way he treated her on their wedding night. The sight of Caroline sobbing her heart out was not one she would soon forget. And what about the stories that she had heard of him and Lady Owen?

Sally tied to put her energies toward making

her mistress appear at her best, but her mind was working even more than her hands.  After she helped her out of her clothes and into her night rail, she brushed her hair until it shone and tied it back with a pink ribbon to match the trim. When she was finished, she looked at her mistress sitting there, the happy anticipation shining in her eyes, and could not hold back any longer.

"My lady?" she ventured.

"Yes, Sally?"

"I could not help but notice your choice of night rail."

"Yes, Sally."

"I – Well, I thought that you were never going to wear it."

"It was for my wedding night. I said that was the only time I would wear it," she said with a dreamy smile and a sparkle in her eyes.

The air hung heavy with the import of those words. "Are you--"

"That will be all, Sally," Caroline said, saving her from embarrassing herself.

"Yes, my lady." Sally gave her dear friend and employer a tremulous smile, and exited the room, leaving her to her fate.  Praying it was a good one but having serious doubts.

Edward walked into his bedroom twenty minutes after his wife went to hers, his blood pumping with excitement. He had never felt this way before. It was not just the fact that he was going to be with *a* woman that made him feel this way, but because it was *this* woman. *She* made the difference. Suddenly the truth hit him with a force that took his breath away. It was not that they were friends, it was not his desire, though both of these had an impact on the way he felt. The truth was, he loved his wife. He laughed, joy bubbling out of him as he saw it clearly for the first time.

He didn't care if she never produced an heir. It was enough that he had her. He loved the way she smiled, and the way she cared so much for others. He loved the way she stuck to her values and the way she could be so childlike and yet so proper at the same time. He loved the way she wrinkled her brow in concentration as she read the morning paper. Her face was the face he wanted to see at the breakfast table every single morning of his life and in his bed every single night. He wanted her so badly, not for what she could give to him, but what they could give each other, not just joined bodies, but joined hearts.

He began to remove his jacket, which was quickly followed by his cravat and waistcoat. He unbuttoned the top buttons of his shirt, and then sat down to take off his boots and stockings. After completing his tasks, he sat back and tried to relax. He ran his fingers through his hair and leaned his head back against the chair with a smile, thinking that the woman he loved would be running her fingers in the same places soon, and more.

He heard the click of the door latch and raised his head to look at the door that adjoined his wife's room.  The smile he wore changed to look of confusion when he saw that the door was still closed and his wife was not there.  He swiveled his head to look toward the door leading to the hallway.  There in the doorway, wearing a white silk wrapper with red rosebuds, was Sarah.

Edward just stared, his jaw slack, while his heart dropped to his stomach.  Sarah began to sway into the room, a sensual smile on her lips.

"Hello Edward," she said

He rose out of his seat.  "Sarah," he said eyes wide with shock, "what are you doing here?"

"You seemed lonely at dinner, I thought that perhaps you needed a woman's attention," she said, walking further into the room to stop at the bedpost.

"I don't need your attentions, Sarah."

"Oh Edward, I feel so awful for you to have to live your life with a woman you cannot possibly love."

His expression darkened.  "You know nothing about me now, Sarah. Please go back to your room."

It seemed as if time slowed down. He was frozen in place feeling like a mouse in the gaze of a snake. His heart was rapidly sinking. Sarah ran her fingers over the bedpost. "I know how much you loved me once, and I know you are a loyal man.  You could not just throw a love like that aside.  You love me still. You just need to be reminded of how good we could be together."  She began to undo the sash of her wrapper and walked toward him. "I never loved my husband, Edward. I loved you.  The minute I was married, I regretted my decision, but now we are both in a position where we can act upon that love."  She let her wrapper fall and stood before him in a nightdress so sheer you could see her every curve beneath its gauzy whiteness.

He turned his eyes away from her nakedness and that's when he saw it. That sparkle of blue around her neck. *It's the necklace! How—*

Edward could not make a move, still rendered motionless by fear. He had to get her to leave. Caroline could come in any minute. He felt sweat begin to form on his brow and upper lip.  He heard himself say, "You must leave now, Sarah."

Sarah pouted, "How could you leave me like this.  I have been aching for you ever since my husband laid his cold clammy hands upon me.  I dreamed of this moment.  Please, please let me love you," she whispered and wrapped her arms around his neck entangling her fingers in his hair. Sarah pressed her body against his and pulled his head down to hers and that was when he heard a gasp come from the direction of his wife's bedroom.

That gasp was the key that unlocked the heavy bonds of dread that had been impeding his movements. Edward wrenched his head up and pushed at Sarah who fell against the bed. Then he turned panicked eyes to his wife who was standing just inside their adjoining door and froze once more. She was wearing a white nightdress with pink ribbons, extremely modest compared to Sarah's, but he never thought he had seen a woman so desirable. Then he looked into her eyes, and the pain and humiliation he saw in them cut him to the quick.

"Excuse me." Caroline said turning to exit the room as quickly as she had entered.

"Caroline wait," Edward said in a strangled voice and moved toward her. She stopped and turned to look at him, her hurt and bewildered expression overwhelming his senses. "I--" he began and realized he didn't know what to say.

"I don't understand, Edward," Caroline said softly. "I can understand you still wanting Lady Owen, she's beautiful. I can't compare. But I'd hoped that if I let you see the real me, that I wasn't just a silly little girl, I was a person, with dreams and opinions and – well, I mistakenly thought if I let you see the real me, you might fall in—," she stopped, took a deep breath, and stiffened her back, ramrod straight. "But I guess it doesn't matter. I just wasn't enough."

"No, you—" began Edward

Caroline shook her head and interrupted. "Your feelings for me are apparent, but what I can't understand is why you revealed them in such a way. Why did you make me feel the way you did? Why did you make me think you cared? That you wanted me? Was this all an elaborate plan to humiliate me? You could have just told me you didn't want me, why make me think you did?"

"I do want you," Edward insisted.

Caroline shook her head again and looked toward the ceiling trying to stop the tears that were forming in her eyes. "No, Edward, you don't want *me*. You want an heir. But something has to die within me before I can enter that kind of relationship. You have mortally wounded it. Now, I just need to be alone so it can die in peace." She turned and opened the door to leave, but before she exited, she turned her head back in Edward's direction. "You know, Edward, for the past few months I've had the strange feeling we've been performing a country dance. We come together, touch hands and push away, only to come back together again, but you obviously had no problem turning to another partner." Caroline looked toward Sarah, who was still on the bed, and then back at him. She pressed her lips together and took a deep breath to help gain control. "I'm sorry Edward," she said, her voice void of expression, "but I've become terribly weary of dancing with you."

Edward reached out his hand toward her. "Caroline, let--," he began, but Caroline turned and walked through the door. The click of the lock punctuated her words with an awful finality.

Edward stood for a moment, hands hanging loosely at his sides, staring at the door. Then he closed eyes and let the air out of his lungs.

"You don't need her, Edward. It's so much better this way. You don't need her. It can just be us. We were meant to be together." he heard from behind him.

He turned to find Sarah lying on the bed behind him in a pose which most men would probably find seductive, but he found left him cold. He clenched his jaw and strode toward her. He looked down at her lying there, disgust in his gaze. Then he picked her up, threw her over his shoulder, carried her to the door, opened it, and deposited her none too gently on the floor of the hallway.

"Edward!" she shrieked.

"Lady Owen, I almost let you destroy my life once. I pray that you didn't succeed this time. If you ever come near me or my wife again, you will regret it."

"But Edward --," she began.

"Lord Montgomery to you," he said before he closed the door sharply in her face, and turned the lock.

Sarah heard the lock turn and sat in the middle of the hall trying to understand what just happened. How could her Edward not love her anymore? He had always been there loving her, always been there for her to fall back on. She didn't want to believe it, but he had made his feelings perfectly clear. He did not want her anymore. She felt totally alone for the first time in her life,

Slowly. she became aware of her surroundings and looked around her. A number of guests had come out of their rooms to ascertain what the noise was about. Her eyes darted down and she realized that her wrapper was still in Edward's room. She took a deep breath. She couldn't ask for it back without embarrassing herself further, so she stood up and with head held high, began the seemingly endless walk to her room, sensing the men's lustful eyes upon her and the women's whispers of speculation every step of the way.

As soon as she reached her room, she rang for her maid and told her to begin packing. She must hurry to the Melbourne's house party as soon as possible. Lord Grimley was there and she had to get him to propose before the news reached him. Her stomach turned at the thought, but it was really the only thing left to her now.

"Hurry up, Mary, you lazy girl" Sarah snapped, "And make sure that good for nothing Jack is readying a conveyance for us."

She looked at the young woman who was packing her trunks carefully.

"Hop to it, or you will be looking for a new job without a reference when I become Lady Grimley."

Mary began packing as quickly as she could without completely crushing her employer's dresses. She did not enjoy working for her, but to be let go without a reference was worse. She would never get another job without it, and her family needed the money. Everything was quickly packed, Jack was alerted, and all the trunks loaded into the rented carriage. Before dawn broke, they were on their way.

Edward tried for hours to get Caroline to answer him. He leaned against their adjoining door and talked until his voice was hoarse, but he still heard no answer from within. Finally, in frustration, he threw himself down on his bed and though he thought he would never succumb to sleep, he soon did.

He awoke to find sunlight streaming across his bed. He rubbed his eyes with the heels of his hands and sat up throwing his legs over the side of the bed. He sat for a moment blinking away the last vestiges of sleep, until the memories of last night and had him jumping up from the bed and walking to the door to his wife's room. The handle turned when he tried it, so he pushed it open and entered her room. He was not surprised to find her room unoccupied and was about to go look for her when he realized that her trunks were gone. He strode over to the wardrobe and threw open the doors, no dresses!

He rushed back to his own room, buttoning his shirt and tucking it into his pantaloons. He pulled on his stockings and boots, threw on his waistcoat and jacket, and strode out of his room without buttoning either. He walked down to breakfast, buttoning as he went. He slowed his pace as he reached the doors of the dining room, and tugged at his waistcoat and jacket to make sure he was decent. He realized than that he had forgotten his cravat in his hurry, but that couldn't be fixed.

He walked in at a leisurely pace, and slowly scanned the room. It was still early, only nine o'clock, but because they had retired early, there were already a few guests present. He found the person he was looking for, Emily Whithers. She was sitting halfway down the left side of the table picking disconsolately at a plate of food. He went to the sideboard, loaded some food on his plate, and moved toward her.

"May I?' he said, inclining his head toward the chair on her right.

"Of course," she replied, though she looked as if she would have liked to refuse.

He set his plate on the table and seated himself beside her. When he looked up at Miss Whithers, he found her to be staring at his plate with somewhat bemused expression.

"I see you are a hearty breakfast eater," she said.

He looked down and found that in his haste, he had heaped his plate with bacon, ham and smoked kippers. He actually put some of those nasty things his wife favoured on his plate. His stomach turned a bit, so he quickly turned his gaze back to Miss Whithers.

"Er, yes," he said, feeling a fool. "Have you seen my wife this morning?"

'Miss Withers' face became shuttered as she stopped eating her toast in mid bite, and placed it back on her plate.

"Yes."

"Would you tell me where I could find her?"

"No."

"No?"

"No, Edward. She told me what happened, and if she hadn't, I'm certain that I would have heard it from one of the guests who witnessed the event. She doesn't want to see you, and I cannot blame her. I don't understand why you would want to hurt her like that."

Tears began to fill her eyes and she got up

intending to leave, but Edward grabbed her arm and held her back.

"Please," he said he had to let her know how desperate he was. "Please tell me where to find her."

She turned to look at him. He saw something in her eyes soften. She sat back down and removed his hand from her arm, as if she were willing to listen, but unwilling to forgive him for hurting her friend. "What do you want?"

"I need to talk to her. I need to explain what happened."

"I believe it is rather clear what happened."

"No, it isn't," he cried in frustration. "I had nothing to do with that...that...travesty that took place in my room last night."

"Apparently you had something to do with it, as you were found holding my cousin in your arms."

"She threw herself there! I was trying to push her away!"

"On to your bed?"

He rolled his eyes. When would this ever end? "That just happened to be where she landed. I... I...," he stopped and took a deep breath to calm himself. "I love Caroline. I don't think I fully realized that till last night. I couldn't wait to be with her, to tell her how I feel. Then Sarah walked into the room and everything fell apart."

Miss Whithers studied Edward for a minute.

"I could wring my cousin's neck," she declared.

Edward smiled wryly.  "So, could I.  In fact, I may have hinted at the fact that I might, if I ever saw her again."

They sat in silence for a moment.

"She needs time, Edward."

"I just want to explain.  I need her to know that I love her and would never purposely hurt her.  Where is she?"

"I don't know."

Edward's face fell.  He rubbed his hand across his forehead and dragged it down his face.  Then he took a deep breath.

"I'm sorry, she would not tell me.  She just said she needed to go away for a while.  She said she needed a safe place to go to make some decisions."

Edward closed his eyes, bowed his head and emptied his lungs.  He felt completely defeated, without hope.

"I am certain this will all turn our alright.  Caroline has always been sensible. I know that she will listen to what you have to say.  She just needs time."

Edward nodded his head. "Has Lydford arrived yet?" he asked.

Miss Whithers looked at her plate. "No.  I fear he may not come."

"He will be here.  He had to attend to some business at Blakemoor Hall.  It must have taken longer than he had assumed.  Could you let him know that I will be at Brookstone Manor? I am afraid I cannot stay here under the circumstances." He rose and then turned back to Miss Whithers, "And if you hear anything from Caroline, please send word."

"Certainly," she looked at him as if she wanted to say more, but didn't know what to say. "If there is anything more I can do, please let me know."

"Thank you," he said, and walked from the room.

Miss Whithers sat and stared down at her barely touched plate of food for a while, then got up with a sigh and did the same

# Chapter 21



Caroline had spent the first half of the night shedding copious amounts of tears, while trying to block out the sound of Edward's voice from the room next door. The second half, she spent trying to decide where to go from here. She did not know if she could face Edward ever again. She knew for certain that she could not in just a few short hours. She had to leave, but where could she go?

She did not want to return to her parents'

house. She needed to contemplate her future, and yet didn't want to be completely alone as she would be without her parents there. She needed some wise counsel. Her mind was beginning to dull from the strain of the past few hours, when suddenly it came to her with a jolt, Great Aunt Mathilde.

Great Aunt Mathilde was a woman of certain age who had the positive outlook of a debutante. She had been married young and was widowed five years after. Since then, she had traveled extensively and had a keen sense of adventure. Even a walk down a country lane could be an adventure with Aunt Mathilde, but of the utmost importance to Caroline at this point was that she contained a heart of gold. She did not judge. She would offer counsel and then allow you to come to your own conclusions. This was exactly what Caroline felt she needed at this point.

Once she had decided on her destination, Caroline began putting her things in order. It made her feel better to be working toward a goal. When she heard the servants beginning to stir, she rang for Sally. She arrived silent and grim, having heard the news from the other servants, and together they finished packing her trunks. By eight o'clock, they were ready to go, but Caroline still had one final task. She needed to inform Emily of her departure.

"Sally, could you have Miss Whithers' lady's

maid inform her that I would like to request an audience with her as soon as she awakes?  Also, please arrange to have my trunks brought down to the hall."

"Yes, my lady." Sally said and hurried off to do her mistress's bidding.

After Sally left, there was nothing more for Caroline to do.  She found herself pacing the floor. It seemed forever to her before Sally returned to tell her that Emily had awoken early and was waiting for her in her sitting room.  She quickly went down the hall and into her friend's sitting room.

Emily was surprised to see Caroline dressed in her traveling clothes.  "Caroline! What has happened?"

Caroline related the past evenings events to her. Emily's room was located in the right wing of the house and so she had not been a witness to the event which had taken place.  Caroline was glad that she was the one to enlighten her friend instead of her hearing second hand from one of the guests.  Who knew what kind of things would be said that morning at breakfast.  She was glad her friend was forewarned.

"So, you can see why I must leave immediately."

"Yes, of course," answered her friend, "but, where will you go?"

Caroline frowned, "I would rather not say.

Please do not take this personally, but I would rather not be found for a while. Suffice to say, it is a place where I will have plenty of opportunity to think, and will receive excellent counsel."

A look of horror passed over her friend's face. "You are not going to a convent!"

Caroline smiled. "No, it is not that bad. Anyway, they would not accept me since I am married."

"You were not married in the Catholic church, so it would not be recognized."

"I do not plan on leaving the church of England. However, I do need a quiet place to go to make some decisions, which may affect the rest of my life, and I think I know of the perfect place." She rose to her feet to go.

"Thank goodness it's not a convent! I had an aunt who went a convent after she was jilted at the altar. She never left. No one in the family speaks to her now." Emily rose and gave her friend a quick hug. "I hope all goes well with you. Please send a letter to let me know you have arrived safely. I shall worry if I don't hear from you for too long."

"I promise. I do have one last favor to ask of you. Could your carriage take me into Newbury to hire a post chaise? I am embarrassed to say, I had only thought of removing myself from this situation and where I was to go, not how I was to get there."

"Absolutely, I shall have it prepared for you immediately.  Have you enough to pay for your journey?"

"Yes, I shall need to economize, but I should have sufficient funds."

"If you need anything--."

"Thank you, Emily, the use of your carriage for about an hour should be enough."

The carriage was secured, Emily reluctantly said goodbye, and Caroline was packed into the carriage and on her way before her husband began to stir.

The day was bright and sunny with a slight crispness to the air and a smell of fall waiting to come.  The workers were in the fields cutting hay.  It was an idyllic scene which would have pleased her immensely, if only her heart were not so heavy, and her thoughts troubled.  She reached Newbury within twenty minutes, where she promptly hired a post chaise and began her long journey to Aunt Mathilde's.  She could have taken the mail coach and arrived faster, but she had never traveled the coach alone and wasn't certain she wanted to brave traveling with strangers.

Aunt Mathilde lived in Pickering which was about three hundred miles away.  She would have to go back to London and then head north.  She hoped to make it in three days, if the weather held.

The weather had been unusually dry that summer, but one never knew when nature would decide to act upon a whim and send three straight days of downpour, which would render the roads impassable. The weather did hold for the first part of her trip. The days were pleasant after the hot summer, and she thanked God that he had at least spared her the misery of a stuffy carriage or bad weather.

The first morning she spent staring unseeing out the window unable to sleep, even though she did not sleep the night before, because of the thoughts running through her head. When they were a few miles on the other side of London, they stopped for a light dinner and to change horses. After fortifying herself with a nice mutton pie and a glass of wine, she began to feel drowsy. She fell asleep soon after beginning the second part of the day's journey. She had to be awakened by Sally, when they reached the inn where they were to stop for the night.

Caroline had never had to get a room at an inn before. Her father had always taken care of such things, and she was unsure of what to do. She remembered Sally's words to her early in her marriage about needing to show who was in charge, and summoned her courage. She held her head high as she walked into the inn and tried to act as if this were a common occurrence for her.

"I would like a room for tonight."

"Certainly, my lady," said the innkeeper, who knew quality when he saw it. "Would you like an extra pallet placed in your room for your maid?"

"Yes, please, and would you have a light refreshment and some water for washing up sent up immediately?"

He looked toward the woman who was standing in the doorway listening and jerked his head to signal her to do her bidding. He turned back to Caroline and Sally to offer to show them to their room. The water and refreshments arrived faster than she had supposed. After washing the dust off her face and arms, she and Sally partook of the bread, cheese, and fruit which the servant had brought. They then promptly went to bed to fall asleep immediately.

Caroline awoke in the morning to find that Sally had her clothes laid out and was ready to help her prepare to go.

"It doesn't look like the traveling is going to be good today, my lady," Sally said with a grim expression.

Caroline looked out the window. The sun was rising into a clear sky. It looked as if the day was going to be as pleasant as the day before.

She turned away from the window and looked at the lady's maid. "What do you mean, Sally. Have you looked outside? It seems to be a perfect day for traveling."

"I was talking with John Coachman this morning, and he said his knee was aching something terrible and that always means a bad storm is coming."

"Well, perhaps that storm will not come until we reach Aunt Mathilde's. If we leave as soon as possible, perhaps we can outrun it."

Sally looked doubtful, but quickly put up Caroline's hair, and after a light breakfast, they were on their way.

The morning started out as beautiful as Caroline said, but unfortunately, in the afternoon, dark clouds began to gather on the horizon. The day became still and the birds quieted. Then the wind came up suddenly and the rain began to fall in sheets. By four o'clock, her traveling was done. The rain was coming down so hard, the driver could barely see and the carriage was becoming mired in the muddy roads. John Coachman pulled into the next inn he reached. It did not look like the most respectable inn, but as cold and damp as she felt, she was thankful for it.

When she entered the inn, she found it to be small, but extremely clean and she felt that at least she could put her mind to rest about adding small passengers to her person. The innkeeper was a jolly rotund fellow, who was pleased to be harboring a member of the quality at his inn.

"Nasty day to be traveling, if I may say so, my lady."

"Yes, I fear we won't be doing any more of it today. I do hope you have a room available."

"Of course, my lady, we are more crowded than

usual because of the storm, but we luckily have one last room available. Even if we hadn't, I am certain one of the men would have given theirs up for you."

At the mention of men, Caroline became aware of the sound of men coming through the doorway off to the left. She hoped not to come across any strange men. What might they think of a young woman traveling alone? "You do have a private parlor, do you not?"

"Why yes, my lady, I will have your dinner laid out for you there at seven o'clock, would that be acceptable? Or do you dine on town hours?"

Caroline breathed a sigh of relief, "Country hours are perfectly acceptable, now if you could show us to our room and send up some water so we can prepare for supper."

She asked Sally to come eat with her. Though it was unusual, she felt her circumstances warranted the situation. Supper was a pleasant surprise. Apparently, both this innkeeper and his cook took pride in their work.  The meal was simple, but delicious, much better than she expected to find at an inn this size.  I began with eel soup, followed by broiled sole with sauce, venison, boiled potatoes, green peas with cream, artichoke pie, and broccoli.  It ended with a dessert of baked custard, fruit and nuts.

Unfortunately, her sorrow dimmed the excellence of the repast, but after such a fulfilling meal and two glasses of wine, she felt a welcome languor come over her and decided to go to bed early again that night, determined to get an early start in the morning. She and Sally went upstairs and fell asleep as soon as their heads hit the pillows. Caroline woke with the dawn and the unfortunate sound of rain still pounding on her window. It did not seem to have slowed during the night at all. Apparently, John Coachman's knee was correct. This was a bad storm.

Caroline spent the morning sitting in her room watching the rain and willing it to stop. Apparently, she held no sway over the weather, because if anything, it seemed to get worse. She began to think once more of her husband and soon her cheeks were as wet as the trees outside. This is the state Sally found her mistress in when she came to call her to luncheon.

"My lady," she said, anger and bitterness in her voice, "I cannot stand to see you like this. He is not worth all your tears. I never felt he was good enough for you, I tried to tell you that night, but even I did not think he would stoop so low. To have another woman in his room at one of your best friend's houses, and in a room right next to your own it is unthinkable! You should not spend one more minute in this room wasting your tears on him. Do you suppose he is spending his time like this?  Of course not, men do not feel the same as women.  As long as their needs are met, it does not matter by whom.  At least you know what to expect now before you have given your heart away."

This impassioned speech, which Sally had meant to alleviate her mistress's pain, only worsened it, and Caroline began to sob in earnest. Sally's eyes widened in alarm.

"My lady," she said, "Please forgive me, I have spoken out of turn.

Caroline just shook her head and cried more. Sally was completely taken by surprise.  She had always found that a good bout of anger lessened her sorrow.  She had just wanted to help.  She couldn't understand why it didn't work.  Then slowly it began to become clear.  Her shoulders drooped as she looked pityingly upon her sobbing mistress. It didn't work because it was too late. Her mistress had already given her heart away and there was nothing she could do to help her now.

Caroline had a good cry and then sat by the window watching the rain fall until she could take it no more. She turned to Sally who was sewing in a chair by the fire. "I don't think I can take the boredom anymore. I think I'll go downstairs to ask the innkeeper if there are any books or cards to be had."

Sally began to put her sewing to the side.

"No, you don't have to stop your sewing, Sally. I'll just ask my question and pop back up."

Sally looked disapproving. "I've been sewing for a while. It is no problem to take a break."

"No, Sally, I know you wanted to finish that dress for your sister's wedding. It's in two weeks, correct?"

"Yes, my lady."

"Well then, you'd better keep working. With everything that has been happening you must be behind. I've kept you away from your work long enough."

"It's alright. I don't know if I will be able to go anyway," Sally said looking down at the half-finished dress in her lap."

"Nonsense. Once I get to my aunt's house I'm sending you on the first mail coach home."

"My lady —"

"No, you have done more than your duty for me. I insist. You are going."

Sally smiled, "Yes, my lady, I will," her eyes snapped back to business. "But only after you are settled. This journey has been quite exhausting. I would also appreciate a break from traveling for a few days."

Caroline smiled," Of course you would lie a rest. I'm sorry Sally I wasn't thinking. I'm not myself. Now, I'm going to take myself downstairs and leave you to your sewing."

"Yes, my lady," said Sally. "But if you are not back in ten minutes, I'll be coming down to find you."

Caroline laughed. "Yes, my Sally," she said and slipped out the door. Within ten minutes she was back with a gothic novel and a deck of cards. Thus, both of them had something to occupy them until well into the afternoon. Caroline found that she could not keep her mind on her book, but it made a good screen she could cry behind so Sally would not worry.

The rain let up that afternoon and by the next morning, the roads were dry enough to travel. Caroline's heart and head ached from crying and lack of sleep, but she was determined to make good time. The cold air had come with the rain, so the air felt quite chill, and the dampness lingered, settling down into one's bones. John coachman's bones apparently were feeling better though, so they got an early start.

They were making good time and had almost reached Doncaster, when they hit a rut in the road and damaged one of the carriage wheels. The next posting house was only a mile away, so, John Coachman slowed the horses to a leisurely walk and prayed they would get there before it broke entirely.

Providence was with them and they made it, but were told it would be two hours before it could be fixed and they could continue traveling. Caroline felt this journey would never come to an end.  It seemed like a month ago that she had decided to depart for her aunt's house.  She was weary to the bone, every joint in her body ached from the jolting of the carriage, and the headache she had awoken with became worse.

She shook her head, "What else can happen?"

Sally started to open her mouth but Caroline held her hand up stopping her. "Wait. Don't answer that."

The two were sitting in a small parlor partaking in a light meal while waiting for the coach to be fixed. Sally looked over at her employer who was picking at her food.

"Do you feel alright, my lady?" she asked.

"Fine. I just have a little headache."

Caroline ate a small piece of potato to show that there was nothing wrong.

"We could stay and get some rest and start out again tomorrow."

Caroline ran her fingers from the bridge of her nose along her brows and ended at her temples. "No, I just want this journey to be done. I'll be fine."

There was a tap on the door and the innkeeper opened it to let them know their coach was ready. Caroline quickly paid for the meal and repair and within minutes they were on the road again.

They were only a few miles down the road when

Sally noticed an increase in Carolines pallor.

"Are you alright?"

Caroline couldn't answer. The pain and nausea were coming in waves so large they were very close to engulfing her. Sally's eyes widened in alarm. She banged on the roof of the coach for John Coachman to stop. The second he did, Caroline lunged for the door, and before she could get to the ground, relieved her stomach of its meager contents.

When she was finished Sally handed her a handkerchief. As she was wiping her mouth, Sally said, "We are stopping at the next inn for the night. I knew you were worse than you said. There is no point in going on."

"I am fine," Caroline said right before her knees began to buckle under her. Sally grabbed her by the waist and called for John Coachman who jumped down and assisted her. Together they settled Caroline back into the coach.

"There should be another inn about five miles down the road, but I am not positive, or we could go back. Which do you want me to do?" John Coachman asked.

"Keep going," Caroline said weakly. She looked up at Sally who was looking at her in disapproval. "I will stop at the next inn, but I am not going back."

Sally looked at her a second longer, then turned and nodded at John Coachman who shut the door.

They felt the carriage tilt slightly as he pulled himself up onto the seat, then a jolt as they began to move forward. Caroline closed her eyes against the pain and thought she had never been in such misery. Would this horrible journey ever end?

Two days later they were once again climbing into the coach, this time it was with the rising sun, and the hope that this would be the last day of travel. Though Caroline was not happy that they had to stay two nights, she was feeling much better, at least in her physical body. Internally, she still felt the continual heaviness of heartbreak.

They pushed through with minimal stops and no mishaps. Just as the sun began setting, the post chaise pulled up in front of her aunt's house. Caroline stumbled out of the carriage and began to walk up to the front door. When she had almost reached it, the door was thrown open and Aunt Mathilde rushed out to meet her.

"Caroline! I had no idea you were coming for a visit. Your letter must have gotten lost in the mail." She looked at Caroline's exhausted face, "Oh dear child, come in, come in. You look as if you could use some hot tea, a bath, and a bed.

"Thank you, Aunt Mathilde," she said gratefully. She felt her body begin to relax. She didn't realize what a strain it was to travel alone. Having to make all the decisions, and look as if one knows what one is doing. It felt good to let someone else take over.

Once they were inside, Aunt Mathilde had what seemed to be the entire staff rushing to make her comfortable. A chamber was being made ready, and a bath drawn. Tea was to be brought to the morning room.

"I thought it would be more comfortable in here. I find it the most comfortable room in the house. Also," she said smiling, "it happens to be where I was sitting before you came so I had a fire made up. It is bound to be the warmest room in the house. It's been quite chill the last few days, but I'm sure you know that better than I do."

She ushered Caroline to one of the chairs before the fire. Caroline sank into it gratefully and stretched her stiff hands and feet toward its warmth. Within the last hour it had gotten quite cold, and it felt good to let the warmth sink into her bones. The tea was brought in and Aunt Mathilde poured her a cup. After handing it to her, she poured one for herself and sat down in the chair across from Caroline.

"It is good to see you, my dear, but I have a feeling this is not just a social visit. And, if I am not mistaken, there was not really a letter lost in the post."

Caroline looked up to see the sharp blue eyes of her aunt studying her. They seemed to pierce right through a person and see to their very soul.

Strangely though, it was not unnerving, more comforting. Now she did not need to feel uncomfortable broaching the subject of her unexpected arrival. Caroline sighed.

"No Aunt Mathilde, I did not come for a social visit. I came because I felt this was a place I could do some searching of myself and make some decisions, decisions that could affect my entire life."

"Oh dear, that is serious. Well, if you need an ear to listen, I've heard I have a fairly good one. Though I'm afraid it doesn't hear quite as well as it did when I was your age." She said with a chuckle. "Drink up my dear," she said as Caroline began to wilt in her chair. "Your bath will probably be ready now. We can talk tomorrow. Our problems always seem a bit more manageable after a good night's sleep."

She rose and Caroline struggled to her feet. They both walked to the door.

"Sleep well, my dear. Don't worry about a thing. You're with Aunt Mathilde now." She smiled and gave Caroline's shoulders a quick squeeze. "Now off with you," she said and gave her a little push out the door into the hall, where a maid was waiting to show her to her room.

Caroline barely noticed her room, all she had eyes for was the bath full of steaming water. Sally helped her undress and she slipped into its warmth. Her entire body began to relax as the warmth seeped into her bones.  She began to feel as if she was floating toward the ceiling, when she was wrenched back to earth by the sound of Sally's voice.

"Do you need any help, my lady?"

"No, not quite yet," Caroline answered as she reached for the soap thinking how glad she was for Sally's presence.  If she hadn't spoken, she would have surely spent half of the night asleep in the bath.

After Caroline finished bathing, Sally brushed her hair dry and helped her get ready for bed.  She slid between the sheets, smiled contentedly for the first time in days, and fell asleep.

# Chapter 22

A wise woman never yields by appointment
It should always be an unforeseen happiness.
-Henri Boyle

The next morning, Caroline awoke feeling remarkably fresh. When she had first opened her eyes, she felt as if she was a child once more. This had always been her room when visiting her aunt, and little had changed over the years. The crisp white muslin curtains still hung on the windows, and the yellow walls still brightened her morning. A touch of sadness touched her when she thought of the morning room she loved so much in London, but she pushed the thought away. Instead, she thought of her visits here as a child. They had always been some of her fondest memories.

Aunt Mathilde never seemed to mind if a young girl became a little mussed. You were always expected to try to look your best for company, but if you happened to rush in the door with sticks stuck in your hair and grass stains on your dress, only to find a group of ladies had come to call, aunt Mathilde would just smile, give you a wink, and discretely slip you a cookie before sending you off to tidy up.

Many was the time when Aunt Mathilde would take Caroline to fish in the stream or walk in the woods. Sometimes, while off on these adventures, Aunt Mathilde would get as dirty as the child she was with. They would lose all track of time and miss tea completely. She would just request that supper be moved up an hour and come back from the kitchen with some scones hidden in her dress, as if she had to sneak them. Her eyes would twinkle like a mischievous child's as she shared them in the garden. All of these wonderful memories wrapped around her like a comforting blanket helping to dull the pain in her heart.

Caroline rose and rang for Sally, then picked the dress she wanted to wear. It was light pink with a square neckline. The long sleeves were banded around the upper arm with dark rose ribbons, which also trimmed the neckline. It had a dark rose overskirt, which scalloped, with pink roses at the points. It was one of her favorite dresses. She felt pretty in it, and she needed to feel pretty today. For a moment she thought of the blue dress that was her husband's favorite. She wondered if she would ever wear it again. Then Sally walked in the room, and she pushed the thought aside.

Sally helped her dress and arranged her hair as quickly as she could. It was not fast enough for Caroline who bore it impatiently and the moment she was released hurried down to find her aunt.

Great Aunt Mathilde was in the dining room eating scones and fruit compote with relish, a small plate of scones and a pot of tea sat on her right.

"Good morning my dear, you look much better this morning.  Come, sit.  The compote is heavenly, and I do not have to tell you about cook's scones.  I usually eat rather simply for breakfast, although, if you would like something else, it would be no trouble."

"Fruit and scones sound wonderful," Caroline said and began to fill her plate.  After pouring herself a cup of tea, she asked, "Have you any plans for today?"

"I was going to walk to Pickering to get some thread for my embroidery.  I seem to use so much green.  I am always running out. Would you care to go?"

"Yes, I would love to, but I am afraid I will have to change, this dress is not much of a walking dress.  I'm not quite sure why I wore it anyway."

Aunt Mathilde smiled. "Sometimes, my dear, I wear a dress only because I want to feel pretty. I assume that was your purpose for that dress today, for you look wonderful in it. It makes me quite envious you know. I would love to wear a dress like that, but who ever heard of an old lady wearing light pink."

Caroline looked at her aunt and tipped her head thoughtfully. "Aunt Mathilde, I believe you are the only woman of your age who could wear a dress like this and look right somehow. There is just something about you that is so young."

Her aunt snorted, "I wish you would tell my bones that, but I imagine if you took away all the wrinkles and white hair, I might look young at that."

They chatted through the meal and when they were finished, Aunt Mathilde rose and said, "I was going to go through my box to see if I needed any other colors while we were out. Would you like to join me?"

"Yes, I'd like to help."

They repaired to the morning room and began the slow task of sorting threads. When they were finished with the task, Aunt Mathilde sat back in her chair and asked, "Are you ready yet?"

"Ready?"

"Yes, ready to tell me your reason for this visit. I don't mean to distress you after this pleasant morning, but perhaps it would do some good to speak of it."

Caroline sighed, "Perhaps it would," she said and proceeded to tell her the whole story, from her fears before the wedding, to the events at Emily's house party. Aunt Mathilde just listened asking an occasional question. When Caroline finished, she looked at her aunt expectantly. After a minute, Aunt Mathilde shook her head and said, "The poor boy can't seem to do anything right can he?"

"Excuse me?"

"Well, it's perfectly apparent, isn't it? The boy has no idea of what he is doing." She tsked and shook her head again. "No idea of what to do with a woman."

"Aunt Mathilde!" Caroline protested. "Lord Montgomery is no mere boy. He is a twenty-eight-year-old man, a man with a reputation of a rake at that. I'm sure he has plenty of experience with women."

"There is experience, and there is experience. The boy obviously has never been in love before. He probably doesn't even know it's what it is he is feeling, and he definitely doesn't know what to do about it."

"But he knows love." Caroline insisted. "He has been in love with Lady Owen since he was a boy."

"Pooh," said Aunt Mathilde with a wave of her hand, "nothing but calf love. This is much different. At least he had the brains to fall in love with a woman of character."

"Who?" asked Caroline, confusion wrinkling her brow.

"Why, you of course, child."

"Me?"

Aunt Mathilde nodded.

"He doesn't love me! Did you not hear a thing I said when I told you how he treated me?"

"Every word."

Caroline's emotions began to get the better of her. "Then how could you possibly think he feels anything except contempt for me? I am nothing to him but a brood mare, he said so himself." She cried in frustration.

Aunt Mathilde looked at her with those all-knowing eyes and said calmly, "He is afraid."

"Afraid?" Caroline cried. "Afraid of what?"

"He is afraid of two things, responsibility, and love. When a man gets married, it is much different than it is for a woman. If he is a good man, he takes his vows seriously and assumes responsibility for his wife. He now must be concerned with her welfare as much as his own, not to mention children when they come. He cannot be a child himself anymore. That can be very hard adjustment. Some men do not go into it easily. It didn't help that he didn't know you better. If he had fallen in love with you first, we would not be talking right now. But I think the fates knew they had to force you together for him to see your worth."

At this point, Caroline started to interrupt, but Aunt Mathilde stopped her with a wave of her hand. "I know he didn't make the effort beforehand, if he had, it may have prevented all this, but that is neither here nor there. He didn't want to be married, he didn't feel ready, but he is one of the good men. He knows in his heart what a good man and husband should be. When he decided to at least attempt to be friends with his wife, he found himself falling in love. He wanted to be with you, and then would push you away. He wanted your love, but was afraid you would reject him. If you look deeply, you will see I am right."

"But, what about the night at the house party?" Caroline asked, beginning to choke on her tears. "How can you explain that?"

"I do not know for certain, but I would say he was as surprised as you to find that woman in his room."

"Are you just saying this to make me feel better?"

"Why do you ask, because you love him too?"

Caroline looked at her aunt, her eyes wide and jaw slack.

"Don't look so surprised. Did you think that from your story I could surmise all that about him and nothing about you?" Caroline blinked and closed her mouth. Before she could speak, Aunt Mathilde shook her head and began again. She leaned forward and put her hand on Caroline's. "No, my dear, I am not just telling you what you want to hear, that would never make you happy. I sincerely believe that you love each other deeply. I think that it is unfortunate that two people who love each other have to go through so much, but perhaps that is what makes love stronger."

She removed her hand from Caroline's, patted her knee and rose from her chair. "Now, you just think on that for a while. You are welcome to stay as long as you like, but I don't think you want that husband of yours to suffer any longer than necessary, do you? I must go talk to Mrs. Perkins about a final airing and cleaning of the house before the air gets too chill. I will be walking to Pickering at two o'clock, if you would care to join me." With that, she left the room at her usual brisk pace.

Caroline stared at the floor still trying to comprehend all that her aunt had said. Could it be true? Did Edward truly love her? Her heart leapt at the thought. She began to review all the things which had transpired between her and her husband since their marriage, but with different eyes. As she did, she began to see the sense in her aunt's words. Mathilde had to walk to Pickering with a maid that afternoon, for two o'clock came and went and Caroline had barely moved an inch.

That evening, Caroline sat at the desk in her aunt's library and penned a letter to her friend

Emily as follows:

*My Dear Friend,*

*I am writing as I have promised to inform you of my safe arrival at my destination. I now know that I have done the best possible thing. I am at my Great Aunt Mathilde's house near Pickering. My aunt has helped me tremendously with my troubles. She is an excellent judge of character and quite knowledgeable in the ways of human nature. I have explained my situation to her and she has brought to my attention certain things which upon reflection, I found to be perfectly sound. I now know what I must do.*

*I also write to inquire of the whereabouts of Lord Montgomery. I do not know if he still resides with you or has taken himself elsewhere. If so, do you know of his destination? I am most anxious to find him, for you well know once I have set my plans, I like to act upon them immediately. Please ease my mind as soon as possible and send your reply in care of Mrs. Mathilde Haddon, Pickering, Yorkshire.*

*I would also be very interested to what happened after my departure. If you could include some of the details, I would be grateful. Please reply quickly, I beg of you.*

*Ever Your Friend,*

*Lady Caroline Montgomery*

# Chapter 23



When he first arrived at Brookstone Manor, Edward was full of promise. He was happy to find the house in good condition. It needed some decorating, but the building was solid and there wouldn't be many renovations needed.

The servants had not had time to get things fully prepared, but at his arrival they apologetically began in earnest. The rooms were aired and dusted, flowers were picked and arranged, fires were lit in the principal rooms and cook began baking enough for an entire house party. He was expecting to hear from Miss Whithers at any moment that all had been explained and forgiven. Then the days began to pass. Every one seeming to pass slower, until he felt as if a month had passed instead of a week, a week in which he had not heard a single word from Miss Whithers. He hoped that his words had not fallen on deaf ears. That she had heard from his wife and was not telling him.

He paced back and forth in the study running his fingers through his hair. Finally, for the first time since he had arrived, he walked over to the table that held the brandy decanter. The sun was beginning to set. Another day was almost over, and he had no hope of his wife coming now. If ever.

He poured himself half a glass and downed it, then poured himself another and drank more slowly. How unfair. Just when he finally realized he had fallen in love with his wife, he lost her. Damn, Sarah for ruining his life again.

He shook his head and sighed. He couldn't blame Sarah. He couldn't even blame her for ruining his life the first time. It was all his own doing. He was the one who threw his life away because she refused him all those years ago. He did not have to become the wastrel he was.

He shook his head as he took another drink and

added to the burn moving slowly outward from his chest. He was blind and wasted half his life mourning the loss of a dream. Now, he knew what love was like in reality, and once again he ruined his own life, but this time he also hurt the one he truly loved in the process.

He should never had gone to see Sarah that day in the park. Never had kissed her when his wife was sitting at home. Why, when he knew he did not want to be with her, didn't her tell her so? Thank God, he had not been foolish enough to take her to bed. He could never have forgiven himself if he had. But Caroline didn't know that. She thought the worst of him. He didn't blame her for leaving.

He poured himself another drink. She deserved better. He had done so many things he now regretted. She was better off without him. He would stay away from her. Let her live where she wanted and get what she wanted. If she spent every cent he had, it could not make up for the things he had done.

There was a light tap on the door before it was opened by Jenny the housemaid.

"My lord, supper is ready when you wish to eat."

"I don't want any supper. I need another bottle of brandy." Edward said raising the bottle he didn't remember emptying, but obviously had. "Do we have more in the house?"

"Yes, my lord, in the cellars."

"Good, good. Then be good girl and bring me one...eh...two bottles. Go on now," he said waving his hand dismissively at the girl standing in the doorway.

"What should I tell cook about supper?"

"Tell her to enjoy it heartily, but don't forget the brandy."

"No, my lord," she said and quickly closed the door.

Edward leaned back in his chair, drained the rest of the brandy in his glass, leaned his head against the back of the chair and stared at the ceiling. His thoughts returned to his wife and he felt the prick of tears start behind his eyes.

What would he do without her? Wallow in drunken misery that's what. It was different with Sarah. He had been so angry, and why? Now he realized it was just his pride that had been hurt. Now he had no pride and his heart truly lay in pieces. Now he had come close to heaven on earth and destroyed it all because he was a coward. A coward that didn't understand what true love was. Now he did, and he realized that meant that if she didn't want to come back to him, he had to let her go. Just the thought brought a sob up from deep within him and he covered his face.

"My lord?"

Edward took a deep breath and dropped his hand to see Pinkerton, the man who had been hired to serve as butler, in the doorway with two bottles of brandy. Edward sniffed and passed his hand over his eyes to remove any vestige of tears.

"Thank you, Pinkerton. Bring them in. Set them here on the desk. Do we have more?"

"Ah...yes, my lord. Your grandfather always kept the cellars well stocked," he said with a note of disapproval in his voice. Perhaps he had more in common with his grandfather than he thought.

"Good to hear. Good to hear. That will be all."

"My lord--"

"I said that will be all, Pinkerton. Thank you."

"Yes, my lord." Pinkerton said, threw one last look of concern his employer's way, exited, and closed the door behind him.

Days later, Edward was wrapped in a deep cloak of misery. Caroline was not coming. He had sent the servants home after asking Pinkerton to bring most of the brandy up from the cellar and sequestered himself in the study. He felt entirely empty. Empty of anger, empty of tears, but mostly he noticed the emptiness in his chest where his heart used to be. He hadn't eaten in days, didn't remember when he had stoked the fire last, and he had finished the last bottle of brandy a few hours ago.

He sat in a chair before the cold fireplace, his body numb. He felt himself fluctuating between dreams and reality and had begun to not be able to tell the difference. More than once, he was certain that he heard Caroline's voice, but when he rushed out of his chair to find her, all he found was an empty house. Just now he thought he heard Lydford say from somewhere far away, "Well, this explains the smoke. Someone must have been here and not put out the fire before leaving." He didn't even make the effort to get up, it was just a dream.

Just like the gasp he heard that sounded like a woman. If only it were true. If only it were Caroline. He began to wonder about his sanity when he felt someone grasp his hands and begin to rub some warmth into them. He thought he heard Lydford's voice again, but it was too far away. He couldn't understand him.

He continued to hear the murmur of voices and a sharp curse. Soon light seemed to flood his being and he began to hear a woman's voice, not Caroline's, speaking slow and with a slight quiver, "Well now, Lord Montgomery, we'll have you right and tight in a few minutes. Can't let that fire die down, can we?"

He began to feel this might not be a dream after all. The voice continued, "Perhaps you could use a nice hot bath. I know when I am chilled, it always seems to help me." There was an uncomfortable pause and she went on briskly, "Of course, men seem to put stock in brandy, perhaps nice toddy will fix you up...or perhaps not."

The voice. It was familiar. "Perhaps tea, a nice hot cup, mmmm, doesn't that sound good?"

It was Miss Whithers! Perhaps she had come with news! He felt her come near. She bent down and wrapped a throw around his shoulders. He couldn't let her go, he had to know if she had heard from his wife. He reached out and grabbed her hand before she could disappear. Her hand stayed in his. It was real! He focused intently on her face which floated above his.

"Caroline?" he said hoarsely.

"No, it's Emily, Miss Whithers."

He closed his eyes and exhaled, "I know that." He opened his eyes again, "Do you know where Caroline is?"

"I'm afraid not, Lord Montgomery."

He dropped her hand, closed his eyes, and breathed shakily in and out, trying to hold on to his control.

I don't know if I can live without her," he said finally, his voice cracking as he spoke.

"Of course you can," she said in her sick room voice once more, "everyone does. My aunt was crushed when my uncle passed, but it has been two years now and she is in Italy with plans to tour as much of the continent as possible."

He shook his head, "I've seen Italy." He looked at her once again with an intense look trying to see into her very soul. "Would you wish to go on without Lydford?"

She stared at him. Their eyes stayed locked like that until, finally, she looked away. "What a silly question to ask."

"Is it?"

Miss Whithers grew flustered. "Yes, of course. Lord Lydford and I are friends. He is just helping me. That is all."

Edward smiled sadly. "Oh yes, the list. Has he showed it to you yet?"

"No, not yet."

"Huh," Edward nodded. "He will," he said, then stared at the fire as the smile slowly faded from his face.

Miss Whithers walked between him and the fire and stood there until he looked at her. "Listen to me, Lord Montgomery, you cannot sit here and give up. You still have a chance. Caroline only went somewhere to be able to think clearly and make good decisions."

Edward stared at her and said slowly, "And what if her decision is to leave me for good?"

His question hung in the air. Miss Whithers had no answers.


Lydford returned bringing hot tea, cold meat, and dry bread. Edward knew he had eaten much better meals, but none that fulfilled him as much as this one. As he ate, Lydford and Miss Whithers tried to convince him to return to Hampstead

House with them, but he was adamant.  He would not go.

"If you will not go, then you must promise me to take better care of yourself.  Do not send away the help Pinkerton will rehire for you."

Edward tried to smile, "Alright Lydford. You always did like to tell me what to do.  I guess it's good to know some things will never change."

Lydford looked out the window at the sun getting lower in the sky.

"We must go Edward, but I will return as soon as the Whithers' house party is finished at the end of the week. I expect you to be looking much better when I arrive."

Edward smiled again and nodded his head as Lydford led Miss Whithers out the door. He sat in the now warm room with the sunlight streaming in on him. He felt the block of ice in his chest begin to thaw. The food cleared his brain, and he began to think of what Miss Whithers had said. He did still have a chance and, miserable worm as he was, he was going to take it when it came.

*Chapter 24*

*Love rules the court, the camp, the grove,*
*And men below, and saint above,*
*For love is heaven, and heaven is love.*
*-Sir Walter Scott*

The days spent waiting for a reply to her letter, were some of the most trying of Caroline's life. She deplored waiting for anything, but this was unbearable. In order to rid herself of extra energy, she took many long walks. The worst days were the ones when it rained, which, being October, it did with increasing frequency. If it were a light, or even a moderate rain, she walked anyway, but for the last two days it had rained so steadily, she had to remain inside.

Aunt Mathilde was a very good hostess, but Caroline couldn't help feeling restless and distracted.

It had been another rainy day. The evening was spent, like most, in the morning room with her aunt playing cards.

"I should have let you wager your pin money rather than just pins.  I could have lived comfortably for the rest of my days on the amount I have won from you today alone," Aunt Mathilde teased, after winning yet another hand.

Caroline sighed.  "I'm sorry Aunt Mathilde, I just don't know where my mind is."

"I do. Unfortunately, sometimes we must wait, dear.  I know how you feel, for I have always been a woman of action myself, but perhaps this time doesn't have to be spent just waiting. Perhaps you could use this time to great profit."

Caroline sat up straighter, "How, Aunt Mathilde?"

"I'm sure I don't know my dear, but perhaps if you reflect a while, you might find that *you* do." She began to rise. "Now I must get these old bones up to bed."  She gave Caroline a pat on the shoulder before quitting the room.

Caroline sat and wondered what it was she could do to use this time to her advantage.  She went to her own bed an hour later, still no closer to finding her purpose.

The next day dawned as dark and dreary as the

previous two. The rain still came down in sheets. Though the weather was dreary, Caroline was not. She awoke with a purpose. Though she did not know what that purpose was, that did not deter her. She was determined to know what it was before the day was out.

She dressed quickly and went downstairs to breakfast with her aunt.

"My, you seem cheery today," her aunt remarked as she walked through the door.

"Yes, at least today is not as bad as yesterday."

Mathilde glanced toward the window, where the rain was pouring down and then back to her niece who was asking if cook would mind preparing her some poached eggs, kippers, and toast. A smile slowly broke across her face.

Caroline spent her day in thought. As she thought, she worked on her stitching, helped her aunt pack up some old clothing for charity, and polished the silver. Not a job she would have usually done, but she offered to do it to have something to do with her hands as she thought, much to the delight of Ann who the job usually fell to.

At the end of the day, she was still no closer to finding a purpose for her time. But though she felt slightly disturbed, as if she were missing something, she had no trouble falling asleep for the first time in days.

The next morning, she awoke to sunshine

streaming in her window. It was as if the sun had awoken from a three-day long nap and was well rested. She dressed and went to breakfast determined to find a good use of her time once again today.

After breakfast, she went for a walk in the garden to think. The sunshine cheered her a bit, but she felt no closer to reaching her goal. She began to feel frustrated once more. After her walk, she met with her aunt in the morning room for tea. As her aunt poured, she said, "I have been thinking ever since you talked to me the other night, but I still cannot see how my time might be used for good as I wait."

"But my dear, yesterday was an extremely profitable day, was it not?"

"Perhaps to you or Ann, whose job it is to clean the silver, but certainly not to me."

"And did I say to whom your time would be profitable?" Mathilde said with a smile. "Dear child, I knew you needed something to occupy your mind and make you feel as if you were working towards something. Think of how tortuous that last day would have been. And it always helps one to get out of misery by helping relieve someone else of theirs."

"I suppose so, but eventually we will run out of silly little tasks for me to do and I will go back to dwelling on how little I can do and feel frustrated once more."

"Well, the weather has broken, so at least you can walk off some of your frustration." She looked away and took a sip of tea. "And, also, there is a letter for you in the hall which I feel may be the cure for your malady."

Caroline jumped up from her chair. "Aunt Mathilde, why didn't you tell me?"

"I wanted you to get some tea in you before you ran off willy-nilly, child. Now go, see what your friend has to say."

Caroline ran to the hall table, snatched up the letter, quickly broke the seal, and began pacing the hall as she read:

*Dearest Friend,*

*I am happy to hear that you are well and have been able to make your decision. I do not know what that decision is, and I do not wish to confuse you further, but I would like to speak, or in this case, write. a few words in Lord Montgomery's behalf.*

*The morning you departed, I met him in the dining room over breakfast. I, understandably, did not want to speak to him, but he compelled me to stay and hear him out. He confessed his love for you and said he could not remain at the party without you, but would repair to Brookstone Manor.*

*On Saturday, Lord Lydford and I drove up to see how he was faring. When we arrived the house looked deserted, but Lord Lydford insisted we check. As it is, I am glad we did, for I am not certain Lord Montgomery would have lived if he had been left in this state for long.*

*He was half frozen, sitting beside a dying fire and hadn't eaten in days. But worst of all, was the look in his eyes. Caroline, if you have any compassion in your heart at all, you will go to him. He could not be a more broken man had you died.*

*Brookstone Manor is outside of Whitchurch. If you stop in the village anyone can tell you how to get there.*

*Your Dear Friend,*
*Miss Emily Withers*

Caroline's face broke into a smile and she ran down the hall to her aunt.

"I can see by your face, it is good news," her aunt said as, as Caroline entered the room.

"Oh, Aunt Mathilde!" she said, her face glowing. "He does love me! I must leave immediately. He is at Brookstone Manor, just outside of Whitchurch, and is miserable without me. Oh, I'm so glad Sally hasn't left for home yet. I must tell her to begin packing, and I need to hire a post chaise as soon as possible."

"Fiddlesticks child, you will do no such thing."

"Aunt, I value your opinion, but surely you

must see that it is imperative that I go to him as soon as possible."

"Of course you must child, it was the post chaise I was speaking of.  I have perfectly good transportation right here.  Now, I have a light carriage, which will get you there faster, but may shake your teeth out, or the larger carriage which is slower but much more comfortable.  Which shall you have?

"Oh, the light one of course, I need to get there as soon as possible."

Mathilde's eyes twinkled.  "Just as I thought. I had Tucker prepare it for a journey as soon as I saw that your letter had arrived.  I also had Sally pack a small trunk with enough clothing for three days.  I think you will find you only need to pack your necessities and be on your way.  I will send Sally home in the larger carriage, and she can continue on to you after her visit with the rest of your trunks."

Caroline hugged her aunt and began to thank her profusely.

"Get along girl," Mathilde said, pushing her lightly toward the door, "the faster you go, the faster you will get to that husband of yours and put him out of his misery."

She was off within the hour. The day was bright and sunny and Caroline could not help but compare this trip to the one she had started on over two weeks ago. This time her spirits were as bright as the day.  She was going to her Edward, who loved her.

They changed horses often to make good time. At one of the stops, Caroline had a supper of cold collation, but she ate as quickly as possible, so as not to lose a moment of travel time.  The skies continued to remain clear and as the moon was full, they traveled until late in the night.  They finally had to stop at an inn for some rest.  It was difficult for Caroline to stop at all, but she knew that Tucker needed to rest in order to continue to drive safely tomorrow.  If they left early, and the weather remained favorable, she could reach her destination by tomorrow evening.  If not, she was prepared to drive through the night. She was so excited she didn't think she could sleep, and was surprised to be awakened by a knock on her door the next morning.  It was the chambermaid informing her that Tucker was ready to go whenever she was.  She looked out the window and thanked God for the continuing good weather.

The chambermaid looked at her with disapproval, after all what kind of lady would travel without a maid. Caroline did not care what she thought.  She was on her way to see Edward. She swallowed her pride and asked if she could help her with her hair, and dressed as quickly as she could.  After a quick breakfast, she was once more on her way.  Her excitement built with every mile they traveled, until she could barely keep her seat.  Soon, soon, she kept telling herself, soon I will see him again.

Edward sat in the same chair, in the same room he had been in when Lydford and Caroline's friend Miss Whithers had come, but this time it was completely different.  This time there was a merry fire crackling in the grate.  There was a lamp burning, which had been lit by the maid before she left for the night.  There were no empty bottles lying discarded by his chair.  All in all, it was a picture of contentedness, the only thing that remained unchanged was the look in Edward's eyes.

After Lydford and Miss Whithers had left, he had begun to rekindle some hope.  Miss Whithers was right, as long as Caroline was alive, there was hope she would come back to him.  He wanted to be prepared to leave if he heard any information about her whereabouts, so he got up each morning and dressed and shaved.  He had a bag packed so that, when he discovered her whereabouts, he could leave at a moment's notice, and refrained from drinking a single drop of alcohol so that he would have an alert mind at all times.

As time passed, and he sat alone in his readiness, his hope began to fade once more.  He had not touched any brandy for at least a week, but it was beginning to seem like a good way to quiet his morose thoughts and help him sleep, so he could escape for a while. He had tried to read, but his mind kept wandering and he would find himself staring at nothing once more. That is how Caroline found him, sitting with an open book in his lap, staring at nothing. The firelight danced on his dark curls and across the planes of his face. Caroline felt she had never seen such a beautiful sight and her heart leapt in her chest.

"Edward?" she said from the doorway.

His head jerked towards her and he stared at her incredulously. "Caroline?"

They remained like that, staring at each other for what seemed like forever.

"Are you alright?" she asked stepping further into the room.

He continued to stare at her a moment longer, then rose unsteadily and began walking toward her. When he reached her, his eyes searched her face and his hand came up to cup her cheek. "I had to see if you were real. I have been dreaming of your face for weeks."

"Oh, Edward," she said, leaning her cheek into his hand.

"You certainly feel real," he said, caressing the side of her face, "but I have one final test."

He brought his lips down to hers and she thought her heart would burst. She could feel his body shake, whether from emotion or restraint she was not sure. His kiss was infinitely tender, followed by two more before he pulled back to look at her.

"Caroline, I don't deserve you. I love you. I need you. But I don't deserve you." Edward said. Then he took a step back and ran his fingers through his hair. Caroline could feel the tension building in him. "I was going to tell you all this at the house party, but then—"

Caroline stepped forward and reached up to put a finger across his lips, "Ssshhh."

Edward stilled and fell silent, looking deep into her eyes.

"It is over, let's leave the past in the past," she said.

She felt the tension leave his body and he smiled a crooked smile at her, "I told you I didn't deserve you. Lydford said I keep throwing away all the most precious things in my life. You were on that list. I'm sorry for treating you like something not worth keeping. Caroline, if you will come back to me, I will always treat you as my most precious possession. Will you come back to me?"

Caroline smiled, joy filling her heart at the sound of the words she longed to hear. "I already have. I'm here, aren't I? And trust me it was not an easy trip. Oh, Edward, I was miserable these weeks without you. I was so hurt that night at Emily's house party, I didn't know what to do. I just knew I couldn't face you the next day.  Then suddenly, I thought of my Aunt Mathilde, so I went.   After telling her my story, I found her feeling sorry for you!  I felt rather betrayed, but then I realized I had not given you a chance to explain.  I knew I cared too much to just walk away, I needed to see if you felt the same."

Edward stepped back towards her and put his hands around her waist, pulling her toward him. "Now that you are here, what do you think?" he asked.

Caroline gazed into his eyes.  The love and passion she saw there made her heart surge in her chest. "I think," she paused a moment, her hands slid across his chest and grabbed the edges of his shirt to pull him closer. "I know, I love you."

Edward, smiling tenderly, began to lower his head, and she knew that he would touch his lips to hers once more.  She felt her breath quicken in anticipation and her knees go weak.  She sagged against him and brought her arms up to tangle her fingers in the soft curls at the nape of his neck.

Then his lips met hers and the tenderness she had felt in them before was overlaid with an urgency.  His lips were hard on hers.  He opened his mouth and nibbled on her bottom lip.  She gasped, and when she did, he claimed her mouth fully.  Caroline answered by opening herself fully to him.  He groaned and ran his hands down the sides of her body, brushing the sides of her breasts as he did so.

Every place he touched her body it tingled, and it seemed that his hands roamed everywhere. Soon, it was like he had lit a spark and her entire body was consumed by fire. Her kisses became as urgent as his as she yearned for something she didn't know.  Her hands seemed to move of their own accord.  She ran them down his neck and began pushing aside his cravat.

Suddenly he pulled away.  She was stunned for a moment. What was it? Had she done something wrong? Her cheeks flamed.  It must be wrong for a wife to act in such a way.  What had come over her?  Her eyes flew open just as she felt him place his hands behind her knees and lift her up into his arms.

"I'm sorry," she said.

She felt Edward stiffen.  "For what?"

Part of Caroline wanted to hide her face in his shoulder, but she knew that she could be stronger than that.  She had changed. She was not a girl anymore and was not going to act like one.  She lifted her chin, looked into his now stony face, and said "For my improper behavior."

His face softened and a smile tugged at his lips. She felt his body relax and once again it was as if they were melting together.

"You should know by now that I don't set any store in proper behavior."

"Then why did you stop me?" she asked wide

eyed.

"Because, as delightful as I find your exuberance, I do not desire, my dear wife, for our first experience together to be on the floor of the library, do you?"

The grin on his face and the twinkle in his eyes put her at ease, and brought out the mischievous side of her. "I don't know," she said beginning to unbutton the top buttons of his shirt and running her hands over the triangle of flesh exposed, "It could be rather fun."

Caroline could tell by the look in his eyes that he wanted to drop her right there to show her just how much fun it could be, but he steeled himself and carried her out the door and up what seemed to an extremely long flight of stairs. Caroline passed the long journey exploring the space from his collarbone to his ear with her tongue.

He pushed open his bedroom door with his shoulder, carried her inside and shut it with his foot. Then, he strode to the bed, unceremoniously dropped her on it and began to show her that it was not nice to tease her husband in such a way...or maybe, perhaps, it was.

Hours later, they lay, legs entangled. Edward's arms around his wife, her head on his chest.

"So," Edward's voice rumbled beneath her ear, "what do you think of the house?"

"Well, I can't say I've seen much more than the study and the bedroom since I've been here," she looked up through her lashes at Edward who grinned back, "but though it could use some decorating, it seems nice. Did you rent it for the winter?"

"No," Edward said.

"Oh, well, will we go back to London then?"

"No," Edward said with a smile.

"Oh," Caroline said, confusion in her voice. After a pause she asked, "Where will we spend the winter?"

"Here."

"I thought you said you didn't rent it." Caroline said.

"I didn't."

Caroline lifted herself up, leaned on her elbow, and looked at her husband who was grinning like a child with a Christmas present.

"It's ours," he said.

"Ours?" Caroline repeated, eyes wide.

"Yes, how do you like your new home, Countess?"

"But I'm not," Caroline's face fell "Your father--"

"Is fine." Edward said running his hand along the side of his wife's face and pushing her head down lightly back onto his chest. She snuggled down closer to him and he continued. "It was a strange thing. My father sent me a letter soon after our marriage and I put off opening it until just before the Landry's party. In it was a letter that was sent to Kendleston Hall. It was from the solicitor of my grandfather's estate. I didn't really know my grandfather. He was not around much when I was a child, and after my mother died, he became a recluse of sorts and I never saw him again."

"How sad."

"Yes, well, it seems he passed away this February and I was his only living blood relative. I inherited his property and title. So, you are now a countess."

Caroline laughed. "And I had barely gotten used to being a viscount's wife!"

"Are you happy?"

"Yes. Very. But not because I am a countess."

She wrapped her arm across his chest and snuggled closer. They lay in silence listening to the sound of the fire crackling in the grate.

"You know," Edward said, his voice rumbling once again beneath her ear, "I don't think I have felt this peaceful since my angel spoke to me."

"Angel, what angel?" Caroline asked.

"When I was ill, I found myself deep in the middle of a nightmare reliving some rather painful moments of my life.  I had reached my lowest, when I felt a cool hand in mine and heard a voice telling me it would be alright.  I felt such a peace in my soul, I felt as if I had been visited by an angel." He looked down at her. "I have tried to find that peace for a long time, but have never felt it again until now, with you."

Caroline pushed against his chest so she could raise her head up, and looked at him with wide eyes. "But Edward, that was me. I was the one who held your hand that night, it was no angel."

Edward's eyes warmed as he looked at his wife. He pushed a strand of hair back from her face and cupped her cheek in his palm. "Oh yes it was. You *are* my angel. You saved me from the hell my life had become, and made it heaven on earth. I love you, Caroline."

He pulled her down on top of him and kissed her tenderly, then proceeded to gently show her once again, just how heavenly love could be.

## The End

Dear Reader,

I would like to thank you for reading my book. It has taken many years to finally get it out into the world and I hope you enjoyed it.

I understand that some people feel that Edward is an ass, and he is, but in the words of Monty Python, "he got betta". This is not to say that all men do, and I just want you to know that in no way am I justifying his behavior. Nor, am I saying that someone should stay with an abusive partner just in case they might "get better".

There are some people who act out the way they do because of past hurts. Edward is one of them. I didn't pick Edward, he picked me. He and Caroline wanted their story told and I obliged. Please don't shoot the messenger. Ultimately, I do believe that their story is one of redemption, and the power of love and determination, and hope that you see it that way too.

If you do like my book, it would help a lot if you would leave a review on Amazon or Goodreads. Not only will it direct others to a book you found enjoyable, but it will help me know that my brain child is liked. Also, if you would like to find out what happens with Caroline's friend Emily, look for my book coming in the summer of 2025, The Marquess List.


Yours in Creativity,
Cary Harter

Coming Summer 2025

# *The Marquess List*

The second book in the
Sisters for a Season series
Emily's Story


Turn the page for a sneak peek of
The Marquess List

Emily stood and watched the dust motes dance in the shaft of sunlight that peeped through the crack around the far door of the barn and touched the golden hair of the man grooming the horse before her. She smiled, knowing his brow would be creased with concentration like it always was when he groomed her horse. She felt a bit regretful interrupting his task, especially knowing why she came.

"William?" she said taking a step closer to him.

The curry comb in his hand stilled and she watched him take a deep breath. It seemed to her as if an entire minute passed before he turned to look at her, but when he did, there was hurt written in his face. He looked her in the eye and with a blank expression said, "Yes, Miss?"

Emily dipped her head down closing her eyes for a second then looked back at him. "Don't do that, William. We've used our given names since we were children."

"Yes, but I guess we're all grown up now," he said turning away to brush the horse again.

"And we weren't three weeks ago? You called me Emily then."

"Three weeks ago, I didn't even know you were leaving. You didn't even bother to tell me."

Emily sighed. "I know. I'm sorry. I just didn't know how to tell you."

William turned back around to face her. "How about, William, I don't have time for you anymore.

I have to go to London to fetch myself a rich husband with a title so I can be Lady La Di Da.”

“Don’t be silly. You know it is all my mother’s idea. I don’t like being in society. I’ll be back, you needn’t worry about that. There isn’t a chance that anyone would offer for me. I won’t take. And I could hardly fit the part of Lady La Di Da, look at me.”

William looked at her. She was barely five foot high in an old dress with an apron covering most of it. Her dark hair was tied back in a kerchief. Her face all dark eyes with a smudge of dirt on her snub nose. He smiled, “Well, you do look rather more like Mary the kitchen maid.”

Emily laughed, “Exactly. And I have no desire to be Lady La Di Da or Lady whatever. I’m happy just where I am.”

The horse nudged William from behind as if to remind him that he stopped in the middle of a good brushing. He smiled and gave her a pat before leading her over to a stall, putting her inside, and giving her a scoop of oats. Then he came back out, closed the gate, and walked over to Emily. He leaned his forearm against the post next to her and asked, “But what about your parents? They want you to be a part of society. They certainly wouldn’t approve of you associating with kitchen maids and grooms.”

Emily looked into the eyes of the man towering over her and said, “No. but I know they love me and they will come to understand that I truly don't belong in the world of society and my heart lies elsewhere."

"I hope they do understand. You have a very good heart and I'm glad it lies where it does." He sighed and shifted so he could lean his back against the post and crossed his arms over his chest, "I'm sorry for getting so upset about you leaving, it's just that everything was going so well, and then you stopped coming to the barn and now you're leaving."

"You must have more confidence. You will be fine on your own." Emily's heart melted at the forlorn look on William's face. "Would it help if I wrote?"

He looked back up at her with a smile and a shine of hope in his eyes. "It sure would." Then the smile and the hope dimmed. "But what would your parents say about you writing the groom. They probably think I can't even read."

"Don't worry, I'll take the letters to the post myself and will send them to your parent's house. I'll let you know where you can send replies once I'm situated in London. I'd like to know how you're getting along. Just don't let this set you back."

"I won't, too much is at stake, but I wish there didn't have to be so much secrecy. Why don't we just tell your parents?"

Emily sighed. "You're right, of course. I just

don't feel like it is the right time. After the season, when we come back, then I can tell them."

The groom before her relaxed. "That would make things a lot easier. I'm so close. I just need a little more time and I feel confident I could get a job as a bookkeeper,"

"I promise I will give you all the time in the world, when I come back and I'm sure you'll make a wonderful bookkeeper."

William bent down and picked up a piece of hay and began twirling it between his fingers. "I like working with the horses, but a bookkeeper is a more respectable job. I could get a small house, and be in a better position to marry." He stopped a moment lost in the dream, then said, "Emily I have to—"

He was interrupted by an insistent voice calling, "Emily! Emily, where are you?"

William straightened so he was standing beside the post, as Emily looked flustered, "I'd better go. Don't worry it will all work out," she said and turned to exit the barn. Just then the door was opened by a girl at least a head taller than her. She stopped in the doorway and looked from Emily to the groom and back.

Emily gave her younger sister an overbright smile, "Oh, come along, Jane, I was just heading back to the house."

Jane pursed her lips and narrowed her eyes, "Mama's been looking for you everywhere. What are you doing out here? You're supposed to be packing."

"I was just saying goodbye to the horses."

"I guess that also explains why you've spent hours out here the last few months. You definitely have developed a love for horses lately."

"Yes, I have. Now let's go," Emily said brushed past her and headed toward the house.

"Uh—huh," Jane said and shot one last look at the handsome groom leaning against the post before following her older sister back to the house.

# About the Author

**Cary Harter** has had an interest in writing since the first grade and has the many illustrated books her mom saved to prove it. When she's not writing or working her full-time job, she likes to sit on the front porch of her northeast Ohio home playing guitar with her dog at her feet. Unless, of course, it's winter, which she doesn't want to talk about because if you can't say anything nice you shouldn't say anything at all. You can find her on Facebook or the website caryharter.com.